Photography by Adi Simion

George Chittenden was born and raised in Kent, and is the youngest of six children from a working class family. He loves to travel and spends several months a year exploring faraway lands and fuelling his imagination. When at home George teaches local history in the medieval city of Canterbury.

THE BOY WHO FELT
NO PAIN

I dedicate this novel to all the children that died at the hands of industry in Britain's past and all the children who continue to suffer across the world in the present day. You all deserved so much more.

George Chittenden

THE BOY WHO FELT NO PAIN

AUSTIN MACAULEY
PUBLISHERS LTD.

A CIP catalogue record for this title is available from the British Library.

ISBN 978 184963 448 9

www.austinmacauley.com

First Published (2013)
Austin Macauley Publishers Ltd.
25 Canada Square
Canary Wharf
London
E14 5LB

Printed and bound in Great Britain

Chapter One

The Town of Deal 1778

Oil lamps hung in several doorways casting an eerie glow over the narrow street, as the smuggler crawled around on his hands and knees and struggled with all his might to rise to his feet and face his foe. As his enemy's shadow cast darkness over him once more, Billy Bates glanced up at the goliath that towered over him. Standing at six feet eight inches and built like a shire horse Bill took in the man's features, the freckled cheeks, dimpled chin and the nose that bore the scars of countless brawls. In the end, Bill concluded that he looked far removed from the out of control teenager that had been forced out of the town several years before. Finding his feet Bill attempted to climb up from the cobbles, but received a heavy kick to the guts that sent him sprawling to the ground once more.

Laughter filled the empty street and echoed off the walls as Billy Bates rolled over onto his back and stared up at the starlit sky. Memories of his youth, his best friend who he'd lost and a life spent standing up to his enemies flashed before his eyes as Billy Bates thought of all the people he'd helped over the years. His heart sank. *'Where are you all now?'* he wondered to himself as Ronnie Jenkins pulled a rusty looking dagger from a sheath around his waist and stepped forward.

"You know Bill, I admire you in many ways, you're not like the rest of this town, you've got courage and brains to boot, but thinking these peasants would stand up against me was a huge mistake! The respect they have for you would never outweigh the fear they have of me," Ronnie said, stepping even closer as Billy Bates crawled along the ground in a futile attempt to escape.

"When it comes to the crunch, fear is a much more powerful tool," Ronnie continued. "My father taught me that."

Billy Bates turned and faced his enemy, staring deep into Ronnie's eyes. "Fear only gets you so far in this world, Ronnie. Your father knew that only too well and let's face it Ronnie, he despised you!" Bill said in that croaky voice, as he continued to stare at the huge thug that had murdered his bodyguard and friend. "Just like everyone else in this town."

Ronnie Jenkins turned a shade paler and gritted his teeth furiously as he stepped even closer with the rusty dagger gripped tightly in his hand. "Any last words Billy Bates?" he asked, and as both men stared at each other neither saw a flicker of movement from further down the street, as a wooden bat was picked up by a man who began creeping along in the shadows in the pair's direction.

Unaware of the newcomer Ronnie Jenkins grinned as he stepped within striking distance of the smuggling leader, who over years had managed to undermine his entire clan's grip on the town.

"See you in hell, Bill," Ronnie said, as he stepped forward to plunge the dagger deep into the smuggler's chest, but suddenly at the very last moment he was hit on the back of the head with such force that the bat broke into two pieces that clattered down onto the cobbles.

Ronnie's eyes rolled in his head, as he was knocked unconscious for the first time. He staggered forward before collapsing in a heap on top of Billy Bates.

The smuggler struggled with all his might to roll the giant off him, but as Billy Bates climbed to his feet ready to congratulate the man who'd saved his skin, he found himself all alone with the only sound coming from boots hitting the cobbles as his saviour fled the scene. Billy Bates wondered which of his men had rescued him and why they'd run away, a mystery that would keep him up at night for many years to come.

Chapter Two

Eleven years earlier on the Kent coast

The young man was standing alone in the darkness on the shingle beach several miles up the coast from the town of Deal, a dangerous place full of sailors and cutthroats where survival was a daily challenge. A bolt of lightning lit up the sky as deafening thunder filled the air, but the man continued his vigil as he stood staring out at the English Channel and braving the heavy wind that had whipped her up into a fury.

Suddenly, the moon appeared through a break in the clouds which lit up the beach revealing the seventeen year old with his black pony tail blowing in the wind and his most distinguishable feature, his pitch black eyes that were busy scanning the treacherous stretch of water that separated England from the continent. The stretch was only twenty-two miles long but so dangerous it had claimed thousands of ships over the years with its hidden sandbanks that lay just under the surface waiting for the next unsuspecting vessel. Finally, the young man's heart began to race as he made out the ship he was searching for on the horizon battling its way towards the Kent coast as waves crashed around her, then the thick clouds covered the moon once more and the channel fell into darkness.

Billy Bates smiled to himself. Navigating the channel in the darkness was difficult enough but in conditions like this it was an act of suicide for even the most experienced of sailors, but not for Bill's best friend and the man who had taught him everything he knew about the sea.

His friend Benny had grown up on the channel, and had worked on the fishing fleet from the age of eight. Benny had first taken the ship's wheel at the age of ten and had steered such an impressive course the fishermen he worked for began training him in navigation that very day. Eight years of steering through the shifting sandbanks on a daily basis had taught Benny the locations of every wreck and safe passage the treacherous sandbanks had to offer. Benjamin knew her so well he could literally navigate her in the dark.

Billy Bates had been friends with Benny since the first day he'd gone to work on the fishing fleet three years ago. At fourteen Bill had been abandoned. He was young and desperate. Benny who was the same age had taken him under his wing, teaching him how to tie knots and sew nets. Within weeks, Bill was up to scratch and manning the decks of the ship they worked on. The pair came from similar backgrounds; they'd both been born into poverty. From that first day, they'd been inseparable and for years, they'd worked like dogs for a pittance.

It had been Bill's idea to start smuggling merchandise across the channel in the dead of night; he'd always been smart and ambitious and was keen to put Benny's unique skills to use. Benny himself was less keen but after weeks and weeks of Bill's pleading the young fisherman had finally given in.

The pair had been patient and had waited until a dark and stormy night when they knew that nobody would be out at sea. Conditions out on the channel were terrible, and yet perfect to bring their first cargo of smuggled goods into the country.

Bill glanced up and down the empty beach all too aware of the risks they were taking, if they got caught smuggling they'd both face hard justice from the law, but that wasn't what scared him. If anyone in the town's dangerous underworld found out the two young scallywags were running cargoes they'd face an even harder backlash for not returning a share of the profits to the ruthless Jenkins clan, a huge gang of thugs currently running illegal activities in the town.

Billy Bates however didn't fear the Jenkins clan. Like his friend Benny, Bill had his own set of skills. The young man with jet black eyes was manipulative, calculating and completely ruthless. He feared nothing in life and believed he could easily outsmart the clan and land cargoes without their knowledge.

Scanning the English Channel spread out in front of him in the darkness, the young smuggler could make out several ships on the horizon anchored up, waiting out the bad weather. Only one was making a course for the coastline. Confident they were alone on this dark stormy night Bill pulled out a small brass lamp that he lit and used to flash a signal to the only person he trusted in the world. A few moments later, he observed the small fishing lugger that was hauling the pair's first cargo shift direction as his friend altered its course.

Bill smiled to himself, confident that the plan they'd discussed for weeks in whispered tones whilst out fishing on the channel was running like clockwork.

Suddenly though Bill heard a creak somewhere behind him and the young smuggler spun around and pulled a dagger from his waistband in one swift movement, whilst he scanned the clumps of bush. His heart raced as he stood ready to do battle, but after a long moment he concluded he was still alone and he breathed a sigh of relief.

Turning his attention back to the task at hand, he watched as a small rowing boat made its way from the ship to the shoreline. Finally, Billy Bates marched down the shingle as pebbles crunched under his feet. The rowing boat pulled up onto the beach in silence and Benny climbed out whilst his shoulder length blond hair blew in the wind. Another man was sitting ready to row the boat back out to sea. He was a good navigator, but nowhere near talented enough to steer a course in the dark. He would remain at anchor off the coast until dawn broke and he could sail away in safety. Meanwhile Benny and Bill began to unload the rowboat in silence; they hauled out bales of tobacco and barrels of brandy. The whole process only took a few minutes and before they knew it the small boat was rowing back out to sea, leaving the pair alone on the beach.

"Safe journey?" Bill asked the man who'd taught him virtually everything he knew, as Benny laughed to himself.

"You've seen it out there, Bill," he said nodding towards the channel as the wind nearly blew them both over and huge waves crashed down onto the beach. "Let's just say the journey had its fair share of scary moments."

Bill turned to his friend and fixed those dark eyes of his on Benny. "Don't worry my brother we made more money tonight than we normally do in weeks. Now let's get this cargo stashed before we get our necks stretched," he said in that croaky voice of his, and with that Benjamin Swift strolled up the beach with Billy Bates, best friends and partners in crime, a partnership that would last a lifetime... or so they both thought.

Chapter Three

Early the following morning when the first rays of sunlight broke through the small window of the old shack Benjamin had lived his entire life, the talented navigator woke immediately. Feeling exhausted he yawned to himself before climbing to his feet. Bill was still in a deep slumber on the floor where he'd slept every night since the day Benny had taken him in years before. Bill's mother had passed away when the young smuggler was only fourteen years old, leaving the pauper with nobody. Luckily, Bill had secured a job working on the fishing fleet.

Benny yawned again and rubbed his eyes. Stacked neatly on the floor of the shack were the bales of tobacco and tubs of brandy the pair had spent the early hours transporting. Looking them over Benny couldn't help but exhale a lungful of air. The highly skilled navigator, who loved taking risks out at sea with a wheel in his hands and a vessel under his feet, had far greater reservations about taking risks on land. Feeling nervous young Benny wanted the cargo out of his house; he'd agreed to go along with Bill's plan in the end after weeks of his friend's nagging. He'd agreed because he wanted to prove to himself that he could take anything the English Channel could throw at him, but he wasn't so sure he wanted to become an actual smuggler. Benny was confident that his role in the partnership was risk free. It was his task to get the cargo across the channel and he knew that if anyone ever gave chase he would just cut through the Pegwell Channel, a small stream of water running between the main sandbanks and littered with countless wrecks under the waterline. Benny knew that no sailor in his right mind would follow his course and if they did it would be at their own peril.

What concerned Benjamin Swift most was his friend's share of the partnership. It was Billy Bates' task to sell the merchandise and collect the money from a crooked merchant over in the port of Sandwich.

The merchant knew only too well that the pair were operating without the consent of the Jenkins family. He'd agreed to adjust the figures of the goods he brought into the country legally. According to Bill the merchant was trustworthy and they'd never be caught, Benjamin wasn't so sure.

The Jenkins family were led by a man named Dale, who was an ex-prize-fighter with a fearsome reputation. Dale Jenkins was very smart and controlled the area with ruthless efficiency. The man had connections everywhere and it was well known that he paid generously for information. Many people were eager to impress the Jenkins family's leader. Benny Swift was concerned the merchant would cheat him and Bill knowing they could do nothing in return, or even worse sell them out to Dale Jenkins and his clan who'd crucify them both just to set an example in the town's cobbled streets.

Suddenly Benny was pulled from his thoughts by a loud noise and he glanced down at his friend who was still asleep on the floor and snoring loudly. Benny leant down and shook Bill who opened one of his beady dark eyes and stared at him, causing them both to laugh. A moment later Billy Bates was climbing to his feet and dusting himself off.

"God I'm exhausted. We must have had two hours sleep at most, come on let's take the day off, we can afford it," Bill said in his croaky voice, knowing his friend would disagree.

Benjamin Swift turned to Bill and fixed him a serious look, causing Billy Bates to raise his hands in surrender. "Okay, okay, we stick to the plan," he muttered.

Benny sat on a tub of brandy whilst he pulled his boots on. "You know if we act out of character, take too much time off or flash money about we'll attract the attention of the Jenkins clan. Dale will send his henchmen after us without a second thought," the young navigator said. "And I only agreed to bring the goods over if nobody apart from me, you and your merchant friend knew about it."

Bill tied his black hair back in a ponytail and chuckled to himself. "Don't worry Benny old friend, I'm in agreement," he said, but deep down Billy Bates hated having to tip-toe about for fear of the Jenkins clan, who he regarded as a bunch of dumb in-bred thugs. "We'll get today's shift over with, then tonight we'll get this stuff out of here and over to Planter's warehouse," Bill promised.

A short while later they left the small shack, beginning their walk to the wooden jetty at the forefront of the rough and ready fishing town. Passing through the labyrinth of narrow cobbled streets, they watched the town come alive as sailors shook off the grog from the night before. Eventually reaching the jetty they climbed aboard the lugger, they were destined to spend another day working like slaves on for very little in return.

Hours later, after a long day out at sea and the sun had dropped from the sky, the pair struggled through the wind and rain hauling the smuggled cargo over to the docks at Sandwich where Robert Planter's headquarters were. Normally the merchant's warehouse was locked at such a late hour but on this dark night Bob Planter was there to meet Bill. The young merchant was only a few years older than Bill, but was already very successful in his own right. Robert Planter came from a long line of merchants who'd been trading on the banks of the Stour for generations. Bob had followed in his father's footsteps and taken over the family business. The merchant was true to his word and when Billy Bates left the warehouse and met his best friend, they stared in shock at the wad of money they'd made. Neither had ever been so wealthy, but as far as Bill was concerned it was only the beginning. The young man with eyes as dark as a moonless night had experienced his first taste of the life he dreamed of living, and as far as the young smuggler was concerned nothing, not even the Jenkins clan were going to stand in his way. But it wasn't going to be as plain sailing as Bill thought and before he achieved those dreams, a life would be lost.

Chapter Four

As the days passed into weeks and the weeks into months Billy Bates and Benjamin Swift landed a cargo roughly once every week in conditions that would make most sailors shudder.

The daring pair of young smugglers were very cautious and particular about what nights to land their cargoes. Every time they heard word of bad weather whilst out fishing on the channel or drinking in the town's shady taverns they'd share that knowing look.

Traffic out on the English Channel was high and ships of all different shapes and sizes sailed out of the royal ports littered along the south east coast of England, bringing goods to and fro from far off lands the young smugglers could only dream of.

Bill's friend, the merchant, Robert Planter was true to his word and bought every cargo the pair could land. Bob Planter was a good businessman and was making a good profit out of the pair of brave smugglers who were taking all of the risk.

Billy Bates and Benny were making good money, but they'd yet to spend a single penny of the profits they'd made. Underneath Benny's shack the pair had dug a deep hole in the ground where they'd wrapped up their money in linen cloth and hidden it. The pair often debated about what to do with the money. Bill was keen to start bringing in larger loads and use the money to hire some help to carry the cargo. He'd had enough of living like a peasant and wanted to expand. Bill wanted the town to know he was a somebody and didn't care about the consequences.

Benjamin Swift thought very differently. In many ways he admired Bill's courage, but he knew his friend's fearlessness would only land the pair in hot water when it caught the attention of Dale Jenkins and his gang. In .the end, Benny would always convince Bill to keep quiet about their night time activities.

Billy Bates knew that without Benny there would be no profit whatsoever. Bill could never borrow one of the fishing ships like his friend could, let alone sail her, so in the end he always agreed with his best friend, but deep down Bill knew that his friend couldn't restrain his ambition forever. On the other hand, Benny knew that his friend with the dark eyes and croaky voice had no problems about going to war with Dale Jenkins and his entire family who were nearly one hundred strong. Sometimes Benny would catch that glint in Bill's eyes and that crooked smile. During those moments the boy who'd grown to become one of the best navigators on the English Channel was certain his friend was actually looking forward to taking on Dale Jenkins and it scared Benny Swift more than anything the English Channel could throw at him.

Whilst the south coast of England was hit full force by a cycle of bad weather, unknown to the pair another threat emerged, a threat that could prove far more deadly.

Chapter Five

The storm raged on through the moonless night, whipping the English Channel up into a fury of white crested swells. Benjamin Swift gripped tightly onto the wheel of the ship and laughed like a maniac as the small lugger reached the top of another swell and plunged into a deep trough, before a huge wave broke over her deck covering Benny in freezing water that sunk deep down to his bones. Flicking back his blond hair with one hand the young navigator studied the coastline that lay ahead in the dark through those bright blue eyes of his. Smiling to himself, he was confident he had his bearings and in that moment of calm he reflected on the treacherous journey he'd made. A journey that had forced him to use all of his skills to make it this far with the ship still in one piece. The storm, that was blowing a gale and trying without mercy to tear the lugger to bits, had forced all other vessels caught in it to drop their anchors and sit the bad weather out. The channel was littered with dozens of ships that were out there hidden in the dark, and coupled with the dangerous sandbanks and the storm itself Benjamin Swift's skills were really being put to the test. Benny took a deep breath before the lugger was struck by yet another huge wave that washed over her deck as he clung on for dear life. Suddenly though fresh hope was restored as he caught a clear view of the Kent coast, instantly recognising the outline of the chalk cliffs that ran from Dover all the way along to Kingsdown, where a shingle beach ran several miles to the estuary of the River Stour. Studying the coastline Benny told himself that the hard part was over. He made slight alterations to his course, a course that would sail his ship all the way to the stretch of beach where he knew his friend Bill would be waiting. But on this particular night, the pair of young smugglers had much more than just a storm to worry about.

On dry land, several miles along the coast at least three dozen of the Jenkins clan were crowded around a blazing fire trying to gather warmth as the men passed around a bottle of rum. The Jenkins shared that same look with freckled cheeks, dimpled chins and broken noses. The scars they bore from the countless fights over the years being their only distinguishable features.

Stood alone staring out at the English Channel and being battered by the wind was their leader Dale Jenkins, with his bushy beard and wide shoulders. At forty years, he was the oldest of his nine brothers, but it wasn't his age that determined his leadership. Nearly two decades earlier when Dale was in his early twenties his clan had lived out in the countryside, a fair distance from the coast. The rough and ready family had lived off the land and traded with travellers. They had rarely left their camp. The drought of 1758 had caused their crops to fail and their entire family faced starvation, but young Dale who was built like a packhorse and as hard as nails hadn't been willing to let that happen. One night Dale and a handful of his younger siblings had marched into the port town of Dover, a dangerous place where sailors fought and drank in the countless drinking dens that littered the shoreline, where pickpockets roamed the streets lightening the pockets of merchants and ladies plied their trades through the night. Dale Jenkins was a desperate man; he had the survival of his entire family on his bulky shoulders. He was completely fearless and knew his brothers were not only tougher than most men but would follow his every word. Reaching a particularly rough pub known as The Bulls Head, a shady place near the docks packed full of the toughest sailors and bandits the county had to offer, the clan had marched straight into the main bar with Dale leading the way with a look of determination on his face. The new arrivals had caught everyone's attention as most of the tavern had stared in shock at the Jenkins clan. When Dale reached the bar he had smashed his fist down on the timber. That's when the cutthroat sailors and thieves had put down their tankards and silence had filled the tavern.

"So who is the toughest man in this town?" Dale had shouted at the shady crowd who eyed him with caution. After a long moment, a huge man with a nasty scar running from the corner of his eye all the way down to his chin had risen to his feet as people gasped in anticipation of trouble.

"That'd be me!" the man had growled at the intruders who'd invaded his territory. Dale Jenkins had strolled up to the man casually and swung a devastating right hook at the man's chin. Dale's fist had connected and a loud crack had echoed around the tavern, before the man hit the deck with a thud.

The crowd had let out a gasp before Dale Jenkins turned on them. "Anyone else think they're tough enough to fight the Jenkins family?" he had roared, but nobody gathered even had the courage to look him in the eye. Dale had stared at the crowd, happy that he'd achieved his aim. "My name is Dale Jenkins and from this day forth this town belongs to me!" he had stated before turning and marching out of the tavern with his brothers following him.

Over the following weeks, Dale and his clan had roamed up and down the coastline leaving a trail of destruction in their path. Dale was smart and understood the power of fear, but unlike his brothers Dale had control of his temper at all times. As months passed, the Jenkins clan had established themselves in towns up and down the coast, as rumours of their viciousness spread like wildfire. Dale began demanding protection money from known criminals. Eventually everyone who chose to live on the outskirts of the law paid a percentage to Dale Jenkins, whether you were a pickpocket, prostitute, bandit or smuggler. This 'donation' as Dale liked to call it not only guaranteed the clan wouldn't put you in a box but also provided protection from any other criminals muscling in on your patch.

Over the years, Dale built a sizable empire and created a huge revenue stream. The Jenkins bred like rabbits and over the years their numbers swelled in size and power.

Now as Dale Jenkins stared out at the English Channel on this stormy night he wondered about who would take charge of his family once he was gone. The gang leader turned and stared at his brother Samuel who was busy telling a story around the fire. Sammy was next in line to fill his boots. He was reliable and thought the world of his family. One day he'd make a good leader. Dale's mind wandered to his kids. The leader of the Jenkins clan had four boys, but it was his youngest Ronald that came to mind. The boy was only ten but already towered over his older brothers and sisters. He was really smart too and more often than not outsmarted his cousins. When that didn't work young Ronnie had no issues throwing punches. One way or another his youngest always got what he wanted. Deep down though Dale knew something wasn't quite right with Ronnie and it concerned Dale greatly. His youngest was unnecessarily cruel and way too aggressive. A few months earlier Dale had caught the boy beating a stray dog with a stick. By the time Dale had intervened the dog was half-dead. For Dale Jenkins aggression and violence were tools of his trade, but for Dale it was always business. That day when he'd asked his son why he'd beaten the dog young Ronnie had simply shrugged before replying "for fun".

A mighty gust of wind pulled Dale Jenkins from his thoughts and he buttoned his coat up and rubbed his hands together as he watched the channel and the outlines of countless vessels at anchor in the dark. Suddenly he spotted movement and he pulled out a small brass telescope and peered through its lens. Battling through the storm towards the coastline was a small ship. Dale watched it for a moment admiring the captain's bravery to sail in such treacherous conditions before turning towards the campfire.

"Sammy," the leader roared, silencing his younger brother who was still telling his story. Samuel Jenkins rose to his feet and joined his brother.

"Who's landing cargoes tonight?" Dale demanded as he continued to peer through his scope at the vessel sailing towards the shore several miles up the coast. Samuel Jenkins pulled out his ledger and began flicking through its pages. It was Sammy who was responsible for the smuggling arm of the family business.

After a few minutes Samuel looked up from the ledger at his older brother. "Nobody had any plans for landing tonight," Sammy said looking over at the stormy channel. "And who'd sail in that?"

Dale Jenkins gritted his teeth and watched as the ship made its way out to sea once more, before turning to his brother. "Speak to your people and find out if anyone decided to run a cargo at the last minute. If they didn't then someone's landing on our shores without consent. If that's the case then I want to know who. Put the word about town that we'll pay handsomely for any information," Dale ordered before the gang leader turned and strolled back over to the campfire leaving his younger brother staring out at the English Channel alone.

Samuel Jenkins swallowed down his anger as he stared at the vessel barely visible out in the darkness. Somebody had just made him look a fool in front of his big brother and by God would Sammy punish them for it.

Chapter Six

Local smuggling boss Harry Booth was sitting in his favourite tavern The Seagull, a small drinking den only a stone's throw away from the shoreline, waiting for his weekly sit down with Samuel Jenkins, a meeting he dreaded. Every week Samuel, who he'd been doing business with for years, always smiled and pretended they were great friends as he extorted money from the smuggler whilst Harry played along in fear of the repercussions. Secretly Harry hated the Jenkins clan and everything they stood for.

The Seagull itself was a rough place. The sort of place you went to escape life's problems and drink yourself into a stupor on cheap liquor that Harry's gang supplied. Many of The Seagull's patrons would drink until they passed out, only to wake up with a sore head and a crooked neck and begin the cycle once again. For Harry Booth The Seagull was a place to discuss shady business in safety, away from prying ears and unless you were known and trusted in the town's criminal underworld then your presence in the pub wasn't welcome.

Harry had been smuggling his whole life. Over the last twenty years he'd built a strong crew numbering nearly two dozen and landing several cargoes week in week out. Like everyone else in the town that made a living on the wrong side of the law, Harry paid a sizable percentage of the profits to the Jenkins family. The smuggler resented giving away such a substantial share of his income but he'd realised a long time ago that he had little choice. Once the Jenkins clan was making money from you then retirement wasn't an option.

When Harry met with Samuel the pair would discuss the smuggler's plans for the upcoming week. Sammy would interrogate the smuggling boss, demanding to know what nights Harry was landing cargoes, where and exactly what merchandise was being brought in. Samuel would then record all of this information in his ledger before calculating how much money he figured the smuggler owed his family, a figure Harry could never argue over.

Harry Booth had realised many years ago that Dale Jenkins wasn't just a vicious fighter but a very clever man who cross-referenced all of the information his family was fed from all of their sources. Every night he made his family sit around the fire and explain what they'd been told and from whom. Dale had managed to keep his family's grip on the area for so long because he knew everything about everyone. If you lied to Dale Jenkins he'd find out one way or another, and then you'd have to pay the price.

When Samuel Jenkins marched into The Seagull with half a dozen of his men the smuggler knew something was up immediately. Harry smiled as Samuel slumped into a chair opposite him, but Sammy Jenkins just glared in return. An awkward silence filled the air as seven sets of eyes peered at the smuggler.

"Is there a problem Samuel?" Harry finally asked. Samuel pondered this for a long moment before rubbing the stubble on his chin. Two cups of brandy were placed on the table whilst Sammy just stared into Harry's eyes, making the smuggler feel very threatened. Eventually Samuel picked up his brandy and drained it in one gulp. Feeling on edge Harry Booth followed suit and then finally Samuel Jenkins spoke.

"Yeah I believe we do have a problem. Did you land any goods last night?" he asked the smuggler who was looking very puzzled.

"Last night," he exclaimed. "It was blowing a gale, of course I didn't."

Samuel Jenkins gritted his teeth, like most of his family the man was well known for his outbursts of violence.

"Nobody would sail in that," the experienced smuggler continued, as Sammy studied the table looking deep in thought before glancing up and looking Harry in the eyes.

"Someone was! Dale saw it with his own eyes," Sammy informed Harry who'd been running cargoes on the channel his whole life. The smuggler thought back to the storm the previous evening.

"It can't be," he muttered.

Suddenly Samuel Jenkins exploded in anger. "Are you calling my brother a liar?" he roared as one of his clan stepped forward and pulled out a dagger.

"No, of course not," Harry pleaded, "but I don't sail in conditions like that you'd have to be crazy."

Samuel Jenkins stared for a long moment at the smuggler he'd been doing business with for nearly two decades. "Nobody sails during a storm and that's why they ran a cargo, Harry," he finally hissed through clenched teeth. "Someone's operating without permission, on territory my family have given you exclusive rights to. This is just as much your problem as mine. I suggest you figure out who this gutsy individual is; otherwise we'll start charging you extra to cover the cost of their shares too. You understand?" he warned.

Harry Booth nodded. "I understand Samuel and believe me I'll look into it," he promised before the pair got down to the upcoming week's business.

When Samuel Jenkins marched out of the tavern with his foot soldiers in tow Harry Booth sat and pondered the situation for a long while. In the end he dismissed it as nonsense. The experienced smuggler had seen the weather the previous evening and doubted that what Dale had seen was even possible. *'Dale Jenkins must have been mistaken,'* Harry thought, but the smuggling boss couldn't have been more wrong.

Chapter Seven

Within days Harry Booth forgot all about Samuel's bizarre claim. The town's top smuggler reasoned that Dale Jenkins had been mistaken and Samuel would eventually calm down. Blessed with good weather Harry concentrated on the task at hand and over the next week he brought a wide selection of goods over from the continent. His men smuggled barrels of brandy, bales of tobacco, French lace and great sacks of tea aboard his ship.

Then suddenly out of nowhere the weather changed. The wind picked up and a storm hit the small coastal town as rain lashed from the sky and cleared the cobbled streets, filling the town's drinking dens to the hilt with sailors whose ships were sitting at anchor off the coast waiting for the storm to pass.

Being a hardworking man Harry Booth hated waiting out bad weather. The smuggler sat in his local tavern with his men, a rough and ready bunch he'd spent years putting together. The Seagull was doing a roaring trade. Harry stared out of a bay window at the stormy channel and the ships bobbing around on her surface, whilst wind and rain shook the pane of glass. It was only when one of Harry's crew cracked a joke about sailing through the storm that the smuggler was reminded of the previous conversation he'd had with Samuel Jenkins and began wondering if there was any truth to it. After several more pots of ale curiosity got the better of Harry Booth and he decided to go for a walk along the shoreline to investigate the Jenkins' bizarre claim.

The smuggler staggered along the beach as shingle crunched under his feet and the wind and rain battered him. Occasionally he would pause and stare out to sea; thick storm clouds had covered the moon and stars so effectively that Harry could barely make out a thing. He stood on the beach and laughed to himself for giving any credit to the Jenkins' claim and not staying in the pub out of the wind and rain. He was just about to turn back and return to The Seagull for a nightcap when the storm clouds broke for a moment and the English Channel lit up before him. Smiling and breathing in a lungful of salt air the smuggler admired the sight in all its glory. Suddenly though a flicker of movement caught Harry's eyes and took his breath away. Focusing on the horizon Harry made out the outline of a small ship at full sail heading towards the coast where he stood, the coastline he had exclusive rights to smuggle on! He stared in shock for a long moment before anger took hold of him, anger because somebody was stepping on his toes and smuggling on his patch, but also because the Jenkins had been right and he'd been wrong. With a head full of ale he wasn't thinking clearly and leapt into action. The experienced smuggler raced along the shoreline towards the wooden jetty where his clipper was moored.

Harry clambered onto her already drenched deck and rushed around setting her off. A moment later he raised her main sail, which snapped in the wind, and without a cargo weighing her down she flew out into the channel. With a belly full of ale and twenty years' worth of smuggling on the coast behind him Harry Booth was confident he could chase the ship down. Now as the anger began to subside it was replaced by fear as Harry's clipper was hit from all angles and waves washed over her deck. The old smuggler instantly regretted the drunken decision to launch his vessel in such terrible conditions; he'd been spurred on by the sight of the phantom ship that was still making progress towards him. Harry Booth had thought that if anyone could sail in this then he could, but he now knew he was wrong. Whoever was navigating the mysterious vessel wasn't just crazy they were incredibly skilled. More skilled than anyone Harry Booth knew and he knew them all.

Meanwhile in the midst of a hellish storm Benjamin Swift clung to his ship's wheel for dear life. He'd had to put all of his skills to hand just to get over the channel and unknown to the young navigator his journey was far from over.

Turning to his deckhand Benny Swift ordered a depth reading only to hear the bad news he'd been expecting. The hour was approaching low tide, which meant the hidden sandbanks were even closer to the surface, and posed a far greater threat to the hull of the old fishing lugger, a hull that would split like matchwood if Benny made the slightest of mistakes. Another wave broke over the deck and Benny wondered if things could get any worse and then fate answered his question as he spotted a rival ship racing towards him. The young smuggler knew straight away that the ship out there in the dark belonged to the town's smuggling boss Harry Booth, an ally of the Jenkins family, and Benny also knew that the only reason it was sailing was to catch him red handed. Benny's heart began to race and a new type of fear flooded through him. All the storms in the world couldn't match the fear of Dale Jenkins and his clan who'd tear Benny and his best friend Bill Bates to pieces. The young smuggler took a deep breath of salt air and stared at Harry Booth's vessel. The ship was a clipper, the ship of choice for smuggling and much faster than the lugger Benny sailed. He knew the smuggling boss had spent a lifetime on the channel and had a lot of experience under his belt, but could Harry's skills match his own he wondered.

"You want me, come and get me," Benny muttered as he swung his ship portside and altered his course, turning his ship away from the wide stream that ran between the two main sandbanks and into a slipstream called the Pegwell, which at such low tide and in such harsh conditions was a suicidal move even for him.

Harry Booth was making progress towards the mysterious vessel and was confident he'd be able to sail close enough to get a good look at her. That was all the old smuggler needed to do. He'd been sailing for decades and knew every ship in the area. Tomorrow Harry would go pay the men who were threatening his livelihood a visit, backed up with a dozen of his toughest men. Suddenly Harry was pulled from his thoughts as the phantom ship abruptly changed its course and sailed straight into the most dangerous area of the entire English

Channel, an area so treacherous it had claimed hundreds of ships and countless lives over the years. For a moment Harry Booth stared in shock before he smiled to himself.

'So you don't know these waters,' he thought, confident his rival had sealed his own fate and solved Harry's problems for him. Harry knew the Pegwell Channel through the sandbanks was a minefield even at high tide. Dropping his mainsail Harry Booth laughed to himself as he slowed his ship ready to watch the phantom ship flounder and sink.

Benny Swift took some deep breaths as adrenalin pumped through his veins and he gathered his bearings, focusing his mind as he pictured the layout of the sandbanks below his feet. A moment later he swung his wheel forty-five degrees to the right and his ship answered him immediately. Watching the dark churning water passing by the young navigator calculated his speed in his head and held his course for a long moment whilst his deckhand clung on for his life looking pale, terrified, and knowing that if he disturbed Benny in his work they'd both die in the water within the hour. Then Benjamin Swift swung the wheel to the left sixty degrees and instantly his ship swung bow side. Below his feet the vessel's hull missed a sandbank by mere inches. A huge wave rose out of nowhere, thrown up by the hidden sandbank and it engulfed the small lugger. For a long moment Benny thought she'd topple and it was all over but suddenly the wave washed over her deck and the ship was upright once more. Staring at the chalk cliffs in the distance Benny gathered his bearings by locating the remains of several wrecks protruding above the waterline. Then he steered the ship through a handful of crazy manoeuvres before the highly skilled young man who'd been sailing since he was ten years old finally reached the other side of the Pegwell Channel and entered safe water where he breathed a sigh of relief. After gathering his breath the young smuggler began sailing further along the coast where he knew of a natural inlet he could drop anchor. Benjamin Swift wasn't too worried now; he knew the immediate danger was over. He'd planned with Billy Bates exactly what to do in a situation like this and Benny knew that his best friend would have witnessed the chase through those dark eyes of his. Benny would rendezvous with Bill later in a different spot and the young navigator was certain his friend would be there. Billy Bates would never let his friend down, Benny knew that and it was that very fact that made the decision he'd made that much harder. The only thing that concerned Benny Swift was telling his friend that he could no longer sail smuggled cargo. Tonight's events had taught Benjamin that the risk was far too great.

Peering through his telescope out into the darkness Harry Booth watched in absolute shock as the mysterious ship began sailing from left to right in a slalom through the Pegwell Channel. The old smuggler watched in admiration as the ship carried out the most impressive feat of navigation Harry Booth had ever seen. As the vessel avoided every obstacle in its path Harry knew two things, firstly someone with immense skill that easily outmatched his own was smuggling in his territory, and secondly Harry could never mention the evening's events to Samuel Jenkins who would go berserk and punish Harry in the process. The old smuggler watched the mysterious vessel vanish into the distance before turning his ship back towards the coastline. Sailing towards the town and safety, Harry's ship was battered by everything nature could throw at her but the man behind the wheel had far bigger problems than the storm to worry about.

Chapter Eight

After that disastrous run across the channel, Benny Swift and Billy Bates argued for days on end.

Benny wanted to take a long break from smuggling. "We nearly got our necks stretched Bill," he shouted at his friend during a particularly bad argument. Bill understood the risks, but he really didn't care about getting caught. Bill liked the idea of living on the edge and watching his back constantly.

"Look at us Benny," he'd shouted back, indicating the ramshackle home where they lived. "We have nothing in this world and nothing to lose. Don't you want more out of life?"

Infuriated Benny turned on his friend. "Of course I do Bill, but life isn't fair. If we carry on smuggling we will get caught, you know that," Benny fired back at Bill who glared at him before storming out of the shack.

In the end Benny refused to sail any more cargoes until the end of the year. Bill sulked for a few days but eventually the pair made up and went out for a few drinks in the town.

The pair were sitting in The Black Horse, a huge tavern with room to seat a hundred. The place was packed out with men drinking and gambling their wages away, whilst an old sailor played a battered piano in the corner. Billy Bates tucked a strand of his shoulder length black hair behind his ear and raised his beaker to toast his best friend.

"Well we had a good run, Swifty," he said in that croaky voice of his. "To catching fish," he finished and they both laughed. Benny clinked his beaker against Bill's before taking a big gulp of ale.

Finally he fixed those blue eyes of his on Bill. "It could have been a lot worse my brother, and one day when they've forgotten all about us we'll land a few more," he whispered. Bill smiled before hitting his beaker against his friend's and taking another gulp. The pair were in good spirits having laid their recent arguments to rest.

Suddenly the atmosphere changed in the tavern as the piano player stopped playing mid song and hushed tones filled the drinking den, as Dale Jenkins himself walked in the doorway. Billy Bates watched the man whose reputation as a fighter was unmatched by anyone in the area. Dale stood there with his greying hair and beard blowing in the wind from the open door, his eyes taking in the tavern and the men gathered. Bill could see the man was past his prime but his shoulders and arms were still ripped with muscles. Dale had lost little of the bulk he'd had and was still a man to be feared. Billy Bates smiled that crooked smile of his as he watched Dale Jenkins march in the tavern like he owned the place. The Jenkins clan always travelled in numbers and tonight they were at full force and at least forty strong, filing through the door one after another. A dozen men rose to their feet to greet the gang leader who strolled to the bar, flanked by several bodyguards as he shook hands with sailors and criminals alike.

"Stop staring," he heard Benny whisper, but Bill paid little attention. He watched Dale in admiration hoping that one day the town's people would greet him with as much respect. Bill had been born and bred in the gutter and unlike Benny had no intention of dying there. The young man with eyes as black and shiny as wet ink was willing to do whatever it took to be a 'somebody' in the town's cobbled streets. Eventually he looked away and smiled at his best friend who took a big gulp of ale.

"Let's get out of here," Benny said, "before we get ourselves in trouble." Bill smiled and finished his drink before the pair rose to their feet and began making their way across the crowded bar. They reached the door and were just about to step outside when one of the Jenkins foot soldiers stepped in their way blocking their path. Benny's heart missed a beat whilst Bill simply stepped forward so that his nose was only an inch away from the man and he fixed him with those dark eyes of his.

"Do we have a problem?" he asked in that croaky voice. The foot soldier took a step backwards without realising it.

"My Uncle Sammy wants a word with you two, follow me," he ordered, before marching across the crowded bar. Bill glanced at Benny and shrugged his shoulders. He had that carefree look in those dark eyes of his and Benny thought that look scared him even more than Dale Jenkins.

Bill leant in close. "Let me do the talking," he said as he turned and followed the foot soldier over to a large wooden table where Dale and Samuel were sitting talking to several shady characters, whilst a dozen of the Jenkins clan were crowded around the table protecting their leader from any threat that could arise. When the pair of young smugglers approached the table the Jenkins bodyguards glared at them. Benny Swift looked down at the floor trying to avoid eye contact at all costs. Billy Bates on the other hand marched over as bold as brass and even returned the glare much to the Jenkins' obvious anger. Dale Jenkins looked up at the pair as the man who'd blocked the doorway interrupted Samuel's conversation. Bill tipped his head at the clan's leader who returned the gesture with a look of curiosity on his face. His younger brother Samuel dismissed the men he'd been talking to.

"Sit," he ordered as the pair sat down on wooden stools.

"So what can a pair of fishermen like us do for a man like you?" Bill asked, showing his lack of fear which was instantly taken as a sign of disrespect by every member of the Jenkins family that were present. Out of the corner of his eye Benny watched Dale Jenkins smile at his friend's boldness.

"You boys have been working out on the fishing fleet for years," Samuel said before turning his attention on Benjamin Swift, "and some say you know the sands better than anyone," he said before turning his attention back on Bill. "Someone's been smuggling goods across the channel without my family's permission and whoever it is knows that channel," Samuel finished, letting it hang in the air.

A silence fell over the table for the briefest of moments before Bill began laughing much to everyone's surprise. "You think me and Swifty here are smugglers?" he asked but didn't wait for a reply. "Look at us!" he demanded pointing at the rags they both wore. "We work all the hours God sends us and we can barely afford to eat," he said glaring at Samuel Jenkins, and his family didn't like it one bit. Benny watched several of the bodyguards step forward ready to attack Bill for disrespecting their family.

Benny rose to his feet and intervened at the very last moment. "Listen Mr Jenkins," he said to Samuel. "I apologise for my friend, he's had too much ale. We are just poor fishermen. We wouldn't dare smuggle, let alone on your doorstep. We haven't missed a day's work in a long time, you can check with our boss," he pleaded.

Samuel Jenkins looked Benny Swift up and down and regained a little bit of his composure. "You know lad, you're a lot smarter than your friend here," he said, nodding at Bill.

"For what it's worth I've already checked with your boss, but I thought it's time we had a chat anyway," he stated as he leant in close to Benny. "You see lad, only a handful of sailors are skilled enough to navigate the channel in the dark and unfortunately the word on these streets is that you're one of them. I'm just making sure that you two are not my family's problem. Now take your friend and get out of here," Samuel said. Benny nodded and went to walk away; hoping that it was over but Bill Bates held his ground. Immediately one of the Jenkins pulled out a dagger and looked at Dale for permission to use it, but the gang leader was sitting nursing his beaker of ale with a smile on his face.

"Lad you've got a lot of guts I give you that and it's a quality I admire in people, but you should listen to your friend more," Dale said casually. "Now get the hell out of here before I give the order and one of my men kills you where you stand."

Billy Bates nodded before he turned and followed his best friend out of the tavern, completely unaware of the man who stared at him in admiration from the other side of the bar for standing up to the Jenkins gang. That man was local smuggling boss Harry Booth who'd been pushed around by Sammy Jenkins and his thugs for way too long.

Chapter Nine

That night in the tavern changed everything for Billy Bates and Benny Swift who'd grown into men at each other's sides. It had confirmed all of Benny's fears and cemented his decision to give up smuggling once and for all. The young man who could sail through any storm admired Bill's fearlessness, but knew it was a quality he lacked. Time passed by and the young man with eyes like lumps of coal struggled day in, day out, repairing holes in the nets and reeling in the catch trying to forget his dream and bury the ambition that burned away within him whilst he slaved away out on the channel.

Autumn turned to winter and young Benny still refused to sail any smuggled cargoes, much to his best friend's despair. The pair would go out in the town's cobbled streets and get drunk in the shady drinking dens once every week. It was on one of these occasions that Benny Swift met Anna Harrison for the first time and the young navigator fell head over heels in love. Anna was a little younger than Benny and had long blonde hair down to her hips. For a living she would dig for lugworm along the sandy beach near the estuary of the River Stour. It was hard work but it earned Anna enough money to put food in her mouth and clothes on her back. Bill had never seen his friend so happy before and even though he was pleased for him he couldn't help but feel threatened. Billy Bates had nobody in the world but Benny Swift. The pair were like brothers and now that Benny was spending so much time with the woman he loved Bill felt alone once more, just like he'd been when his mother had died years before. Anna loved Benny in a way that Bill never could. She adored his best friend too and understood that Billy Bates would die for Benny without a second thought, but she also knew that one day Bill would get him into trouble and Anna loved Benny too much to allow that to happen. Anna was against smuggling from the start and always discouraged Benny from agreeing to his friend's demands.

When the pair were out on the channel fishing Bill found he daydreamed more and more about becoming a smuggler and landing goods every night, whilst Benny would talk non-stop about Anna. During these moments Bill would always grit his teeth and look away out at the channel so his closest friend wouldn't realise his true feelings, feelings Bill felt ashamed for even having.

One evening Bill strolled into the shack and was greeted by Benny who had a huge smile on his face and Bill could have sworn those blue eyes of his were sparkling more than ever. In the end curiosity got the better of Bill.

"So what's made you so happy?" he asked in that croaky voice, as he watched Benny turn and face him.

"Anna's expecting, I'm going to be a father," his friend exclaimed and Bill grabbed hold of him and hugged him tightly before the pair toasted the good news with a cup of brandy. Then they talked long into the night and Bill informed his friend that he would move out of the shack in the next few weeks.

"You don't have to do that," Benny argued, but Bill wouldn't listen.

"You're going to have your own family now, my brother," Bill said, and even though he was really happy for his best friend, Billy Bates knew that the dream he'd shared with Benny for years was finally over and Bill felt more alone than he'd ever felt.

A few days later Billy Bates moved out of the shack he'd shared with his best friend for years. The young fisherman rented a room in a rundown house overlooking the sea. It was expensive but for Bill it was only temporary. When Anna was nearly due to give birth Benny Swift, who had financial concerns, finally succumbed to his friend's pleading and agreed to land one more cargo.

"I'm not landing anywhere near this coast. I'll sail into that small cove in the cliffs on the other side of the estuary," Benny said, as Bill pictured the inlet where he'd met his friend on the evening that Harry Booth had nearly caught them. It was miles from the Jenkins territory and perfectly suited for the job.

Bill nodded in agreement. "We have a deal, my brother," he said excitedly.

A few days later they landed the largest cargo they'd ever smuggled. There was so much merchandise that Bill had to borrow a few horses from a farmer he knew to transport it all back to Planter's warehouse. The pair made a healthy profit and hope was restored in Bill's dream. That crooked smile returned to Bill's face and it looked like everything was going to work out just fine, but things were not destined to be that way.

Chapter Ten

Many miles away from the town's cobbled streets, across the open fields and flat landscape of Kent, an agricultural fair was taking place. It was a huge event that attracted farmers from all over the country who came to trade horses and livestock and meet up with friends and family from neighbouring counties. One of the biggest attractions though was the bare-knuckle fights in an arena made from bales of hay; this particular event brought tough gypsy fighters from all over the south of England to the Kent show. The gypsy travellers were tough people who lived off the land. Most were handy with their fists and eager to prove it.

When the Jenkins clan marched into the fair one hundred strong they caught the attention of everyone and the atmosphere changed in a heartbeat. Dale and Samuel led the way, closely followed by their fighter for the day, Ronnie who at sixteen years old stood at 6 feet 3 inches towering over the rest of their clan. With huge shoulders that rippled with muscles, Dale's youngest was a force to be reckoned with. Marching towards the arena like their own private army the Jenkins clan passed pens of cattle, whilst farmers nudged each other and glanced over at Ronnie before whispering amongst themselves.

They all knew of the notorious Jenkins family, a name that put the fear of death into even the most hardened of men. Many years before, Dale Jenkins had carved himself a reputation with his fists, fighting at fairs like this one. Now it was his son's turn to uphold the family name, but that wasn't the only reason Dale had put his son in the ring. Dale had been teaching his youngest to fight for years in the hope it would install some sort of self-control in the boy. So far Dale had failed but the leader hoped today would be different. Ronnie was huge, quick on his feet and fearless like his father. Dale had high hopes of victory for his son and the family expected to make a lot of money betting on their young fighter.

Approaching the arena young Ronnie was pleased to see a huge crowd of tough gypsies eager to watch some blood be spilt. *'Oh I'll give you a show,'* Ronnie thought as his father was spotted by the crowd. At events like this Dale Jenkins was a celebrity and dozens of men shook his hand and welcomed him, as his family took up their positions ready for the fight.

Dale, Samuel and Ronnie himself were led around the back of the arena where the leader of the clan was greeted by Sean McGregor, an old friend, ex prize-fighter and leader of one of the largest gypsy families in the country.

"Dale Jenkins, it's been too long," the gypsy said before they shook hands. Standing by him was his own fighter who Ronnie eyeballed.

A moment later a short man who was refereeing the bout joined the group. "Good afternoon gentlemen," he said. "This fight's under Broughton's rules, I don't want to see any low blows, eye gouging or biting or you'll be disqualified, understand?" he asked and they all agreed. Then Dale led his son aside to prepare him for the bout.

"Sammy, go and place the bet," he ordered his younger brother, who turned to him.

"All of it? Are you sure? Their fighter looks tough," he said, causing Ronnie to grit his teeth. The young fighter and his Uncle Sammy rarely saw eye to eye.

"Yes all of it," Dale demanded, before Sammy walked away leaving Dale and his son alone.

"Now listen to me lad. Today you play by the rules, understand?" Dale ordered, Ronnie grunted as he warmed up for the fight. "You need to learn to control yourself. If a fighter's getting the better of you then you be patient and bide your time, okay?" Dale continued.

"I get it! Now lead me to the ring so I can tear that guy apart," Ronnie spat.

Dale chuckled. "That's my boy," he muttered as he began making his way towards the arena.

Entering the arena the crowd cheered at the sight of Dale and his youngest son. Ronnie entered the ring, joining his adversary who flashed him an evil glare. The man was at least a decade older than Ronnie and was far more experienced, but that meant nothing to Ronnie who was focusing all his anger and hatred on the man in front of him. He could hear the cheers from his family who made up a large proportion of the crowd, but Ronnie didn't take his eyes off his opponent.

Suddenly the bell rang and the gypsy ran at Ronnie, throwing a barrage of wild punches that Ronnie easily avoided. Hearing his father's words clearly, 'Duck and weave boy', young Ronnie impressed the crowd with his footwork as he avoided a left hook and a savage uppercut. Ronnie was focused and wanted to win the fight his father's way. Impressing Dale Jenkins meant more to Ronnie than anything. In the past when he'd been hit he'd lost his temper and all self-control. Young Ronnie wasn't going to let that happen today. Seeing an opportunity the young fighter threw his first punch, a body shot to the chest that stopped his opponent in his tracks, then Ronnie tried to follow it up with a punch to the head but the gypsy ducked out of Ronnie's range at the last moment.

The pair circled each other like animals as the crowd roared. The gypsy leapt forward and faked a dummy punch with his left, a split second before he threw a hard right hook that connected with Ronnie's jaw. The young fighter sprung into action and returned a barrage of blows that the gypsy easily avoided. The gypsy was using all his years of experience to his advantage as he moved around the ring. Ronnie was following his father's advice and being patient, slowly circling the gypsy and waiting for that moment when he'd strike and knock the man unconscious with a shot to the jaw. The gypsy wasn't stupid though. He was weary of Ronnie's sheer size and unwilling to present him with an opportunity. Suddenly the gypsy stepped forward and managed a jab that got through Ronnie's defence and caught him straight in the mouth splitting his lip and forcing blood to pour down his chin. The crowd roared as the gypsy threw another punch that caught Ronnie on the temple. Suddenly as the pain registered Ronnie

Jenkins saw red and lost all control. He elbowed the gypsy in the face and followed it up with a head butt that broke the man's nose. The Jenkins clan went wild but Ronnie couldn't hear a thing, the young fighter had zoned out completely and was virtually chasing the gypsy across the ring. Suddenly the gypsy stopped retreating and rushed forward and punched Ronnie with all his might. But it didn't stop the young fighter who rushed forward and grabbed his opponent around the throat. Then Ronnie sunk his teeth into the gypsy's left ear, causing him to scream in agony before the arena erupted into chaos and the fighters were pulled apart. For a moment it looked like the Jenkins clan were going to fight every man present, as they stepped in to protect Ronnie from the gypsies who were outraged by the attack, but it was Dale who calmed things down and dragged Ronnie away. The referee announced the gypsy had won by default and Samuel Jenkins went berserk.

"You imbecile," he screamed at his nephew. "We just lost a fortune thanks to you."

Ronnie was still zoned out with that crazy look on his face as he rushed forward to attack Samuel, the uncle he'd despised his entire life and he would have done serious damage if Dale Jenkins hadn't wrestled his son to the floor.

"Calm down!" he roared. "We don't fight amongst ourselves."

It took ten minutes before Ronnie's anger eventually subsided and Dale got off him and helped him to his feet. "I'm sorry I let you down Dad," he muttered, looking genuinely embarrassed. "I don't know what happens, it's like somebody else takes over."

Dale led him away from the arena and the countless men who would have put a knife in his back if his name had been anything other than Jenkins.

"It's okay son, you did your best," the gang leader was saying, but as they marched out of the fair that day young Ronnie Jenkins' anger and hatred began brewing up against his Uncle Samuel, the man who was next in line to lead his family. *'Not if I have anything to do with it,'* Ronnie thought.

Chapter Eleven

In the early hours of the morning on Wednesday 14 January 1772 Anna finally went into labour and for the first time in his life Benny Swift took a day off work so he could be at his loved one's side. The nurses were called for and the small shack was crowded. They all worked hard to make Anna as comfortable as possible, but it was clear from the start of the labour that something was wrong. Benny Swift tried to be strong and reassure Anna that everything was going to be okay, but deep down he knew that wasn't the case. Benjamin Swift would have sailed a thousand cargoes in the worst storms imaginable or fought a war with Dale Jenkins any day of the week rather than watch the woman he loved in such distress and pain. It was the hardest thing he'd ever had to do in his life. Finally the baby's head crowned and as Benny watched as his son came into the world, the life of the woman he loved was extinguished. The skilled young navigator watched in horror as the baby was placed on Anna's chest and tears rolled down her cheeks as she looked at her baby for the first and last time.

"It's a little boy," the nurse said and Anna smiled, she knew she was dying and so did Benny. She gripped the hand of the only man she'd ever loved. The nurses didn't know where to put themselves and in the end they shuffled out of the shack.

"Promise me you'll be there for him whenever he needs you and you'll never risk that by smuggling. Promise me you'll raise our son on honest money," she asked, her breathing was unsteady and she was clearly in a lot of pain.

Tears flowed freely down Benny's cheeks as he muttered, "I promise."

Anna smiled the sweetest smile Benny had ever seen and as her life left her the grip she held on Benny's hand softened. The fisherman picked up his newborn son and held him closely and as Jacob Swift cried for the first time, his father joined him.

When the nurses returned they tried to console him and explain that they'd organise a wet nurse to feed the boy, but Benjamin was heartbroken and in a state of shock, their words meant nothing to him. They couldn't bring Anna back so in the end he sent them away. Placing his newborn son in a crib and pulling a sheet over Anna's lifeless body, Benjamin sat for hours staring into space trying to deal with his loss.

Eventually Benny was startled by a knock on the door signalling Bill's arrival. His best friend strolled into the shack after a hard day out fishing excited and eager to see his best friend's baby and congratulate the pair for bringing a new life into the world. The man with eyes like lumps of coal had that crooked grin on his face, but he was instantly frozen to the spot by the sight that greeted him.

Bill's best friend was sitting in silence looking like his soul had died and his life had been sucked out of him. The only light came from a flickering candle on the table.

"Benny, what's wrong?" he asked in that croaky voice and his friend who'd sailed in everything nature could throw at him burst into tears. Bill marched over to Benny and threw his arms around him as his friend poured his heart out.

"I'm never smuggling again," Benjamin Swift mumbled through the tears. "I'll never break that promise to her."

Bill gripped his friend tightly and rubbed his back. "It's okay my brother, I'd never ask you to," he said.

The pair talked for a long time about their futures. Destiny had steered them on different paths and Bill wanted his friend to have all of the money they'd earned from smuggling. The bundle of notes were still untouched in the hole in the ground under the shack they'd dug together a lifetime ago.

"I don't want a penny of it," Benny stated. His friend tried to protest but was cut short. "You always wanted to be a smuggler Bill and all I have ever done is hold you back. Use the money and make your dream come true."

Bill stared at his friend, the only person he'd ever had in the world, and the young man with pitch black eyes knew he'd lost Benny forever, and it broke Bill's heart.

Suddenly a high-pitched screeching filled the shack and Billy Bates smiled that crooked smile of his as he wiped tears from his eyes and approached the crib where the baby lay wrapped in blankets. Picking up Jacob Swift Bill laid those dark eyes on the son of his best friend and the man he admired more than anyone in the world for the first time. Unknown to the child he'd taken away Bill's best friend and partner, but the young smuggler didn't blame Jacob one bit. When he placed the baby back down he kissed his forehead. It would be many years before they met again.

That night Billy Bates went for a long walk along the shoreline to clear his head. Now Bill had nobody and nothing to lose. Staring out at the channel and the ships visible in the moonlight the young man made a decision. It was time for Bill to make his smuggling dream a reality; he was twenty-two years old and had wasted far too long fishing for pittance. Billy Bates was turning smuggler and to hell with Dale Jenkins and his gang of thugs. From now on nothing was going to stand in Billy Bates' way.

Chapter Twelve

That night Billy Bates slept fitfully. He tossed and turned contemplating the crossroads he'd found himself at in life and trying to decide which path to take. At the break of dawn the young man who dreamt of being a smuggler was up and out of the house.

Bates strolled along the beach towards his boss' headquarters. Mr Western had employed him on the fishing fleet since his teenage years. He'd been good to him and Bill wanted to say his goodbyes face to face, he owed the man that much.

When Bill handed in his notice the old fisherman scratched his chin looking perplexed. "What will you do to earn a crust?" he asked, and Bill pondered this for a long moment.

"I'm going away for a bit sir," he finally replied. The old fisherman nodded

"Well lad you've been a good grafter. If you ever come back to the area and need some coin you look me up."

Bill shook his hand firmly. "Thank you Mr Western, you've done a lot for me and I'll never forget that," he said before strolling out of the office and towards the beach where he watched the fishing fleet sail out into the channel and eventually disappear on the horizon. Bill smiled that crooked smile of his, before he turned his back on the channel and the industry that had put clothes on his back and food in his mouth for many years as he began marching down into the town's cobbled streets.

Feeling confident and very determined Billy Bates marched through the labyrinth of dangerous streets as the town came to life around him.

Several hours later he was standing in the docks at Sandwich. Through those dark eyes of his he watched men rushing about unloading merchandise from a dozen ships of different shapes and sizes. After a while Bill turned and walked over to the entrance of Bob Planter's headquarters and made his way through the warehouse that was full to the brim with cargoes from all corners of the globe. Suddenly he heard his merchant friend's voice.

"Bill Bates, always a pleasure," and Bill turned and was greeted by Robert Planter who shook his hand before ushering him into his office where they could talk business in private.

Robert Planter descended from generations of merchants who'd traded on the banks of the River Stour for centuries. At twenty-five years old he'd taken over his father's import/export business and was making a tidy profit. Trading commodities was in his blood and Bob Planter knew that good business was wherever he found it.

As the merchant poured two large brandies from a crystal decanter, Bill admired his friend's fancy office. The walls were covered with maps of the English Channel and the mighty oceans, they meant very little to Bill but he knew his best friend Benny would be able to read them like the back of his hand. The thought of Benny was painful and gave Bill a sinking feeling in his guts. The young smuggler forced himself to block these thoughts out and continued studying Planter's office. Several bookshelves were full of manuscripts and as Bill gazed around at the merchant's personal space he vowed to one day have a headquarters like this all of his own.

Finally Robert Planter took a seat and asked the question that would set Bill's dream in motion, "So old friend, what can I do for you?" and Bill wasted no time explaining his dreams of becoming a full time smuggler.

"I need you to take on larger consignments at a much more frequent rate. Can you do this for me, my brother?" Bill asked. The merchant took a sip of his brandy and considered the offer. It had its fair share of risks but Bob Planter trusted Bill completely and he also knew he'd make a tidy profit if he agreed to the deal.

After a long moment the merchant spoke. "Bill we've known each other a long time. I'd be more than happy to help, but no one can ever know of my involvement, not even your own men can be aware that the merchandise ends up in my hands, agreed?" he asked as Bill smiled that crooked smile.

"It's between me and you Bob," he promised in that croaky voice of his as Bob Planter nodded.

"And if the Jenkins ever catch you, you're on your own Bill. You can never mention my name. I'm a legitimate businessman and as it stands Dale and his thugs leave me well alone and that's the way I like it," Planter said raising his glass to which Bill toasted.

"To expansion," Bill said as the pair who had lived very different lives clinked their beakers of brandy. Planter with his privileged upbringing, private education and guaranteed future. Bill with his friend Benny and the rags on his back.

The pair's conversation drifted to ships and the young smuggler confided to his friend that he was looking to buy one. "I'm looking for a clipper. Something fast," he said.

Robert Planter chuckled. "You know Bill I think I may be able to help you with that," the merchant said before telling Bill a story about a captain who owned his own ship but had become a complete drunk. "The man's incompetent and has let so many people down, none of the merchants will hire him anymore," Planter said shaking his head before fixing his eyes on Bill. "But I swear he has one of the quickest vessels I've ever seen. Its sails are rigged fore and aft and it cuts the wind perfectly."

Bill's dark eyes lit up. "But that's not what makes it so special," Planter continued. "Its hull is as smooth as a baby's bottom. It's not clinker built and without the resistance against the water that overlapping the planks creates it cuts straight through the water."

Bill took another sip of his brandy. "He's been offered a fair price for her but he won't sell up. The drunk has his life savings tied up in that ship and he doesn't realise he has a problem, but no one will employ him anymore fast ship or not," Planter said as Billy Bates smiled that crooked smile of his and began hatching a plan.

*

51

Hours later Bill stood in the shadows on the banks of the River Stour staring at the ship Robert Planter had spoken so favourably about. The captain was stood around a small lantern on the teak deck of his clipper slugging from a liquor bottle and muttering to himself. The old drunk had docked his ship a long way upstream from the port of Sandwich where he'd made lots of enemies amongst the men who'd once employed him. It had taken Bill most of the afternoon to track the clipper down, but as Bill gazed at her through those dark eyes of his he liked what he saw.

Slowly Bill crept out of the shadows towards the vessel and climbed onto the clipper's decks without making a sound. The old drunk didn't even notice Bill's presence until the smuggler was upon him, then suddenly he staggered to his feet and raised the bottle he held as a weapon and attempted to threaten Bill with it. A moment later he staggered forwards and fell to his knees on the decking.

Billy Bates casually took a seat and stared into the drunk's eyes, satisfied to see shame, humiliation and fear. After a long moment the ambitious young smuggler finally spoke.

"My name is Bill," he said very slowly and clearly.

"If you're a thief then my cargo hold's empty," the drunk slurred before taking a gulp from the bottle. Bill stared at the drunk for a long moment before he slowly leant forward and took the bottle from the man's hand and threw it over the side where it splashed into the river. The drunk went to protest but then noticed the look on Bill Bates' face and thought better of it.

"I'm no thief," Bill stated glancing around the deck and admiring the drunk's vessel. "I hear this ship's fast," he said. For the first time since Bill had climbed onto the deck the old drunk smiled.

"She's the fastest ship on The English Channel," he said proudly. "So who are you?"

Bill returned his gaze on the old seadog that'd given up on life and tried to find an escape in the bottom of a bottle.

"My name is Billy Bates," he said pulling a large bag of coins from his pocket, which the drunk stared at open mouthed. "I would like to hire you and your ship."

The drunk was speechless for a long moment. "You'll give me work?" he asked and Bill nodded

"I won't let you down sir, I promise," he said as Bill smiled that crooked smile of his.

"Don't worry old timer, I won't give you the opportunity and don't ever call me sir. I work for a living. Now get some sleep. We set sail for the continent at sunrise and then we'll see how fast this ship really is," Bill said.

Chapter Thirteen

Bill woke abruptly on the hard timber of the clipper's deck and sprung to his feet as he gathered his bearings. "Morning," the clipper's captain called out as he rushed around on deck preparing his ship to set sail on the twenty-two mile trip across the channel to France. The captain was hardly recognisable as he raised the anchor and dropped his sails. Sober and in the light of day he was far removed from the desperate, slurring drunk Bill had met the night before.

Pausing from his work, the clipper's skipper approached the young smuggler. "Bill isn't it?" he asked extending a hand, which Bill shook with that crooked grin of his plastered all over his face. "My name's Marcus," the skipper continued. "And we've got a lot of ground to cover, but this wind's in our favour," he said before busying himself casting his ship off from the bank.

An hour later the clipper was cruising out of the estuary into the English Channel at full sail. Billy Bates was stood staring overboard in the ship's wake, trying to work out her speed. The young man who'd spent his teenage years aboard bulky fishing luggers had never seen a ship so fast.

"Impressed?" the skipper asked chuckling, and in good spirits. Billy Bates turned to the man whose drinking problem had destroyed his once impeccable reputation as a sailor.

"Very," was all the young smuggler replied, and then he turned and gazed out at the countless ships in the channel and took a deep breath of salty air. A moment later he turned to the skipper. "Marcus, my friend, I like you already," he said and the old seadog smiled at the compliment. "And I think we can have a long and prosperous partnership, but I've got one rule and it's not to be broken, understand?" Bill demanded fixing those dark eyes on the skipper. The man was busy steering his clipper but he nodded encouraging his new boss to continue. "I don't mind you having a drink when the job's done and we're safely docked on the banks of the Stour, I'll even join you. Tonight when we get back we'll get drunk together," Bill said and Marcus smiled, but Bill could see the man was embarrassed about his weakness for liquor.

"But when you're sailing this ship or when we're docked in Calais I want you sober. I'm going to need to know that I can trust and rely on you Marcus, understand?" Bill asked. The skipper fell into silence and stared out at the sea for a long moment before turning to his new boss.

"It's a deal Bill, but one thing you need to know," he said, looking embarrassed, "sometimes I get sick and it's only the grog that makes me feel better."

Bill nodded. The young smuggler had known his fair share of drunks. "We'll deal with that bridge when we get to it, deal?" he asked and the skipper smiled. "It's a deal Bill, and don't worry I won't break it."

Then Billy Bates offered to fix them both some breakfast and disappeared below deck, but breakfast wasn't his biggest concern. Bill had known drunks before and wasn't prepared to take any risks where Marcus was concerned. The young smuggler was already taking too many bringing goods into the country tax-free and on top of that under the Jenkins' nose, that was enough for him. Bill planned on searching the vessel for any stashes of liquor Marcus may have hidden.

Below decks Bill had a good look at the clipper's cargo hold and was impressed by its size. The young smuggler was planning on investing all of the money he'd saved with Benny on contraband and loading the clipper to the hilt with smuggled cargo for the return journey in order to maximise profits. Bill knew he'd nearly double his money on this run alone. The young smuggler wasn't planning on wasting any more time making his dream a reality and was already thinking about recruiting some men he could trust to help transport the smuggled goods to Planter's warehouse. The young smuggler knew he'd need money to expand. Searching Marcus' belongings Bill quickly found what he was looking for. The skipper had a bottle of rum three quarters full hidden in the back of a drawer. Bill took the bottle and for a moment he considered throwing it overboard, but then he remembered the skipper's admission about getting sick and the smuggler thought better of it. Confident he now had some control over the situation Bill felt better. His worst nightmare was returning back to the clipper after purchasing the cargo from the merchants in France, only to find the drunk he'd met last night staggering around on deck.

After eating a hearty breakfast Marcus and Bill talked for hours about their pasts as the channel flew by below their feet, but Bill's first trip over to the continent wasn't destined to run so smoothly. It was gone noon when trouble first reared its ugly head. It came in the form of a sailing ship on the horizon in the ship's wake. Bill had been observing the countless vessels out on the channel since they'd sailed out of the estuary hours earlier. He gripped an old telescope and stared at the vessels through a dark and beady eye, admiring the huge merchant ships with all their sails snapping in the wind, and the countless fishing luggers as he wondered which vessel Benny and himself would have been aboard if destiny hadn't pulled the pair apart. This ship though made his heart beat faster in his chest. It was a clipper, the ship of choice for smugglers. Even at a distance Bill recognised her. She belonged to none other than Harry Booth.

Bill spun around and faced the captain that most sailors described as a liability. "Marcus, can you get anything else out of her?" he ordered in that croaky voice of his, all too aware that Harry's ship was gaining. Marcus wasted no time as he rushed around on deck tightening his ship's sails. Minutes felt like hours for Bill as he gripped the telescope anxiously, but much to his relief Harry Booth's clipper slowly dropped further back on the horizon. Finally Bill breathed easy once again knowing he'd come close to being caught on his first ever run. The smuggler realised he'd been ill prepared. He'd taken a huge risk and he swore that he'd be more careful in the future. Bill knew it'd only take a handful of words from Harry Booth and all of his dreams would be over. The Jenkins family wouldn't hesitate setting an example in the town by tearing Bill to shreds.

Feeling a little more relaxed Bill continued getting to know Marcus and by the time the cliffs of France came into view the pair were good friends. Billy Bates liked the man. He could see the Marcus had a good heart and had just fallen on hard times. Bill understood. The young smuggler had been through some tough times himself when his mother had died, leaving him alone to fend for himself in the world.

Finally when the clipper reached the docks at Calais Marcus tied his ship up and Bill climbed onto dry land. "I won't be long," he promised, eager to get loaded up and under sail once again. Then he marched to the warehouse that Benny had told him about. A short time later he returned with three men and a cart loaded with small barrels of brandy, but when he reached the clipper his heart missed a beat. Bill could see that Marcus was feeling ill even before the man spoke. He looked pale, clammy and his hands were shaking slightly. Signs Bill recognised. Whilst the men rushed around loading the clipper Bill poured Marcus a generous shot of rum, which the skipper took with a look of embarrassment on his face.

"Thank you for understanding, Bill," he said before draining it in one gulp. Then the captain Bill had met when he'd awoken that morning returned and Marcus raised anchor. Before the pair knew it they were sailing back out into the channel and racing across her choppy surface.

*

Meanwhile though standing on the docks at Calais and surrounded by several of his men, Harry Booth stared through his own telescope at Marcus's vessel as it sailed out of the harbour. He watched both of the men on deck, paying particular attention to one whose black hair was tied back in a ponytail.

"Well, well if it isn't that gutsy fisherman Billy Bates," he muttered, as he let the telescope fall to his side and glanced at his number one bodyguard, a huge African man whose loyalty was unquestionable. "We have a problem that needs fixing," Harry said and his bodyguard nodded.

*

Hours later when Bill and Marcus finally sailed into the estuary and reached the banks of the River Stour they docked miles away from anyone. Billy Bates cracked open a barrel of brandy and poured two beakers. Marcus took his and the pair toasted their first successful run across the channel.

"To many more like it," Marcus said and Bill smiled that crooked smile.

"Aye. Aye Captain," he said in that croaky voice, and the pair drank late into the night, completely unaware of the storm that was brewing.

Chapter Fourteen

The next day Bill Bates woke up on the deck of the clipper for the second day in a row, but this time he had a sore head and Marcus wasn't up and about either. The clipper's skipper was still snoring away sleeping off the grog he'd consumed the night before. Creeping below deck to the cargo hold Bill checked on his merchandise and was pleased to note the clipper was still stocked up with barrels upon barrels of brandy. Billy Bates smiled to himself and rubbed his hands together, happy that his plan was coming together, but now he faced yet another problem. The young smuggler's entire savings were tied up in the smuggled cargo and the man with pitch black eyes had overlooked one really important thing. Bill couldn't transport the entire cargo on his own in one run and Marcus wouldn't dare leave his precious ship unattended. So Bill would have to leave most of the alcohol on board the clipper when he ventured into Sandwich to visit Planter's warehouse. The young smuggler would have to trust Marcus, who he barely knew, with his life savings.

Bill had little choice and had spoken to Marcus the previous evening about the dilemma, during which Bill had made it very clear to the skipper what he'd do to the man if he cheated him.

Leaning overboard Bill splashed water on his face before he climbed onto dry land and began a long journey on foot towards the town of Deal and straight into the heart of Dale Jenkins' territory. Bill was hoping he wouldn't be seen in the town. He knew it wouldn't take long for Sammy Jenkins to figure out he'd quit working the fishing fleet.

He hoped the Jenkins clan would hear that he'd left the area. Billy Bates planned on recruiting several trusted men who'd help transport the cargo and deal with any other business in the town's cobbled streets on his behalf in the coming months. The young smuggler would stay away from the town and assist Marcus smuggling the merchandise into the country as he slowly built his empire.

When he finally reached the outskirts of the town it was early in the afternoon and his feet ached, but Bill knew his long day was far from over. Creeping through the cobbled streets Bill was on high alert, looking out for members of the Jenkins' huge family whilst searching for a young pickpocket he knew he could trust. Henry Cutler had been working the crowds in the town's markets relieving people of their jewellery half his life. Years ago he'd attracted the attention of the Jenkins who'd issued him with a beating for not paying his percentage, something they'd been collecting off the pickpocket ever since. Cutler hated Samuel Jenkins with a vengeance; as a result Bill knew he could trust the young thief.

Strolling through the crowded streets where traders sold their fares, wenches searched for company and sailors drank their weight in rum, Billy Bates' heart missed a beat as he spotted a gang of the Jenkins foot soldiers approaching him. They were in mid-conversation, arguing about something or other and just at the last minute the young smuggler managed to slip out of sight into an alleyway.

He stood for a long moment watching the group march out of sight before Bill himself slipped back into the crowd. Eventually he spotted Cutler. The pickpocket was leaning up against a brick wall staring at the crowd in the town's main market, picking his next victim Bill surmised. The young smuggler slowly crept up on Cutler and prodded him in the ribs with his fingers imitating a knife.

"Money now!" Bill ordered in that croaky voice, a voice the pickpocket recognised instantly.

Turning to his friend Henry Cutler laughed. "Money!" he exclaimed. "Chance would be a fine thing. I haven't earned a penny in days." Bill's eyes followed Cutler's and both men stared at the crowd, searching for anyone with something worth taking amongst the peasants and paupers that littered the towns cobbled streets. For a long moment neither man spoke, it was Bill who eventually broke the silence.

"I may be able to help you there," was all he said, but it was enough to pull Cutler's eyes from the crowd and get the thief's full attention.

"I'm looking for a worker, and I'll pay you well," Bill said, staring at the pickpocket with those dark eyes.

Cutler smiled. "Doing what? Or dare I ask?" he said. Bill nodded.

"What I'm about to tell you is not to be spoken about to anyone, understand?" Bill demanded. Now it was the pickpocket's turn to nod.

"I'm bringing merchandise across the channel and I need help transporting the cargoes," he said. Henry Cutler chuckled to himself for a moment before fixing Bill with a serious gaze.

"You know Bill I always admired your ambition, but do the Jenkins know about this? They'll tax you on that cargo more than the government would," Cutler said laughing at his joke. Bill stared at the young thief.

"No I've no intention of coughing up a penny to Sammy or the rest of the Jenkins gang," he stated in his croaky voice.

Henry Cutler chuckled once more and stared at the crowd for a long moment before turning back to Bill. "Okay, if it's like that count me in."

*

Hours later under the cover of darkness Bill and Henry Cutler returned to the clipper with six mules to help transport the smuggled brandy. Much to Bill's relief the super fast clipper was still sitting at anchor in the cove. The young smuggler believed that trust was something that needed to be earned in life and when he climbed back onboard and was greeted by a sober but shaky looking Marcus, the skipper had earned trust in Bill's eyes.

"Hey Bill, I was beginning to worry," the old sailor said and Bill shook his hand as he grinned from ear to ear.

"Open a tub my friend and have a nip, you deserve it," he said before he began the long task of emptying the cargo hold of its precious merchandise.

It took Bill and Henry Cutler over an hour loading up the mules and even though it was a real struggle they eventually reached the town of Sandwich. The smuggler hadn't forgotten his promise to his merchant friend and had no intention of letting Henry Cutler know about Planter's role in the smuggling operation. Bill trusted Cutler completely when it came to the Jenkins clan but the young smuggler wasn't planning on taking any unnecessary risks. As soon as Bill was close enough to the crooked merchant's warehouse he paid his pickpocket friend and sent the man on his way, then Bill dragged the mules the rest of the way on his own.

Creeping through the dark deserted streets Billy Bates' pitch black eyes scanned every nook and cranny as the mule's hooves clip-clopped along the cobbles. The young smuggler was on edge. He was taking a great risk but he knew it would all be worth it in the end. Reaching Planters warehouse he tapped on the door. A moment later the merchant opened up and scanned the street before ushering his friend inside. Robert Planter smiled and shook Bill's hand as he looked over the mules that were loaded with the huge cargo his friend had smuggled.

"Congratulations old friend. The days of being a poor fishermen are over for you," Planter said as he began un-strapping the four gallon tubs from the first of the mules and stacking them on the floor of the warehouse. "How many did you smuggle?" he asked. .

Billy Bates smiled proudly. "Sixty tubs," he said. "According to my calculations you owe me one-hundred and eighty pounds."

Robert Planter laughed and rubbed his chin. "You done well Bill. If you carry on landing cargoes like this you'll be a rich man real soon. My advice is to save the money and don't go flashing it around. I'd hate to hear that someone had put a knife in your back."

Bill nodded. The young smuggler understood his friend's warning. "Don't worry I'm planning on staying away from Deal and the Jenkins family. I do have one problem though, and I think you can help," he said.

Robert Planter turned to him. "Yeah, let's hear it," he replied.

Bill fixed those dark eyes on the merchant. "I've been doing some thinking and I've realised that I won't be able to bring the merchandise here myself every time. I'm planning on building a crew who can do my legwork for me, and you don't want anyone else to know of your involvement." The merchant nodded, encouraging his friend to continue.

"I figure we need some middle ground. Somewhere my men can unload the cargo safely."

Robert Planter stopped unloading the mules and smiled before strolling over towards his fancy office. A moment later he re-appeared holding a key which he handed to Bill. "You know Billy Bates you're a smart man. This key is to an old building I use for storage. It's down Cotters Lane on the outskirts of town. It's the perfect place for your men to stash up the merchandise and it eliminates a lot of the risks I'm taking by having you bring smuggled merchandise here," Planter said before both men finished unloading the mules. Then Robert Planter pulled a thick wad of notes from his pocket, counted out one-hundred and eighty pounds and handed the huge sum to Bill. The young smuggler held the money in his hands, much more money than he'd ever had.

"This is for you," Bill said, handing back thirty pounds to the merchant who eyed him suspiciously.

"We agreed on one-eighty Bill, three pounds per tub," the merchant said.

"I know my friend, but this is to say thanks. Without you none of this would be possible and I'd still be out fishing for pittance. I want you to know how thankful I am Bob," the smuggler said as he began leading the mules back out of the warehouse. When he reached the door he turned and fixed those dark eyes on his merchant friend. "Check your storage shed the day after tomorrow, okay?" he said in that croaky voice, before disappearing into the night.

Bill spent a few hours dropping off the mules to a young farm hand named Havelock, who he'd borrowed them off and when he reached the clipper and climbed onto her decks

Marcus greeted him warmly. The ship's skipper poured him a brandy and they clinked their beakers together.

"When do we set sail boss?" the ship's captain asked and Billy Bates smiled and took a big gulp of brandy that warmed him to the bones.

"We sail on the first tide my friend," he said in that croaky voice.

Chapter Fifteen

The Whitegate Cotton Mill, On the Banks of the Thames, London

The orphan was alone in the punishment cell kneeling on the damp rotting hay his owners often referred to as bedding, staring at the brick walls that enclosed the small room, walls that trapped the young boy for twenty-three hours of everyday. The orphan was taking short breaths, bracing himself for another wave of pain from the deep whip wounds that criss-crossed over his entire back. A moment later the throbbing pain returned and the orphan felt like his breath had been taken away. When the pain passed the boy was left gasping for air. He struggled to his feet and staggered over to the small barred window, which offered a view out on a world that had punished the orphan since the day he'd been born. Glancing out at the city of London and St Paul's in the distance, partially concealed by the city's smog, he stared out at the Thames and the ships anchored alongside her. Suddenly the orphan clenched his teeth once more as he was hit by another wave of excruciating pain. His legs stiffened and he bunched his hands into fists so tightly that his knuckles turned white. After a moment that felt like a lifetime the pain subsided and the orphan was still locked away, he was still the property of the mill owner and he was still only ten years old. As another wave of pain hit the orphan he gripped the bars of the window to stop himself from collapsing on the filthy floor. As he drifted out of consciousness his mind wandered to the day this living nightmare had begun.

*

It had been a pleasant spring morning over six months ago when Mr Baker first arrived at the Greenwich Orphans Asylum. The man had appeared very kind and good natured. He wore a smart suit and was well spoken; the orphanage's board of directors liked him from the very start. Mr Baker was a businessman and owned a number of cotton mills in the city. He was aware the orphanage was struggling financially and explained that he was always eager for new workers in his mills. Mr Baker quickly convinced the orphanage he was doing them a huge favour by buying their children to work in his mills. He promised good working conditions, money and a future for the orphans.

"At the age of twenty-one they'll be free and wealthy," he'd said.

Now as the orphan clung to the bars in agony he knew he'd never live to the age of twenty-one, and whatever age he reached he'd experience hardship on a daily basis so horrific he'd sooner be dead. The directors of the orphanage had bought Mr Baker's lies though and that spring day he'd been marched in front of the mill owner who sat at a table looking down the end of his nose at his new purchases. A sheet of paper was placed in front of him and the orphan was asked to make a mark on the sheet with a pencil. The young boy wasn't able to write and furthermore had no name. The wardens at the orphanage referred to him by his bedroom number only. He was called Fourteen and had been for as long as he could remember. The orphan marked the paper and was told that he now belonged to the Whitegate Cotton Mill. The young boy was actually excited and happy about leaving the orphanage, a place he'd lived since he'd been abandoned at birth. At the time the boy had fallen for Mr Baker's lies too. He thought the mill owner was a good man. Looking back the orphan realised how naive he'd been. A few weeks later the orphanage was cleared out and the boy was taken to his new home. The Whitegate Cotton Mill was an enormous brick building on the banks of the Thames. The orphan was ushered through the huge gate alongside fifty other children between the ages of eight and twelve. Inside the mill was a hive of activity with workers rushing here and there. The fifty orphans were marched into a huge hall and were made to line up in straight rows. The orphan stood taking in his new surroundings, excited about the thought of work when suddenly a man entered the hall. He had pale skin, a pock marked face and a shaven head. He stood at the front of the hall staring at the orphans with a look of distaste written all over his face. He wore thick leather boots and in his right hand he held a thin wooden stick. The boy wondered what the stick was for. He didn't have long to wait.

The man marched up and down the hall and eyed the new workers one by one. Most of the children stood rooted to the spot, staring at the ground terrified. The young orphan thought he had nothing to fear though and as the man marched past he looked him in the eye. Suddenly the man stopped and stared back at the orphan. The man actually smiled before he moved on. The orphan had re-lived that moment a thousand times in his mind, wishing that he could have changed it. The orphan would have stared at the floor like the others if only he'd known the consequences, but now as he clung to the bars on the cell's window racked with pain from the wounds on his back he knew it was too late. That day the man had turned on the children gathered in front of him.

"My name is Mr Anderson and I run this mill," he roared at them. "All I ask is that you do what you're told. I expect you to work hard, your food and lodgings won't pay for themselves. If you don't pull your weight and earn your keep there'll be consequences, you understand?" he bellowed at the orphans who were now petrified. "I said do you understand?" he shouted once again and this time the children mumbled, "Yes, Sir," in unison. Mr Anderson smiled and scratched his chin. He could see the children stood before him dressed in rags were terrified and it pleased him immensely. Nothing made Mr Anderson happier than flexing his power over the mill's workforce. Within the walls of the cotton mill he was judge, jury and jailor. Nobody defied him and he planned on keeping it that way.

Mr Anderson began marching up and down once more, then suddenly he stopped and glared at the children. "If you fail to carry out your share of the workload there'll be consequences," he said as he stared at Fourteen. The orphan smiled at his new boss but Anderson didn't smile back, instead he raised his hands and pointed in Fourteen's direction. The orphan froze to the spot as two guards seized him by both arms and dragged him to the front of the hall and up onto the stage where Mr Anderson was stood. The boy had no idea what was going on. He hadn't done anything wrong but he was soon to learn that made little difference with Mr Anderson who was a bully and a coward. It was Mr Anderson's job to turn the orphans into a productive workforce, and for that control was required. The mill's warden had learnt a long time ago that fear was the best way of controlling the workers and by God was Anderson going to scare them out of their wits. The orphan he'd singled out had possessed the courage to look him in the eyes, and Anderson was going to beat that courage out of him. The orphan had a square jaw, wide shoulders and looked far tougher than most of the other children gathered in the hall. Anderson thought that the boy looked like he could take a good beating and the sadistic warden was about to give the orphan the hardest beating he'd ever had, for the greater good of the workforce and the Whitegate Cotton Mill. Anderson stared down at the orphan who stared back at him, a huge insult for Anderson.

'How dare this toe-rag defy me!' the warden thought as he gripped the stick in his hand. The orphan clearly had little fear and Anderson was going to do everything in his power to change that.

Turning to the crowd Anderson tried to concentrate on the task at hand. "I want you to remember this!" he shouted. "This is what will happen to you if you don't do what you're told," he said before turning to the orphan and swinging the stick with all his might. The first blow struck the orphan's back with such force it knocked him to the ground. The poor boy screamed, but the scream died away as the vicious warden stood over him and rained down blows with all his might. A full minute later when Anderson had spent all his energy he stepped back exhausted and wiped his brow. The child was lying in a heap shaking uncontrollably and crying as blood oozed out of fresh wounds on his back and arms. Anderson turned to the crowd gathered, satisfied with his work. For a long moment he stared at the children. Pleased to note the terrified look on their grubby little faces. Mr Anderson had achieved his goal of terrifying his new workers. He turned to one of his guards and nodded. A moment later the guard dragged the beaten child out of the hall. That was the young orphan's first day at The Whitegate Cotton Mill, his first run in with Mr Anderson. A man who was destined to make his life hell on earth.

Chapter Sixteen

Early the next day as the first rays of sunshine appeared on the horizon Marcus raised anchor and the old drunk's super fast clipper sailed once again out into The English Channel, on a voyage it was destined to make hundreds of times in the years to come. Bill stood on her decks gazing out at the stretch of water he'd come to think of as home whilst the salty sea air gusted around him.

The following day when his merchant friend Robert Planter marched down the track to his lock-up with a handful of his men, he laughed whole-heartedly when he pulled the shed's doors open to reveal a sheer bounty of smuggled goods. Once again Billy Bates had stepped up his game and this time had brought a huge selection of contraband into the country. There was rum, brandy, tobacco and rolls upon rolls of French lace. Planter chuckled to himself. The merchant wasted no time bringing the goods to market.

Weeks turned to months and Billy Bates worked like a slave far away from the town's cobbled streets and the trouble that came with them. But Bill was all too aware that crossing the English Channel carried its own set of dangers. On several occasions Bill had spotted Harry Booth's ship, but he was always lucky enough to escape capture thanks to Marcus' super fast clipper, that really was worth its weight in gold. The ambitious young man landed cargoes like clockwork with Marcus at his side. Bill and Marcus became great friends and learnt to trust and rely on each other completely. The young smuggler forced the old sea dog to face up to his demons and to finally get a grip on his drinking problem, and in turn Bill earned a debt that the old sailor could never fully re-pay. A debt that would keep Marcus sober and loyal to Billy Bates until the day he died.

On land the pickpocket Henry Cutler was true to his word and slaved away delivering the cargoes, content with the idea that he was helping cheat Samuel Jenkins and his family out of a small fortune.

The young man who had once worked the fishing fleet dressed in rags became wealthy as his empire began to grow. Bill's mind would often wander to his best friend Benny Swift and the young smuggler would force these painful thoughts away. Billy Bates missed Benny Swift more than words could ever express, but deep down the smuggler knew that if he truly cared about the man he had to leave Benny alone to raise his son. For Bill it was the hardest thing he'd ever done.

Meanwhile in the town's cobbled streets and dangerous taverns locals wondered whatever had happened to Bill Bates, the young fisherman that had just disappeared. Just like Bill had planned rumours began to spread that he had upped sticks and left the area. Rumours that were confirmed when people saw Benny Swift and the fisherman informed them that his childhood friend had gone forever.

One face that was being seen around the town's streets more and more was that of young Ronald Jenkins, Dale's youngest son. The teenager who people called 'Big Ronnie' stood at six feet four now, towering over most men and putting the fear of God into every person he crossed. Young Ronnie was a loose cannon and even his own family feared him. It was rumoured that Dale Jenkins was getting long in the tooth and it wouldn't be long before somebody took his place as leader of the clan. It was well known around the town that Big Ronnie and his Uncle Samuel hated each other with a vengeance. It was only Dale himself, who had enough power to keep them from tearing chunks out of each other, but everyone knew that couldn't last forever and there was trouble ahead.

Meanwhile Ronnie Jenkins ran his own gang of thugs, roaming the cobbled streets a dozen strong collecting debts on his family's behalf. The young ruffian was carving a brutal reputation for himself in the town's streets with his bouts of uncontrollable violence. Big Ronnie Jenkins was a savage; he enjoyed inflicting pain and would often attack people even when they paid their debts. Ronnie argued against Samuel, claiming that he was just re-enforcing the Jenkins' reputation and maintaining fear in the town.

"Fear controls people," he'd roar at his uncle during the family's evening business discussions around the fire. Samuel felt differently though and would plead with his older brother to restrain his son. Samuel Jenkins knew that people in the area were starting to realise that being protected by the Jenkins clan didn't actually guarantee your safety anymore. Whilst the great leader and ex prize-fighter Dale Jenkins' health began to deteriorate, the empire he'd spent a lifetime building began to crumble. Dale had kept control of the area for a very long-time because he was smart and knew that aggression alone wasn't enough. The man who had saved his family from starvation many years before knew that neither Samuel nor Ronnie individually had what it took to retain control of their territory. Dale Jenkins also knew that between his brother and son they had all the qualities of leadership. Samuel had the brains and self-control and Ronnie had the brawn. Together the pair had everything it took to continue his family's reign long after he'd gone. Dale Jenkins prayed that the pair would settle their differences in the end.

Then on a cold October morning the great Dale Jenkins passed away and all hell broke loose.

Chapter Seventeen

Billy Bates sat in the corner of a quiet tavern on the outskirts of Sandwich. Wearing a tailored suit and sipping a coffee the smuggler was hardly recognisable to Henry Cutler as he entered, and the pickpocket needed to take a second look to make sure it actually was the fisherman he'd once known. Cutler had been working for Bill, carrying the heavy loads of smuggled goods for the best part of a year and even though the smuggler paid him generously, Cutler still secretly resented the young man with pitch black eyes. Bill had taken a huge risk smuggling, but it had paid off for him. Now Bill Bates had money and power, everything Cutler had wanted for himself. The young thief was very smart and manipulative though and he buried his true feelings deep down before he approached his old friend who looked up from the table where he sat and smiled that wicked smile of his.

Cutler slid into a chair opposite him and ordered a beaker of ale. "So you've heard the news then?" he teased his boss. Billy Bates fixed those dark eyes of his on Cutler and instantly the teasing stopped and the pickpocket got straight to the point. Bill was a good man, but the pickpocket was well aware that his boss wasn't a man to be crossed.

"Dale Jenkins is dead, he snuffed it a few days ago," Cutler blurted out. Bill put down his coffee cup visibly shaken. "Oh my God," he mumbled to himself, as Cutler allowed this information to sink in.

"How have the clan taken it?" he finally asked.

Henry Cutler chuckled to himself. "Well Samuel's trying to retain their control over the area, but as you can imagine they've been seriously weakened. Have you ever met Big Ronnie, Dale's youngest?" Cutler asked Bill, who shook his head.

"Not personally. I've heard a lot about him though; people say he's wild like an animal."

"And that's putting it mildly," the pickpocket cut in. "He was the one who found the body. Rumour has it that he cried like a baby at first, and then he just drifted into silence. For an entire day he didn't say a word, and then yesterday he gathered his gang and vanished. Samuel tried to stop him but Ronnie wouldn't listen, he barely would whilst his father was alive."

"Where's his gang now?" Bill demanded. Cutler took a gulp of ale and shrugged, "Nobody knows but people in the town are really scared."

Bill scratched his chin deep in thought. "Will Samuel be able to retain the Jenkins' control over the area?" he asked, not expecting an answer but Cutler provided one anyway.

"The man's a dog, lowest of the low. He's lived in his older brother's shadows for so long. I would love to think the Jenkins empire would crumble, but they still have far greater numbers than anyone else in the area, and for that reason alone I think he'll weather the storm. That's if his nephew Ronnie doesn't send him to meet his brother in hell."

Bill glanced at Cutler. "I've heard they don't get along too well," he said before lapsing into silence.

Dale Jenkins' death was big news and could change everything for Bill. The young smuggler hadn't ventured into the town's cobbled streets for a very long-time but Bill knew he'd have to watch the situation closely and to do that he'd need to take a huge risk and tread those cobbles once again.

*

Later that night six men marched along the seafront with expressions of anger and determination on their tough looking faces. Faces that bore the same features with dimpled chins and freckled cheeks, making them instantly recognisable as soldiers of the Jenkins family, but it was their pointy noses that sealed the deal, noses that had been broken on more than one occasion. For these men fighting was a family business, a fact of life that was introduced to them at a very young age. Out of the six men, one marched ahead of the pack completely lost in his own thoughts as his cousins battled to keep up. The shock had passed now for Ronnie and the ruthless thug was going to waste no time stepping up to fill the void left after his father's death. Young Ronnie was willing to stand side by side with his Uncle Samuel but as an equal and nothing less. Ronnie knew it wouldn't be easy. He was well aware that his father Dale Jenkins had big shoes to fill, but for now Ronnie concentrated on the task at hand. Big Ronnie Jenkins was in the town to send a message to anyone who doubted his family's strength and like always some poor unsuspecting soul was going to get hurt in the process.

*

Billy Bates crept slowly along the street, pausing from time to time to hide in the shadows. He was nearly in the heart of the town where alleyways criss-crossed in every direction creating a vast network of passages. Suddenly though Bill thought he heard a noise somewhere behind him and he spun around only to discover a mangy old cat scuttling away. The daring smuggler took a deep breath to settle his nerves and pulled the dark cloak he wore up towards his face. The hour was late and the sky was now dark, the only light coming from candle lamps hanging over doorways every dozen or so yards. Again Bill heard footsteps behind him and this time he turned around a fraction of a second too late. Bill made out at least three men, but there could have been more. One of the men was much bigger than the rest and grabbed Bill by the shoulders, gripping him tightly as he brought a knee up which connected with the smuggler's chest and knocked the wind out of him. Bill collapsed to the floor and was dragged out of the street and into a dark alleyway. The young smuggler tried to put up a fight but it took all of his efforts just to draw a breath. His attackers gagged him, bound his arms and feet, then the biggest of the attackers picked Bill up and threw him over his shoulder before marching through the dark streets. Bill racked his brain concluding that there was only one explanation. The men were Jenkins and Bill had landed himself in a world of trouble.

Chapter Eighteen

Over the course of the next few weeks the orphan known only as Fourteen received horrific beatings every other day. Whilst the other children at the cotton mill were put to work, Fourteen would be taken out of his cell only for the purpose of receiving physical punishment in front of the other young children. They would stand in shock, terrified at the thought of experiencing a similar beating themselves at the hands of the sadistic warden, Mr Anderson, who was depraved and clearly enjoyed his violent sessions with the orphan.

When the beating finally ended the poor boy would be dragged away and locked back up in his filthy cell, where he'd lie in agony in the freezing cold wondering what he'd ever done to receive such punishment. Deep down the orphan knew about strengths and weaknesses, and could see Anderson for the coward he was. He knew Anderson relied on him to control his workforce. Occasionally the orphan would hear the guards talking from outside his cell. Often the children whose job it was to roll underneath the heavy machinery and collect the loose cotton would get caught up in the machinery. The children would lose limbs regularly and deaths occurred every other week. When this happened the bodies would be buried in unmarked graves within the mill's grounds. The orphans had no-one to mourn their deaths; they were the property of the mill and for the majority that's all they'd ever be.

For the poor orphan things were changing deep within him. At first he'd been terrified and would lie in his cell dreading the lock being turned and the guards dragging him out to receive more punishment. As the weeks turned into months he noticed that he no longer feared Anderson or any of the other guards. The beatings were agonisingly painful but they happened as regular as clockwork. As time passed the orphan discovered that he no longer dreaded the clink of the lock in the cell door, indicating another beating. The orphan was slowly becoming conditioned to physical pain. The boy had accepted his fate and knew he'd never leave the mill alive. He'd never see adulthood.

The orphan hated Anderson and the other guards, but there was little he could do. They never handled him alone and unarmed he'd never stand a chance against their wooden clubs, but little did the orphan know he could get to them in a way nobody could have ever imagined.

The incident that would be remembered amongst the cotton mill workers until the end of time happened late in October. The mill's workforce hadn't been producing the output Mr Anderson expected for several days and the bald pocked-face warden was livid. All afternoon he'd been screaming at the workers and had even issued half a dozen minor beatings, something Anderson was reluctant to do. The sadistic warden didn't like to injure the actual workers; such a move was never good for production. After all, the warden had the orphan known as Fourteen to take his anger out on. Once again Mr Anderson planned on using Fourteen to scare the workers and improve production. Ultimately the mill's output was the warden's only concern. The fact that he enjoyed punishing the boy was an added benefit, a perk of the job as he liked to think of it. In the late afternoon the sadistic warden sent two of his guards to collect the boy.

This time though as the guards opened the cell's thick wooden door they paused for a moment in surprise. The orphan rose from the straw and stood with a fearless expression on his face totally prepared for his punishment. The guards shared a look before they sniggered at his bravery. Their boss and good friend Mr Anderson hadn't broken the orphan yet, but neither guard had any doubt that he'd succeed in the end. Over the years they'd seen it countless times, and knew that when Anderson singled someone out like he had the orphan in front of them, that person was destined for a short and painful life. Both guards also knew that for some reason their boss hated this one more than most. However what the guards didn't know was that Anderson had never picked a target quite like the orphan they called Fourteen. The boy was very unique and far tougher than anyone that had ever entered the cotton mill before him.

As the guards entered the cell and began shackling the orphan he didn't resist one bit; they'd noticed this for the first time a few weeks back. It was almost as if the orphan had no fear and this angered both of the guards. Deep down it made them feel powerless; both guards looked forward to that moment when the orphan's tough facade would slip. They knew that moment was inevitable for they knew how ruthless their boss could be.

When they'd finished securing the locks and chains the guards led the orphan out of his cell and through a labyrinth of corridors into the great hall where Anderson paced up and down screaming and shouting at the workers. As he entered the hall the orphan glanced at the crowd of his fellow orphans cowering in their rags, and completely terrified. Many looked up at him with curiosity, which didn't surprise him. The orphan was rarely seen by the other orphans and only ever during moments like this when an example needed to be made, and a lesson taught.

Suddenly Anderson turned from the crowd and fixed his eyes on the orphan in shackles. The cruel warden stared at the boy with a look of distaste and for the first time since that first day when he'd arrived at the cotton mill, the boy stared straight back as bold as brass. Mr Anderson's surprise was obvious to everyone gathered and for a moment he was taken aback, and during that moment as the orphan heard many of the children gasp in shock he saw a clink in the warden's armour.

The boy had been beaten severely for months and months. He'd been humiliated and belittled day in day out. Now after all this time the stocky little orphan with the square chin had discovered some sort of hidden strength, some courage hidden in reserve, somewhere deep inside where the sticks and whips Anderson had beaten him with hadn't been able to penetrate.

Gritting his teeth and struggling to control his anger the warden looked up from the orphan and at his workforce. Instantly his heart began to thump in his chest. For the first time the grubby little toe-rags were staring at him and not down at the floor in fear. Anderson could see that the orphan's courage was giving them hope. Suddenly the warden could control his rage no more and he began screaming and cursing at the crowd. Spittle flew from his mouth as he marched up and down. Now none of the workforce was looking him in the eye. Much to Anderson's satisfaction they were scared once more, all but one. Fourteen stood in shackles on the small wooden platform at the front of the hall, surrounded by guards. The stocky little orphan stared at Anderson through those sunken eyes of his and then something happened that sent shivers down the vicious warden's spine and made all the hairs on his body stand on end. Anderson watched open mouthed as a smile crept up on the boy's normally emotionless face and it terrified the warden. He knew in that moment that the child in front of him posed a serious threat to his control over the mill's workforce. Anderson realised he'd been too cruel to Fourteen; he'd tortured the boy so badly it had sent him mad.

Anderson grabbed his cat o' nine tails, a thick leather whip that hung around his waist. Approaching the orphan he tore away the rags that covered his back. Then Anderson began administrating the most severe beating he'd ever given anyone in his life. He swung the whip with all his might and when the whip's nine separate leather cords made contact with the orphan's back a loud crack echoed through the hall. Every child winced as the cords buried themselves deep into the child's back and blood flicked over Anderson and the guards at his sides. Stepping back the warden admired his work. For a fraction of a second he watched the blood oozing out of the thick wounds he'd caused. The orphan was standing covered in dirt and fresh blood, staring defiantly at the workers; he was completely silent as if he couldn't even feel the agonising pain from the fresh wounds that zigzagged over his back like a spider's web. In panic Anderson glanced up at the children gathered. Many had looked up from the ground and were staring at the shackled orphan in complete amazement.

Turning back to the orphan the warden watched as he turned his thick neck and stared Anderson straight in the eye, then much to the warden's surprise he smiled at him.

Suddenly a loud thud filled the hall as Andersons whip fell from his hands and hit the floor. Every single child gathered was staring at the spectacle now. Whilst the blood drained from Anderson's face the warden felt genuine fear for the first time, an emotion he enjoyed inspiring in others but one he hated feeling himself. The other guards were equally perplexed as they stared at their boss for orders. Anderson stood rooted to the spot, staring at the orphan with a look of fear plastered all over his face.

After a long moment he turned to the guards and nodded. "Lock him back up," he mumbled as the orphan known as Fourteen was dragged away, never to be seen by the workforce again. Unknown to him the orphan would grow into a legend amongst the workers at the Whitegate Cotton Mill, for generations they'd tell stories about the boy who felt no pain.

Chapter Nineteen

Whilst the attackers carried their victim through a network of alleyways the young smuggler tried to calculate where he was, but with the blindfold tight over his eyes he was quickly disorientated. After a few more minutes he gave up and just slumped over the man's shoulders accepting whatever fate awaited him. Suddenly the men stopped and Bill heard one of them bang on a wooden door. A moment later when it opened Bill heard a whispered exchange; he strained his ears trying to follow the conversation but couldn't make out more than a few words.

Suddenly he was hauled off the man's shoulders and placed in a wooden chair, and then his arms were tied firmly to the chair. When the blindfold was pulled away the smuggler found he was squinting whilst his eyes adjusted to the dim light. Taking in his surroundings Bill discovered he was in a small room illuminated by a single candle on a table in front of him. Leaning against the walls of the room were four men who stared at the smuggler with hate in their eyes. Billy Bates recognised them all; they were tough characters around the town and men that were not to be messed with if you valued your life. The biggest of them all was an African man named Boseda. He had been stolen from the Ivory Coast by a slave ship when he was only a child. Boseda was a slave no more, but the huge man had a master, that master sat opposite Bill at the table smirking like a hunter that had cornered its prey.

"Well, well Harry Booth, what do I owe this honour?" Bill asked the man who had exclusive smuggling rights over the local coastline and for a long moment Harry Booth just stared at Bill, finally he spoke.

"You know lad, I can't work out if you're really brave or just incredibly stupid. These last few months I've seen you out on the channel most days!" Harry raged at him. Bill smiled and shrugged as if he didn't have a care in the world. Harry watched him and then much to Bill's surprise the smuggling boss' tough facade slipped and he smiled to himself.

Harry's personal bodyguard stepped forward and poured both men a drink. Harry Booth took a nip. "The first time I spotted you I thought you'd be dead within a week. The Jenkins have people everywhere. In my younger years I would have clicked my fingers and had you killed myself, but I'm growing too long in the tooth for all this territorial warfare so I've kept my mouth shut," Harry said, pausing to take another nip of brandy. "So tell me Bill, how the hell are you moving the merchandise without arousing Samuel's attention?" he asked. Bill thought for a long moment about his answer and decided that he would sooner take a knife in the guts than betray his friend Robert Planter.

"The merchandise gets taken straight to London and sold there. I lose some of my profit to transport costs but at least I can sleep easy at night," he finally said.

Harry Booth pondered this for a long moment. "That's a clever move. The Jenkins have no idea. It was very wise not to land on this stretch of coast either. The Jenkins would have dispatched young Ronnie without a second thought and that animal would tear you to pieces without a moment's hesitation," Harry said, taking another sip of brandy. "I admire your courage for living the life I can only dream of, but it ends now lad. You've smuggled your last cargo. Start fishing again, leave the area or you'll end up with a knife in your back. Are we clear?" Harry Booth demanded.

The room fell into silence for a long moment as the candle flickered and both men sipped their drinks under the watchful eyes of Harry's bodyguards. The young smuggler stared at Harry Booth through those jet black eyes of his. "With all respect Mr Booth, I've thought about it long enough and I'll do neither. As far as I can see the only enemies I have in this world are the Jenkins family, and Harry you know as well as I do in truth they're enemies we share," Bill said as Harry spluttered his drink, clearly shocked. "I'm a smuggler through and through. It's my destiny to conquer that channel," Bill stated.

Harry rubbed his chin for a moment before turning to his men. "Leave us," he ordered before his men filed out of the room sheepishly. Only one remained, the huge African rarely left his boss' side.

Bill watched them leave before turning his attention on the smuggling boss, fully aware of Boseda who stood ready to pin him to the decks if he made one wrong move.

"The Jenkins may own these streets," he said, "but they're nothing out on the channel where it actually counts. Harry you're the only person who knows of my antics out there. Ask yourself this, how would it benefit you if the Jenkins found out?" he asked. "The Jenkins are thieves who bleed you dry of virtually everything you earn. You owe them nothing Harry."

The smuggling boss was staring at Billy Bates, and without realising it he was nodding his agreement. "Don't you want more Harry?" Bill demanded. Suddenly though much to Bill's surprise the smuggling boss exploded in anger.

"Of course I do," he roared, "but Samuel knows my operation inside and out. It would be impossible for me to cheat him without declaring all out war with his entire family. Dale Jenkins may be dead, but let me tell you a few things about Dale. I knew the man for nearly two decades and he could be vicious but he always had control of his temper. Trust me his son Ronnie is far more dangerous. These are words of advice you should heed Bill or pay the consequences with your life."

Billy Bates shrugged and fixed those dark eyes of his on Harry, eyes that could penetrate into a man's very soul, and in that moment Harry Booth caught a glimpse of the leader the young man in front of him would one day become. "I will pay you ten percent of the profits from every load I bring across the channel, if you keep your mouth shut about my antics," Bill said as Harry's mouth opened in shock.

"You may not have the courage to cheat the Jenkins Harry, but I do," Bill said before the room lapsed into silence as Harry Booth pondered Bill's offer.

After a long awkward moment Harry finally spoke. "I'm interested Bill, but before we could ever do business together there's one thing I need to know and I promise you it'll never leave this room," Bill nodded for Harry to continue. "Last year I chased a ship and it left me in its wake. I've lived and breathed salt air my whole life and I couldn't compete with whoever was navigating her. It's frustrated me day in, day out ever since. I need to know who was steering that ship, because it certainly wasn't that drunk Marcus."

Bill stared at Harry surprised that the smuggling boss knew of his involvement with Marcus and angered by the thought of his best friend Benny Swift, somebody who Bill missed every single day. "Harry I would never give that person up. I would rather die," he finally said.

Harry Booth stared at the young smuggler for a long time, then smiled and extended his hand. "I admire your courage, but not as much as your loyalty. From this day forth consider me an ally," he said, and from that moment, unknown to the ruthless Jenkins family and everyone else who roamed the town's cobbled streets the young fisherman who'd lived his life in poverty took his first step towards becoming the number one smuggler on the Kent coast.

Chapter Twenty

Samuel Jenkins stood greeting the dozens of people arriving for the funeral of his elder brother, the man he'd admired his entire life. The mourners arrived in droves. Criminals from every walk of life crawled out of the woodwork to say goodbye to the man who'd ruled the area with an iron fist for the best part of twenty years. Gypsy travellers from all over the south coast were there. Many of which Dale had fought and beaten over the years. They'd traded blows, but the man lying in the casket at the front of the church had earned their respect both in and out of the ring. Even the men and women the Jenkins had terrorised for decades turned out in their best clothes to pay respect to Dale, but more importantly win favour with whoever was going to lead his family.

Samuel himself had a terrible feeling deep in his guts. The church was nearly full but there was still no sign of Ronnie. His nephew had vanished days ago and gone to ground with his gang. Samuel hadn't seen him since but had little doubt he'd be here for the funeral. Samuel knew Ronnie was in pain, the teenager had idolised his father. Samuel knew the boy was unstable and unpredictable. He was prone to bouts of un-controllable aggression and during these moments, with his huge stature the boy was a deadly force. Samuel knew Ronnie would kill anyone or anything that stood in his way; he was his father's son after all.

Turning to greet more visitors arriving Samuel was pleased to see the town's new magistrate amongst the crowd. The man was young, twenty or so and fresh out of school. Samuel noted the man's big stomach protruding from the finely cut suit he wore as he stood at the back of the church holding the hand of the young lady he'd recently married. Samuel sized the man up concluding the magistrate had clearly been born into money, but his presence at the funeral meant Samuel could rely on his support and loyalty in the years to come.

Suddenly Samuel's chain of thought was interrupted as one of his men pointed towards the track leading towards the church. Marching along the track was Big Ronnie and half a dozen of his men. They were Samuel's relatives but they were loyal to Ronnie and Ronnie only, they'd made that clear to Samuel as soon as Dale had died. Samuel despised them as much as he despised Ronnie and vowed that one day he'd deal with them all for their lack of loyalty and respect, family or not.

Samuel was a patient man though and he put these thoughts from his mind as he strolled out of the church to greet them. Samuel needed to talk to Ronnie in private. Hundreds had arrived for the funeral and a confrontation between the Jenkins' new leader Samuel and Dale's son Ronnie would be devastating to the clan's reputation. Samuel knew the clan were feared because of their numbers and their loyalty to one another, if you threatened one of the clan then you threatened them all. The clan didn't squabble amongst themselves and especially not in front of outsiders. Samuel approached the small gang who stepped forward and blocked his path.

"Leave us," he ordered Ronnie's foot soldiers who just stared at Samuel with a look of contempt. Ronnie himself looked his uncle up and down before turning to his men and giving his consent. Then Ronnie's foot soldiers marched towards the church leaving the pair alone. A long awkward moment passed before either man spoke. It was Samuel who broke the silence. "I know we've never really seen eye to eye, but we need to work together for the sake of our family. That's what your father would have wanted."

Ronnie Jenkins nodded his agreement; Samuel could see that his giant of a nephew hadn't really come to terms with his father's death. Ronnie had always had that crazy look, but now the teenager looked much worse, haunted even.

"I've never liked you Samuel, I'll admit that much. But I'm willing to work with you for the sake of our family and the memory of my father," he said. Samuel stepped forward and offered his hand, which Ronnie shook before the pair strolled into the church together under the watchful eyes of half the town, as both men wondered if the other had bought their lies. Then the service began and Ronnie Jenkins paid his final respects to his father, the county's most successful gang leader and the man Ronnie hoped he'd one day equal.

*

Later that night Harry Booth sat nursing a beaker of ale in The Seagull alongside Boseda and a handful of his men, hardworking, loyal men the smuggling boss had worked with for many years. The Seagull was lively as usual. A storm was brewing in the channel and countless ships had dropped anchor ready to wait it out. Sailors from every corner of the globe wandered up and down the cobbled streets, boozing in the taverns and spending their hard earned meagre wages on pleasures of the mind and soul.

The smuggling boss was feeling on edge about the deal he'd struck with Billy Bates after spending the day at Dale Jenkins' funeral. Harry Booth could see that burning ambition in Bill's eyes and was confident they'd earn good money together in the years to come, but there were many risks involved, risks that terrified Harry.

Suddenly the tavern's door swung open with a thud and a gust of wind blew in the pub, closely followed by Big Ronnie who as far as Harry was concerned was equally unwelcome. The teenager ducked down to fit through the doorway before he stood upright once more and took in his surroundings. Harry Booth watched Ronnie smiling confidently as he surveyed his territory and the smuggling boss could see that even at such a young age Ronnie was fearless. The town's streets belonged to him now and like everyone else in the town, he knew it. Now Ronnie's gang of thugs entered the tavern and stood by his side, which only accentuated his huge stature. Most of the town's criminal underworld who were drinking in the tavern rose to their feet and approached him, offering their condolences, attempting to win favour in his eyes. Harry rose to his feet ready to go and do just that.

Harry Booth was happy to cheat Ronnie and his family by doing business on the side with Bill Bates, but the smuggling boss was smart enough to pay his respects face to face to the town's new leader. Samuel Jenkins was now leading the clan, but everyone knew Ronnie was calling his own shots. As Harry stood Ronnie spotted him from across the room.

"Harry Booth," Ronnie said towering over him, "I saw you at the funeral, thanks for coming."

Harry shook the teenager's hand, deciding that he was even bigger and uglier up close. "Your father was a great man. We did business together for many years. I'm sorry for your loss," Harry said. Ronnie nodded, pleased with the compliment.

"And many years to come," he said, staring Harry in the eye and maintaining eye contact until the smuggler looked away intimidated. Then Big Ronnie turned his attention to Harry's men and stared them down one after another, finally resting his eyes on Boseda who stared straight back. Harry Booth's heart rate jumped up as Big Ronnie gritted his teeth in anger.

"Boseda isn't it?" Ronnie demanded. Harry's number one bodyguard nodded. He looked far removed from anyone else in the town. Standing at over six feet three inches Boseda wasn't far off Ronnie, but it was his dark skin and plaited hair that set him apart from anyone else in the town's cobbled streets.

"They say that outside of my family you're the toughest man in this town," Ronnie said glancing at the crowd gathered who were hanging on his every word, before turning to Boseda. "I suppose it's true that you get what you pay for," he said referring to Boseda's slave roots. Now it was Boseda's turn to grit his teeth in anger as half of the pub sniggered at his expense. Ronnie glanced around at the pub with a look of satisfaction on his face. The young leader knew he had the power to insult anyone in the town and nobody could do anything about it. Ronnie was enjoying flexing his muscle in the town for the first time and showing off the power his family name brought him.

Suddenly a group of sailors staggered in the door noisily interrupting Ronnie's moment of triumph and the teenager turned and glared at them. The sailors had no idea who the teenager was and were so drunk they paid little attention. Ronnie gritted his teeth and rose to his feet as half the pub held their breath in anticipation. Everyone's eyes were fixed on Ronnie as he marched over to the tough looking sailors. Making no effort to introduce himself Big Ronnie head-butted the first man he came across, who collapsed to the floor. The sailors turned on Ronnie and launched an attack on the giant, but Dale had taught Ronnie to fight before he could even walk. Ronnie ducked their weak punches before throwing his own. When Ronnie's fists made contact with the sailors' jaws the men were knocked off their feet by the brute force. A moment later the teenager was standing over their unconscious bodies sprawled on the floor of the pub. Ronnie laughed and stared at Boseda from across the tavern, before marching out of the door with the rest of his gang.

When the door swung shut everybody breathed a sigh of relief. Harry turned to Boseda, his right hand man and personal bodyguard. Somebody he considered a great friend. The man Harry Booth had shamefully bought a lifetime ago.

"You know old friend you've been a free man for a long time. Don't let that thug's insults get to you," Harry said, as the African who Harry respected more than most nodded. The smuggling boss leant in closer so nobody would overhear.

"Listen we both know he isn't as smart or as powerful in this town as he thinks. One day he'll come unstuck and he'll bring his whole family down with him," Harry said. Boseda nodded but remained silent. Big Ronnie Jenkins had just made a huge mistake insulting Boseda. Dale Jenkins' son had just made an enemy out of Harry's right hand man and Billy Bates had just made a powerful ally. Bill Bates didn't fear the Jenkins and he wasn't alone.

Chapter Twenty-One

Meanwhile in the city of London…

When the orphan known as Fourteen was thrown back into his cell he fell forward and crashed onto the cold stone floor where he passed out. When he awoke he crawled along the floor as he was hit by wave after wave of agonising pain. Eventually when he reached the cell's wall he used it to support his weight as he scrambled onto his feet and stared out at the city of London whilst gasping at the smoggy air drifting in through the small barred window. Anything was better than the foul stinking air in the cell from the rotting hay that covered the floor. Another wave of pain hit the orphan and he gritted his teeth, struggling to remain conscious as his mind drifted. He wondered how long he'd been unconscious on the floor. Staring out at the city he could make out the silhouette of St Paul's Cathedral across the river. It was late at night now, exactly how late the orphan couldn't tell. Suddenly the pain became too much and his legs gave out from underneath him and he collapsed to the floor once again.

*

Meanwhile in a drinking tavern a short distance from the cotton mill Mr Anderson sat with several of his guards drinking and racking his mind for a solution to his problems. The vicious warden was on his sixth pint of ale since leaving the mill earlier in a state of shock. The toe-rag known as Fourteen had created a big problem for Anderson who'd used the boy to control his workers. Now in a complete turn-around it seemed the orphan had the potential to take away that control. Anderson knew the workforce could cause him serious problems if he didn't deal with the situation, and deal with it tonight.

Now with a head full of ale the warden felt marginally better. Anderson knew the boy had to go; he was too great a risk to control of the mill. The warden decided that the only solution to his problem was to arrange a little accident for the orphan. Suddenly Anderson was pulled from his thoughts by one of his guards, a wiry man named Simmonds who raised his beaker for a toast. The warden looked up at his friends and clinked his beaker with theirs.

"To getting rid of our problem," he said to the guards who downed their drinks and cackled; only the warden himself wasn't laughing. "I'm going to teach that boy what fear is," he promised his guards who stopped laughing at their boss' threat. Climbing out of the wooden chair that creaked under his weight Anderson placed a hat over his baldhead. The guards rose to their feet too and followed their boss out of the crowded tavern ready to deliver some justice to the boy who defied them and their control at the mill.

*

The lock clinked and the cell's thick wooden door swung open. The orphan staggered to his feet and stared at Anderson who was stood menacingly with two of his guards, Simmonds and Roberts at his sides. It was clear the men were drunk; all three stared at the orphan through glassy eyes. It was Anderson who stepped forward first.

"Let's see how brave you really are," he snarled as the guards rushed forward and seized the orphan. Simmonds tied a gag around his mouth and pulled an old sack over his head so he couldn't see. The next thing the boy knew he was being dragged forward out of the cell. The orphan racked his brains trying to calculate what time it was but he was confused, disorientated and near exhaustion as he was dragged forward. A moment later the pock faced warden reached an exit next to the river and crept out of the mill. Scanning the surrounding area Anderson was happy to observe it deserted. It was dead quiet as waves lapped on the banks of the river. It was nearly two in the morning and even the drunks and working girls had called it a night.

The orphan was dragged out onto the cobbled bank that led between the mill and the murky water of the Thames. He could feel the cool wind as it hit his skin and numbed the deep wounds on his back, as he wondered where he was being led and how this nightmare of a life would end. Occasionally he could make out the guards talking through hushed tones, from time to time they'd cackle breaking the eerie silence. The orphan could only wonder what they found so amusing.

Eventually the sack was pulled from the orphan's head and through those deep-set eyes he took in his surroundings. Directly in front of him were a dozen steps leading down into the river. At low tide the waves lapped against the steps but this was far from calming for the boy who was beginning to realise what Anderson's intentions were. Suddenly one of the guards jabbed him hard in the back causing excruciating pain and forcing him to bite hard into the rope gagging his mouth. His vision blurred as he stumbled forward and he would have fallen down the steps into the river if it hadn't been for the guards who gripped his arms tightly.

Anderson stood looking up and down the riverside, when a smile crossed his pale scarred face and he turned to his guards. "Down here boys, below that wooden jetty," he ordered before creeping down the steps towards a small pier that darted out a dozen or so yards into the river.

"Boss, we'll get soaking wet," Simmonds protested before all three men cackled once more. Then Simmonds and Roberts waded down into the river and dragged the boy several yards under the jetty out of sight. Both guards were waist deep in the filthy water but it didn't seem to bother them too much.

The water soaked straight through the rags covering the orphan's back and into his wounds, and he let out a gasp before nearly collapsing into the river. "Not yet boy," Simmonds snarled as he tied one of the orphan's hands tightly to the wooden jetty's pylons. A moment later the guards waded back up the steps leaving the boy alone, in agony in the dark.

Suddenly Anderson crouched under the jetty and approached the orphan. The vicious warden bent down so their noses were only inches apart. "Now let's see how tough you really are. When the tide rises in an hour or so this will all be underwater," he snarled. "I'll see you in hell," and with that the mill's warden and the man who'd made the orphan's life hell on earth waded back and disappeared up the steps where he was greeted by his guards who were smiling as they congratulated him on a great idea; both were always keen to earn favour with the mill's top man.

Anderson stared at the waves lapping on the steps, slowly climbing higher and higher before turning to his guards with a smile on his face. "Let's go get a nightcap," he said as he walked away from the jetty, and a problem that would one day return to haunt him.

Chapter Twenty-Two

Billy Bates stifled a yawn as he crept along the deserted lane. It was near dusk and he struggled to make out the bramble bushes on each of his sides as he made his way towards a meeting that had taken days of planning to organise. The hour was getting late as he rounded a corner and spotted the barn. As he approached he observed flickering light at the edges of its thick oak doors and gripped the handle of the dagger he carried even tighter.

It had been another long day for the ambitious young smuggler. Since being kidnapped by Harry Booth's right hand man and personal bodyguard, Boseda, Bill found he had lots to think about. Bill was fearless and had no qualms about using the weapons he always carried, but more importantly he was smart, always analysing every situation before making a decision. Bill was content. He was doing very well for himself smuggling with Marcus and Henry Cutler, but he had a burning desire to escape the poverty of his past and set himself up financially for life. Billy Bates dreamed of owning a fancy office like his friend Bob Planter, with cases of books lining the walls. He fantasised about owning a fleet of clippers that would ferry smuggled cargoes across from the continent and land on the Kent coast day in day out. Bill now knew that Harry Booth posed no threat; in fact the smuggling boss would make a powerful ally and with Dale Jenkins six feet under, the time for Bill to expand his budding empire had arrived. Bill had racked his brain over the situation and had quickly concluded that he would require more help selling his illegal merchandise. His friend Robert Planter had reached the limit of contraband he was willing to mix into his legal stocks of merchandise. Planter was a rich and wealthy man. He didn't need to risk everything he had by getting mixed up in the smuggling trade, but the merchant had shocked Bill by revealing the final card he had hidden up his sleeve and introduced the young smuggler to several of his merchant friends. These friends operated on the banks of the River Medway, a day's ride away from the town's cobbled streets, far from the Jenkins clan's territory and the ears of young Ronnie and his thugs. Bill made mutually beneficial deals with the merchants, deals that would keep the men happy with some extra income whilst setting up a route to move a much greater flow of smuggled goods with very little risk.

Now though, as the soles of his leather boots smacked on the chalk track, Bill thought about the man he was going to meet. The man was dangerous; there was no doubt about it. He'd spilled blood on his employer's behalf countless times since he'd arrived in the town many years before. Boseda was solidly built with wide shoulders and thick black hair that made some of the town's more superstitious inhabitants shiver with fear when they passed him in the street. The man was feared around the town, but in the last few days Billy Bates had come to trust the African bodyguard. Days earlier Bill had been contacted by one of Harry's men and instructed to meet with Boseda. Initially Bill had been suspicious of a trap and had taken precautions but Boseda posed no threat to the young smuggler and was actually keen to help him. The bodyguard who had watched Samuel take advantage of Harry Booth for years had grown a deep hatred for the Jenkins family and especially their unpredictable young protégé Big Ronnie.

Bill and Boseda talked for hours, creating a plan and assembling a selection of reliable foot-soldiers to recruit into the young smuggler's organisation. Harry's right hand man had lived his life in the thick of trouble and was an ally of the Jenkins in the town's eyes. People were terrified of him, and he knew every toe-rag and vagrant that had ever wandered the town's cobbled streets. Most importantly he knew exactly who the Jenkins enemies were, men who held grudges against the clan and would be willing to stand against them. Boseda had marched through the town's labyrinth of cobbled streets and searched the drinking dens high and low for the selected candidates. Times were hard and food was short. Boseda had no doubt the men would snatch up the deal being offered to them.

Finally, Bill reached the barn's door and strolled inside. Boseda stood in the corner leaning against an oak beam whilst four men stood awkwardly in a cluster, all of them dressed in rags and looking half-starved. As Bill entered they looked up and held his gaze. Bill stared at them through those jet black eyes of his and was pleased with what he saw. They were tough, hardworking and desperate, all the qualities Bill was looking for. Glancing at Boseda he complimented him on a job well done and watched as the huge black man nodded before turning to the men.

"Do you know who I am? And why you have been gathered here?" Bill asked, and the men nodded and voiced their support for the young smuggler urging him to continue. "A great opportunity has presented itself for you. For a long time you've suffered in poverty at the hands of the Jenkins. Nobody will employ you for fear of their vicious reprisals," he stated, as he marched up and down like a general on parade. "I'm willing to give you work, put clothes on your backs and food in your mouths," he said to the men who were nodding excitedly at his speech, "but understand this, if you betray me I will cut you down without a second thought." He pulled out his dagger whilst staring at the men one at a time, and watching as they broke away from his gaze and stared at the floor in fear.

For the first time since the meeting began Boseda stepped forward and approached them. "And understand that Bill Bates has my full support," he said menacingly, "from this day forth any move against Bill is a declaration of war against me, and I'll spill your blood without hesitation, understand?" The men nodded, they all understood the consequences of backing out of the deal they were about to make, if they betrayed Billy Bates they would face the death penalty.

Bill approached the first of the men who was only a few years younger than him with short ginger hair. "Why are the Jenkins your enemies?" he asked.

The man rubbed his chin and looked at the floor embarrassed. "I was courting a girl sir, and one of the clan took a fancy to her. I was approached by half a dozen of them who told me they were claiming her before they beat me to within an inch of my life with clubs and bats," he said, finally building the courage to look up and into Bill's eyes. "Then Samuel Jenkins forced my boss into sacking me, he's a good man but he had little choice. I've lost everything including the girl I love. I've barely eaten a meal in the last six weeks," he said, emotionally. "The Jenkins are bullies and cowards. If you are standing against them Bill, I would be honoured to stand at your side." Billy Bates smiled that crooked smile. He knew instantly that he could trust and rely on the man in front of him.

"And your name," Bill asked, extending his hand and gripping the new recruit's tightly.

"My real name is Travis, but people call me Carp," he said.

"Very pleased to meet you Carp, and I promise from this day forth you'll fear them no more. If you are loyal to me I promise you'll want for nothing," Bill said before moving onto the next man in line.

Chapter Twenty-Three

Trapped under the wooden pier in the dark the orphan began to panic as the River Thames rose higher and higher around him. He pulled with every ounce of his might at the thick rope that held his wrist, but it wouldn't give. The guard, Simmonds, had worked on one of the many barges that traversed the mighty river and could tie knots that would impress any sailor. The orphan tugged until the rope bit into his wrist drawing blood, but he didn't care. He was already in agony from the wounds covering his back. Now he was about to drown in a filthy river. He had nothing to lose.

A few minutes later after he had exhausted every option and the rope still held firm he slumped his shoulders and accepted his fate. Through a gap between the planks of the wooden jetty a few feet above him, the orphan could see the full moon sparkling brightly. He stared at its beauty and as the river rose above his chest and began lapping over his wide shoulders, the child who'd been born into a life of cruelty and pain tried to forget about the guards. He tried to forget about Anderson but the man's pale pockmarked face kept returning with the words, 'Let's see how brave you really are'.

The orphan could accept death; it was something he'd had months to prepare for whilst sitting on the cold stone floor in the mill's filthy cell. What the boy couldn't accept was the injustice of the world he was about to leave. It was something that all the time in the world couldn't have prepared him for. Suddenly the first of many waves lapped up and splashed over his face and in that moment he knew that death wasn't far from him. When the first waved dipped the orphan took a gasp of air just in time as another wave hit him. Suddenly he noticed movement behind him and he turned around with fresh hope that the guards had returned. For a brief moment he thought that this had been their idea of a joke, a test to scare him out of his wits, but the orphan's hopes were dashed by the sight of half a dozen rats scuttling along the steps and fighting over a rotten putrid fish that had been washed ashore. Then another wave hit and this time it covered the orphan's entire head. When it dipped, the boy reached over to the steps. Immediately one of the rats bit into his hand but not before he'd grasped the rotting fish. Instantly the rats went crazy and dived into the river, swimming towards him in a frenzy, but the orphan had far greater worries on his mind. With his one free hand he squeezed the rotting fish and as its guts spilled through his fingers. In a last ditch effort he rubbed them all over the rope binding him to the jetty just as another wave rose over his head.

Underwater and in pain the boy wondered if the wave would dip or if this was the end. Was he about to drown? But then it dropped once again and as he gasped for air he caught a glimpse of a sight that made his heart thump in his chest and restore a little hope. The fat greedy rats were going berserk and gnawing at the rope trying to get the most out of the meal the orphan had denied them.

Then hope was taken away by another wave that covered the boy completely. He held his breath but this time the wave didn't dip. The tide had risen and the boy could only wait until his lungs gave out and he would have to breathe in a mouthful of filthy water. Suddenly with that terrifying thought in mind the orphan pulled with all his might at his shackled hand. A fresh wave of pain flooded through him but in his panic and despair he paid little attention, this was his last chance. Suddenly with a snap the rope finally broke and the orphan bobbed to the surface taking in huge gasps of air. The orphan had been in the water for over an hour, and was shaking with the cold as he gripped onto the jetty and gathered his thoughts. The first thing that was clear was that he needed to escape. He was free from the jetty, but now he needed to get away from Anderson and his mill and away from the city of London forever. The orphan knew that the guards would eventually return to check under the jetty. The boy began to panic knowing they could arrive back any minute. Suddenly he leapt into action and crawled up the steps. The orphan stood and stared at the world for the first time as a free man. Taking a few deep breaths he looked around at the city he'd grown to hate. Aided by the moonlight the boy got his bearings before staggering along the banks of the Thames. After a hundred yards or so he came across a huge ship docked against one of the many piers jetting out into the river. Scanning the decks he checked to make sure all lights were out. The boy had very little energy left and knew he needed to rest before he collapsed on his feet. The orphan wasted no more time and staggered along the pier. A moment later he hauled himself overboard onto the wooden deck where he lay in agony for several minutes. Then he crawled along and hid under an oilskin sheet on the ship's deck. Lying there in the dark freezing cold, hungry and in agonising pain the orphan smiled to himself. With the thought that Anderson and his guards would never find him he drifted off into a deep sleep, feeling safe for the first time since he'd arrived at the mill all those months ago.

Little did the orphan know that he'd just jumped out of the pan and into the fire by stowing away aboard a ship captained by the most ruthless pirate to ever sail the high seas. A man who'd spent years plundering the wealth of the rich and evading capture by virtually every navy on earth. A man who'd fought so many battles and survived unscathed that people claimed he had supernatural powers and some even claimed he was the devil himself.

Chapter Twenty-Four

The orphan awoke from his deep sleep disorientated and confused. He opened his eyes suddenly, instantly aware that the ship was moving underneath him. The orphan's heart began to race as he peeked through a gap in the oilskin sheet he was hiding underneath on the ship's timber deck. At least a dozen tough looking men marched around carrying out various jobs under the shadow of huge sails blowing in the wind. The orphan checked the deep wounds on his back. During the night the fresh air had closed them up. They still throbbed with pain and the boy gritted his teeth as he wondered what to do next.

After a long moment the orphan pulled back the oilskin sheet a little and tried to get his bearings. He had no idea how long he'd been asleep but the huge ship was no longer in the Thames. It was out on the sea, sailing along beside what the boy assumed to be the Kent coast.

The orphan lay there for a while longer listening to the sailors' banter on deck and wondering what to do. He was thankful he was out of the city and far away from that savage Anderson and his cotton mill. Lying on his chest and daydreaming, the orphan almost felt relaxed for the first time in a long while. Suddenly though everything changed as the oilskin sheet was pulled off of him completely and the shout of, "Stowaway!" filled the air. The orphan jumped to his feet as the first of many sailors rushed towards him. Without a second thought the orphan swung his wide shoulders and punched the first sailor in the jaw, knocking the man unconscious with one hit. A skill he'd master and depend upon for survival in the years to come.

More sailors attacked him and the orphan swung both fists like a wild animal. For the briefest of moments the sailors froze, rooted to the spot in shock at the boy's courage. Suddenly they snapped into action and quickly over-powered him. The orphan was pinned to the smooth timber deck as the sailors crowded around him. A man with hardly any teeth and a scar running down his left cheek stared at him for a long moment before sneering, "Let's drown him!" which received shouts and whistles of support from his crew. The orphan heard a cabin door creak and suddenly the sailors' behaviour changed and they formed a neat line as a huge figure rose from deep within the ship. The sailors glanced down at the floor. Fourteen had seen this behaviour before and knew the men were scared out of their wits.

"Aye, aye Captain Mudd," the men roared in unison, and now it was the orphan's turn to freeze paralysed with fear. The orphan had heard of Alfred Mudd, the most ruthless pirate ever to sail the seven seas, few people hadn't. The orphan glanced over at the pirate and his heart missed a beat. Captain Mudd towered over his crew and was much taller than anyone the orphan had ever seen. The pirate was so skinny he looked gaunt and had a bushy ginger beard that came down to his chest. He was fairly young too, much younger than many of his crew. According to the stories Fourteen had heard Alfred Mudd had gone to sea in his early teens and had been a mere deckhand when he'd ransacked his first ship, and chose to live the life of a pirate. A few years later he led a mutiny and butchered his pirate captain before taking control of the ship himself. For a few years Mudd sailed the globe attacking only merchant ships and always letting the crews live. One day the navy caught up with him on an island in the Caribbean. Mudd managed to escape but several of his crew were not so lucky. From that day forth Alfred Mudd vowed revenge. For over a decade he'd built a horrific reputation by attacking every ship in his path and torturing any man who stood in his way.

Now Captain Mudd stared at the boy who'd dared to stowaway aboard his ship and the boy stared back defiantly for a long moment that the boy would remember for the rest of his life. In that single moment the orphan regretted everything, even escaping from the mill, fearing an even harsher punishment. Eventually the pirate glanced at the coastline a few hundred yards off the mighty ship's stern side.

"Can you swim boy?" the pirate barked as he twisted the end of his ginger beard. The orphan nodded and the pirate turned his attention back to the coastline. "Throw him overboard, but let him live," he barked at his men who looked surprised by their Captain's leniency. A moment later they snapped into action, picking the boy up and throwing him like a ragdoll into the water.

The orphan hit the surface as agonising pain flooded through him. When he surfaced he lay on his back and swam towards the shore. Reaching the coast he crawled up the shingle beach exhausted picturing the face of the notorious pirate Captain Mudd, a face that would stick in his mind for the rest of his life. Finally the boy sat up and turned towards the town that destiny had brought him to. A rough town littered with cobbled streets where cut-throat sailors spent their wages drinking and gambling. The orphan had arrived in the town of Deal, a place he'd one day think of as home.

Chapter Twenty-Five

Samuel Jenkins took a sip of his brandy and twisted the end of his bushy beard as he waited for the meeting with the thorn in his side, the one person in the town capable of causing problems for his family, his own nephew Ronnie. Since Dale's death young Ronnie had been given, or more accurately had assumed free reign of the town with his small gang of thugs. Samuel had held back and watched, seeing it as an opportunity for the teenager to prove his worth, but all Ronnie had done was cause problems for the clan. Earlier in the day Samuel had ventured down into the cobbled streets to collect a handful of debts and discuss business with several of the town's underworld figures, men who lived on the wrong side of the law and paid the Jenkins handsomely for the privilege to do so. What Samuel had learnt was shocking, even by Jenkins' standards, but it didn't surprise him. Ronnie had been on the warpath once again. Over the last few weeks he'd attacked half of the clan's allies. Most of the time Ronnie had collected what they owed before throwing devastating punches, for no reason whatsoever, apart from the fact the teenager was a sadist and enjoyed inflicting pain. The townsfolk were very confused. If paying off the Jenkins clan didn't guarantee your safety there was very little point paying in the first place. Samuel Jenkins knew that Ronnie was only trying to do some good on his family's behalf, but struggled keeping his temper in line. The huge teenager was trying his best to fit into his father's shoes. Young Ronnie had the brains, Samuel didn't doubt that, but he lacked the self-control his father had and was doing a lot more harm than good.

Finally Ronnie arrived at the meeting, pulling Samuel from his thoughts. He marched into the room like he owned the place, with that look of confidence on his face, a look his uncle had grown to despise, and slumped his huge frame in a chair across from Samuel. All of the elders of the clan were present.

Most of which were Samuel's brothers who'd stood at Dale's side when they'd first ventured into the town of Dover rather than face starvation nearly two decades earlier. Samuel offered his hand, which was quickly lost in Ronnie's grip, as the teenager squeezed with all his might to show Samuel who was in control. Samuel struggled not to react and let on to the other family members of the mind games young Ronnie played.

"Welcome nephew, it's good to see you," he lied.

Ronnie smiled, seeing through it immediately. "And you Uncle Samuel," he sneered before greeting his other relatives.

Eventually Samuel rose to his feet. "As leader of this family I've called this meeting. In the last few weeks people's opinions of our family have shifted somewhat," he stated. "For a long time people have paid us for their safety. A payment few can afford," he said, turning to Ronnie.

"In the last few weeks you've worked hard for this family," he said, trying to appeal to his nephew's better side, "but you need to learn to control your temper. Acts of violence against men who pay for our protection only help to undermine our control of this area. Do you understand that Ronald?" The teenager gritted his teeth and glared at his uncle with hatred in his eyes, but swallowed it down. Samuel watched closely and could see it was a struggle for his nephew. Then Ronnie climbed to his feet and everyone arched their necks to look him in the eye as he towered over them and addressed the table.

"In the last few weeks I've had to throw a few punches to make my mark on this town, which I admit. Now people fear me like they feared my father. I'll do what you ask and restrain myself. You're in charge after all," he said, taking a seat once more and flashing an evil glare Samuel's way. Deep down Ronnie had no intention of restraining himself. Every day he learnt of fresh faces in the town's cobbled streets who dared to cheat the Jenkins out of what was owed and Ronnie had every intention of knocking them all into place. Samuel Jenkins stared at his nephew. The teenager was a savage and wasn't right in the head, his elder brother had realised that when Ronnie was only a child. His nephew presented a huge problem for Samuel Jenkins; a problem that as far as Sammy was concerned had only one solution. The leader of the Jenkins clan hoped for the sake of his dead brother that he'd never have to go that far and call an execution on his own nephew.

*

Meanwhile miles away on the other side of the rough and ready fishing town, the orphan clutched his belly and tried to ignore the pain. He hadn't eaten a proper meal since he'd left the Whitegate Cotton Mill. He was starving in the literal sense of the word. After his lucky escape from the feared pirate Alfred Mudd's ship, he'd found himself all alone once again, but this time in a strange town. The boy who'd been known simply as 'Fourteen' in a previous life had quickly fled the streets and found somewhere safe to sleep under a wooden jetty amongst the rats and other scavengers. Here where men dared not to go he felt safe. The rats meant him no harm, he often watched them scurrying around and thought they had a lot in common with him. Like him they chose to live in the shadows away from humans, and like him they struggled to survive in a world that offered no sympathy. The orphan was aware he needed to eat desperately. The scraps he'd found over the last few weeks had offered little sustenance. It was time for him to take a risk or the pain in his stomach would get worse and he'd die, he was sure of that. The orphan crept out from under the jetty and stared at the lights in the town, before walking towards them.

Chapter Twenty-Six

Billy Bates sat surrounded by half a dozen bodyguards in a drinking den far away from the town's cobbled streets. The smuggler was waiting for a messenger he'd sent into town. Bill had been very busy for several weeks and his hard work was finally paying off. The daring young smuggler had not only added another vessel to his fleet, doubling the amount of merchandise he could bring over the channel, but he'd also purchased another safe house to stow his cargo. It was an old barn in the middle of the countryside, half way to London. It was the perfect place for his men to hide out overnight en-route to meet the merchants Robert Planter had put him in contact with. Bill's crew were now over a dozen strong and growing daily. All the men worked tirelessly at their roles, whether it was Marcus navigating his clipper or the likes of Carp and Henry Cutler loading up mules and transporting the goods. They were all keen to build Bates' empire and a future for themselves in the process, and the man with jet black eyes paid them well for it.

Bill scratched his chin and pulled a fancy watch from the pocket of the fine suit he wore. His friend Planter had taught him that if he wanted to be the boss, then he needed to act like one and look like one too. At first the young smuggler had felt like a fish out of water in such fine clothes, but he understood it was all part of the game. Noting the time Bill grimaced. His messenger was late and the smuggling boss was wondering why. Any other man wouldn't have such grave concerns but the young smuggler wasn't any other man. Bill was a great thinker. He was constantly analysing things. Not just his profits and losses, but everything else, including his workers' behaviour. Ordering another round of drinks for his men Bill sat back and waited. After another half hour or so his messenger finally staggered into the tavern, and Bill noticed the man's split lip and swollen jaw before the man had barely passed through the door. Instantly the smuggler's bodyguards were on edge, rising from their seats and clutching their weapons. The smuggler himself acted composed and ordered the messenger to sit and explain what had happened.

The messenger was shaken up, that was clear for everyone to see. He avoided Bill's gaze and the smuggler wondered if the man was scared or just nervous about delivering a lie to his new employer. Billy Bates wasn't ruling anything out until he'd heard the whole story.

"I was in town strolling up Coppin Street towards the beach when I was attacked," the man said shakily. Whether he was lying or not Bill could see he was scared out of his wits. Bill could also see disappointment in the man's eyes that he'd let his new boss down, which added credibility to his story in the smuggler's eyes. Bill stared at the messenger and didn't utter a word, encouraging the man to continue.

"I was knocked unconscious. When I came around they'd gone," he said. Bill gazed at the man with that crooked smile on his face as he discreetly pulled the dagger he carried with him everywhere from the sheath in his right boot, fully prepared to use it.

"And I assume they took all of my money, these attackers?" he asked calmly, but much to the smuggler's surprise the messenger shook his head.

"No sir, that's the strange thing. They didn't take the money!" the messenger said bringing shocked silence to the table. Billy Bates cocked his head. The crooked smile had vanished as he slid the dagger back into its hiding place without anyone noticing.

"They what?" a bodyguard cut in but the young smuggler raised one of his hands and silenced him immediately.

Bill sat and thought about the situation before he continued. "Did you get a good look at them? Can you confirm they were Jenkins?" he asked. The messenger glanced down at the table, purposely avoiding eye contact.

"No sir, not for certain, truth is I didn't see it coming. I heard a scuttling behind me and as I turned I was hit in the jaw.

It has to be the Jenkins though. It wouldn't be the first time they've attacked me Bill," the man said rather honestly.

Bill glanced at one of his bodyguards. "Get this man a drink," he ordered, before turning to the messenger. "You did well, don't worry," he said before lapsing into silence, wondering whether the clan had discovered his smuggling operation and were delivering a message. Bill couldn't quite figure it out. The attack didn't add up. If someone had betrayed him to the Jenkins clan they'd launch a full scale attack, led by Ronnie and dozens of his foot soldiers, or at least have given a message for the man to pass on to him directly rather than attack one of his men anonymously, that really wasn't the Jenkins style. Attacks happened in the town daily. It was a dangerous place but the fact they didn't search the victim and take the money was crazy. Billy Bates hadn't heard of an attack like it in all the years he'd been alive.

Suddenly he glanced at the messenger who was struggling to sip brandy through his split lips. "Did they take anything from you? Anything at all?" he asked.

The man thought for a moment before nodding slowly. "Come to think of it Bill they did. I had some food, a loaf of bread and some corn. When I came around it was gone," he said. Bill's confused expression increased ten-fold.

"So you had more money in your pocket than most men earn in a month but they left that and took a loaf of bread instead?" he asked aloud to no-one in particular. The smuggler sat back in his chair and took a sip of brandy himself. He didn't think the Jenkins were aware of his operation, but the young smuggler had every intention of speaking to the one person who would know for sure to find out. Either way Billy Bates had to expect the worse and prepare for an all out war with the Jenkins clan.

Chapter Twenty-Seven

Harry Booth was having a pleasant morning sitting in his den calculating the weekly profits for the various smuggling crews that worked on his behalf, when Boseda barged into the room and delivered the news that Billy Bates was here to see him in person. The smuggling boss was genuinely shocked. The daring young smuggler was taking a huge risk even entering the town. Harry suspected that the visit was urgent though and Bill couldn't wait until a meeting was arranged in a safer location. These suspicions were confirmed by the look on the young smuggler's face when he marched into Harry's den.

"Bill, this is a surprise," he said, rising from his chair and greeting the young man who was making a regular and healthy contribution to his retirement fund. Billy Bates shook Harry's hand and wasted no time getting to the point.

"We have a situation. One of my men was attacked last night and I suspect it was at the hands of Ronnie's thugs," he said before explaining the suspicious events of the previous evening. Harry Booth sat back listening intently, shocked by the news. Bill was great at spotting deception and could tell the smuggling boss and so-called ally of the Jenkins family was genuine.

"Your man had over forty pounds on him, a small fortune, and whoever attacked him left the money?" Harry finally asked, looking baffled. Bill nodded. "But that doesn't make any sense," he continued. Billy Bates was just about to voice his agreement when a startled looking Boseda burst into the room for a second time.

"The Jenkins are here!" he hissed. Harry Booth's jaw sagged open as he adsorbed the news.

"We're done for," he found himself muttering. Thankfully Boseda was more productive. The huge bodyguard grabbed Bill around the scruff of the neck and dragged him over to a cupboard where he tossed the young smuggler like a rag doll, before closing the cupboards door firmly. Boseda quickly spun around on his feet and stood with his arms crossed in front of him, his huge bulk blocking the cupboard's door completely. Harry Booth took a deep breath and composed himself just as the den's door swung open and big Ronnie bowled into the room. Harry knew something was up immediately. The huge teenager lacked that smug arrogant expression he normally wore, it had been replaced with a look of hatred as if the thug was about to spill blood right here in Harry's den and it was enough to send a cold shiver down the old smuggler's spine. Harry believed Ronnie would have if he hadn't been followed into the room by Samuel Jenkins himself and half a dozen bodyguards, who quickly filled the den.

"Welcome my friends," Harry said, summoning all of his skills to act as if such visits were a regular occurrence. Deep down Harry's heart was thumping in his chest as he wondered whether or not the clan were aware of his under-hand dealings with their competitor, the man who was half a dozen feet away hiding in a cupboard.

Thankfully Samuel didn't look as upset as his nephew, but it was clear the Jenkins' leader was far from happy. Ronnie himself glared at Boseda through gritted teeth and the African glared back, fighting the urge not to use his fists to knock the youngster down a peg or two like he had to hundreds of others in his long career as Harry Booth's bodyguard.

"We have a problem," Samuel said, before Ronnie cut in and interrupted him.

"Somebody attacked a member of our family a few days ago," the thug spat, "and whoever it was will pay with their life."

Harry Booth remained calm and watched Samuel Jenkins grit his teeth out of the corner of his eye. Harry had known Sammy for a long time and could see the leader was angered by his nephew's interruption. As leader of the clan it was Samuel who spoke with outsiders on his family's behalf. Harry was pleased to note the huge thug was un-controllable, even to his own family.

"Ronnie, silence," Sammy ordered before the teenager flashed an evil look his uncle's way and continued to glare at Boseda. The African smiled at Ronnie just for a fraction of a second, so that only the thug would see. Suddenly big Ronnie exhaled a lungful of air and began clenching his fists, struggling to control his vicious temper. Boseda was ready to spring into action and had no doubts he'd beat the teenager in a fight. Ronnie had been trained by a champion bare-knuckle fighter and had no trouble beating up drunken sailors in the town's drinking dens, but as far as Boseda was concerned he lacked the experience the African had on his side from years of enforcing his boss' smuggling empire.

"Is this true?" Harry asked Samuel who confirmed Ronnie's statement. The smuggling boss' mind was swimming after hearing of simultaneous attacks on both Bill's small crew and the Jenkins family.

"Samuel, nobody in this town would attack a relative of yours, it would be an act of suicide," he said, still trying to figure it all out. "It must have been an out of towner, a sailor from one of the ships anchored in the downs," Harry continued. Samuel voiced his agreement before rising to his feet.

- "Sailor or not, they pay the price. If you hear anything you get in touch, understand?" Samuel asked.

Suddenly Harry felt incredibly uncomfortable as over half a dozen sets of eyes fixed on him. "Of course Samuel, we're on the same side. If I hear anything I'll bring the culprit directly to you," he promised.

Suddenly Big Ronnie turned his attention to Harry. "I want him alive so I can have some fun with him. Nobody attacks our family," he said before the Jenkins filed out of the room as quickly as they'd arrived.

Once they'd gone Harry Booth pulled a bottle of brandy from a drawer in his desk and took a big gulp to settle his nerves. Boseda turned and opened the cupboard door, allowing Bill to stagger out dusting himself off.

"Sorry about that by the way," the African said with a big grin on his face. Bill looked up and glared at Harry's bodyguard before smiling that crooked smile of his.

"What the hell's happening in this town?" Harry muttered.

Bill thought long and hard as he poured himself a generous brandy. "I have an enemy in this town, but at least they're loyal to no-one," he said, pondering the situation a little longer before turning to Boseda. "Whoever the attacker is they are fearless, which makes them dangerous. I want them found and taken alive if possible." he ordered the African who had no issues killing on Bill's behalf.

Boseda nodded. "Don't worry nobody can hide from me in these streets," was all the bodyguard had to say.

Chapter Twenty-Eight

Hours later Boseda was roaming the labyrinth of winding streets searching for the elusive attacker. The town was crowded as usual with stallholders selling a variety of wares. Working girls were plying their trade to the countless sailors who were eager to spend some of their hard-earned money after long voyages to the end of the world and back, whilst pickpockets roamed the crowds looking for that opportunity that would put food in their mouths. Times were hard and the cobbled streets were unforgiving. The town was a dangerous place to be, even during the day. Boseda had nothing to worry about though. It only took one look at the bulky African and you knew he wasn't one to mess with. The locals knew Harry Booth's number one enforcer and knew of his reputation, which made hunting the attacker all the more easier for him. Boseda interrogated every local he came across for information, taking great pleasure out of informing the entire town that a member of the Jenkins had received a beating. A fate they all deserved. Every time Boseda would watch that look of satisfaction on people's faces, a look that would quickly evaporate for fears of reprisals from Boseda himself, who after all was supposedly allied with the clan. The African was enjoying playing both sides and slowly undermining the Jenkins' grip on the town. He knew that locals despised them, not that they'd ever dare voice such opinions about the family who terrorised the town. People had been scared of Dale Jenkins but there was also a measure of respect mixed in with the fear. Where their new leader Samuel was concerned the respect had evaporated. He wasn't half the man his brother was and people knew it. On the other hand people feared Big Ronnie even more than Dale himself, who'd been quite the businessman. Ronnie was unpredictable and way too aggressive. As far as the huge thug was concerned, his family's dominance over the town had little to do with money and everything to do with power.

Every corner Boseda took in the winding streets he came across members of the Jenkins family. He could spot them a mile away with their dimpled chins and freckled cheeks. Like the African they were also turning the town upside down in their search for the attacker, and having about as much luck. Eventually the sun began to set and the streets began to empty. Few dared to tread the cobbles at night. Boseda had spoken to everyone in the town and nobody knew a thing about the attacks. Feeling frustrated the African finally admitted defeat and strolled up towards the shore for a walk along the beach. Harry's bodyguard liked to breathe in the salty air whilst he stared out at sea and remembered a childhood robbed from him a lifetime ago. He often dreamt of returning to his homeland and his people once his boss had retired. Harry Booth had become a close friend over the years and had not only encouraged his bodyguard to return to the African coastline he'd been taken from, but had even offered to pay the costs for the long and expensive trip. Boseda had been touched by Harry's generosity. The smuggling boss was truly a great friend and because of that Boseda had no intention of leaving his side.

Staring out at the English Channel Boseda watched the various clippers on the horizon that were carrying his boss' illegal merchandise amongst many other ships of all shapes and sizes. Suddenly the bodyguard spotted a flicker of movement on the beach. Turning and staring at an old wooden jetty the bodyguard could have sworn he'd seen somebody crawl underneath it. Boseda wondered if it could have been the attacker. It explained why nobody knew anything and either way he needed to find out. He could forgive the man for beating up a member of the Jenkins. In fact he'd shake the man's hand, but nobody attacked Billy Bates' crew, for that they'd pay with their lives. Reaching the jetty he marched along the old weather-beaten timber that creaked under his weight as he stared through the cracks into the darkness below. Suddenly he froze as he came across a set of eyes staring back.

He stood staring for a long moment and the attacker held his gaze. He debated venturing under the jetty himself, but it was pitch black down there and he had no source of light. Remembering Bill's wise words "they are fearless and that makes them dangerous", Boseda decided to raise the alarm and return with some lamps and a handful of men. The African gazed into the attacker's eyes for a long moment before marching off towards Harry's headquarters where he'd send a messenger to fetch Bill. Marching along the seafront Boseda thought about how he was going to punish the man those eyes belonged to.

Chapter Twenty-Nine

It took two hours for Billy Bates to gather his crew and enter the town under the cover of darkness. The young smuggler was taking a huge risk venturing into the town, especially with such a large build-up of Jenkins' foot soldiers in the area. As a precaution Bill posted a handful of lookouts strategically positioned to cover all the streets leading up towards the deserted jetty where the attacker was supposedly hiding.

It was the first time anybody had stepped out of line and the young smuggler was all too aware that his men were watching to see how he would react. He needed to set an example to his men that would stick in their minds, a brutal punishment that would quell any thoughts of mutiny within his own ranks in the years to come. He had these thoughts in mind as he approached the jetty with Boseda and eight other bodyguards at his side, all armed with thick clubs, daggers and lamps so they'd be able to see their prey. Reaching the jetty Bill signalled for two of his men to crawl underneath it and they quickly disappeared. For at least a minute no sound was heard, the only noise came from the waves crashing on the shore less than a dozen yards away. Then all hell broke loose under the jetty as shouts and grunts were heard whilst punches were exchanged. Bill stood with the wind gusting off the sea in his face and blowing his black hair all over the place as he clutched the handle of his dagger, waiting to plunge it straight into the chest of the first man who'd ever challenged his budding organisation.

Suddenly one of his men appeared, dragging the attacker by one leg as he lay on his back kicking and throwing wild punches. Bill's men quickly surrounded him and raised their bats. The attacker rolled over and stared at the men and their looks of confusion before finally admitting defeat. He knew he didn't stand a chance, it was a feeling he was used to. Billy Bates stared in shock before he stepped forward and grabbed a lantern so he could get a good look at the man who'd declared war with the town's two biggest criminal gangs.

"It can't be," Bill found himself muttering as the attacker climbed to his feet and stared straight into Bill's eyes without an ounce of fear. The orphan stood waiting for one of the men to hit him with a club and finally bring an end to the life that had brought him nothing but misery and torture since the day he'd been born, to a mother that had dumped him that very day.

Nobody moved a muscle or said a word; they all just stared at him. The boy stood covered in filth and rags, looking half-starved and near death. Bill stared into his eyes, eyes that belonged to an emotionless face. A knot twisted deep in Bill's stomach as the smuggler saw himself in the boy, and painful memories of years past when his mother had died leaving him alone in the world came flooding back. Eventually Bill snapped into action.

"You attacked one of my men! Why?" he asked. The stocky little boy who couldn't have been older than twelve or thirteen nodded much to Bill's surprise. The smuggler was finding it hard to come to terms with the fact that the boy in front of him could attack grown men and walk away unscathed. "I'm sorry I needed food," was all that the boy said. Bill looked over at Boseda and from the look on his face the huge African bodyguard was equally puzzled.

"Do you have any idea what you've done? Half the town are hunting you down and when they find you they'll kill you," he raged, but the boy didn't react. He just stood there returning Bill's gaze without a care in the world. Bill was astonished; the boy was unlike anyone he'd ever seen. Either he was insane, which the smuggler was considering or he was the toughest person Bill had ever come across. Suddenly the moment was shattered as the missing bodyguard crawled out from under the jetty where he'd been lying unconscious. The man flung himself towards the boy in anger as blood poured from his nose, but was quickly restrained. If punishment was handed out to the mysterious young boy then it would be at the hand of Billy Bates only. The young leader wasn't throwing any punches though, like many would if they'd been in his shoes. Bill was a great thinker and his mind was racing.

"What's your name lad?" Bill asked and for the first time the boy not only broke eye contact and looked down at the floor, but also displayed emotion on his face for a fraction of a second. It was enough for Bill to spot it before it vanished and the smuggler knew that emotion only too well, it was embarrassment.

"At the orphanage they called me Fourteen... before they sold me," the boy muttered.

Suddenly a snigger filled the air from the bodyguard with the bleeding nose. "A slave, eh? It serves you right," he said, realising his mistake as soon as the words had left his lips. The man turned in a frantic effort to plead, but Boseda had no understanding of the word forgiveness. The huge African hit the man with all his might, knocking him unconscious for the second time. Turning and staring at the boy whose past matched his own, Boseda could see that the damage had already been done. Whatever the child had been through it had been horrific and had destroyed part of his soul, leaving a scar that he'd carry forever. Boseda also knew that the boy's lack of emotion made him a natural killer, capable of ending lives without hesitation or remorse. The African knew that one day the child would grow into a powerful weapon.

Billy Bates was rubbing his chin deep in thought. Like the boy in front of him the young smuggler had come from nothing and had done whatever it took to survive. In that moment Billy Bates made a decision that unknown to him would change the course of his life. "Do you want a hot meal and a warm bed?" he finally asked in that croaky voice of his. The boy stared back suspiciously for a moment before nodding. It would take a long, long time before the orphan would ever trust another man again.

Chapter Thirty

That night Bill rode out of the town of Deal and into relative safety with the orphan at his side, taking the boy out of the streets that were as dangerous for him as they were for the smuggler himself. Bill knew that Ronnie and his thugs would torture the boy if they found him, regardless of his age, so Bill took him to the house he was staying in on the outskirts of Sandwich. A short while later a meal was placed in front of the boy and the smuggler watched in amazement as he ate it with his bare hands like a wild animal. The smuggler watched the child with fascination. There was so much Bill could teach him, but the boy would have to earn his keep like everyone else. Bill didn't quite know what role the child could play in his budding empire but the smuggler knew he didn't quite trust the boy and would need to keep a close eye on him. For several days the boy didn't leave his side. Bill took him everywhere and would talk to him constantly and tell him all kinds of stories about storms at sea and wild adventures in far off lands. It was always a one-way conversation and the young smuggler wondered how long it would take for him to open up, but however long, Billy Bates was willing to wait.

Within days the Jenkins clan gave up their search for the mysterious attacker, dismissing it as a one off and assuming it was the work of a sailor who had since left the area. Billy Bates eventually put the boy to work carrying tubs from Marcus' clipper to one of Bill's safe houses with Henry Cutler. After a few days the pickpocket reported good things about the boy, claiming he was as strong as an ox and would carry a tub of brandy on each of his shoulders, shoulders that would slowly swell with muscle. Weeks passed by and Bill watched the boy slowly become more and more comfortable with his surroundings. He was always alert and suspicious of everything, but he was making slow progress. The smuggler's men would often strip to their shorts and dive into the River

Stour but the boy would never take his top off, always opting to stand and watch instead.

One evening Bill sat with the boy in front of an open fire getting warm and preparing to venture back out to meet one of his ships when the boy turned to him.

"Why are you doing this?" he asked the smuggler, who lapsed into silence and placed another log on the flames.

"You mean helping you?" the smuggler asked and watched as the boy nodded but stared at the ground avoiding Bill's eyes. "You know you are not alone in this world. A long time ago I was like you were." With this the boy looked up and stared at Bill. "I had no-one in the world and nothing to eat," the smuggler continued. "I thought it was all over and then I met someone. A complete stranger who took me under his wing and taught me everything he knew. He put a roof over my head and food in my mouth," he said glancing away and wiping a tear from his eye from the painful memories of his greatest friend Benny Swift who he missed every day.

Silence filled the room for a long moment before the orphan looked at Bill. "And what did he want in return?" the boy asked. Bill laughed whole-heartedly, expecting such a reply from the youngster who had issues trusting others.

Finally he stared at the boy straight faced. "He wanted nothing, but I would've given him anything and everything," he said. The boy lapsed into silence and stared at the flames as they flickered around in the fire. "You know kid, you need a name," Bill said and the boy turned to him and smiled for the first time ever. The smuggler was surprised. "Anyone you like, few people in this world are lucky enough to name themselves," he continued, chuckling. "You have a think about it, and in the meantime I want you to know that you can talk to me about anything. I can see you're not ready but when the time comes I'm here, okay," Bill said and watched as the boy nodded and continued to stare at the flames. It would be a long time before he'd be able to face the horrors of his past.

The room lapsed into silence once more and after five minutes or so the boy turned to Bill. "I would like to be called

Thomas," he said and Bill smiled and extended his hand, which the boy gripped.

"Pleased to meet you, Thomas," he said in that croaky voice of his.

Early the next morning Bill met up with Boseda to deliver Harry's share of the young smuggler's profits. Bill had no issues with paying Harry Booth his ten percent, and as far as he was concerned it was money well spent, just for the services and information he received from Boseda alone.

"Bill we need to talk about the boy," the huge African said, catching the smuggler off guard.

"His name's Thomas, he chose it himself," Bill replied. "What does the boy have to do with anything?" he continued. Boseda sat back and explained to Bill what he saw in the child's eyes and how much potential the boy had.

"That boy's a killer, Bill, you need to let me start training him now," the huge bodyguard said. Bill sat back speechless. He wasn't stupid and could see what Boseda could see.

"He's just a kid and I have enough men," the smuggler replied. Much to Bill's surprise and anger the African laughed.

"Men," he said, "they're pickpockets and fishermen. Yes they can carry tubs and transport your cargoes, but seriously Bill when war breaks out with the clan, which it will, and we both know it. Do you think any of them will stand their ground against Ronnie and his thugs?"

Bill Bates gritted his teeth and stared hard at Harry's number one bodyguard. The man was right and deep down Bill knew it.

"You need to think of the future Bill. The day will come when you'll need some capable men at your sides. Men who you can trust and rely on, men who'll spill blood without a moment's hesitation and that boy has more potential than anyone I've ever seen," the African warned.

Bill scratched his chin and sighed. "What do you suggest?" he asked.

Boseda sat back in his chair and thought for a moment. "We'll take it slowly. You let me have him three days a week. I will teach him everything he needs to know. Hand to hand combat, how to use every weapon imaginable and how to move through the streets unseen. Eventually I'll teach him how to kill a man without making a sound and what to do with the bodies, but that's a long way off yet," the African said. Bill thought for a moment before agreeing with Boseda's demands and from that day forth the huge African began training the orphan and turning him into the ruthless killer he'd one day become.

Chapter Thirty-One

On a dark winter night several miles out of town four horses galloped down a hill, pulling a stagecoach along a dangerous stretch of road, a stretch of road that was covered in dense woodland on both sides making it the ideal place for bandits to hide. The coach driver was well aware of the risks and knew that when he reached the bottom of the hill his horses would need rest before beginning the steep climb up the other side. The hour was late and the driver scanned the tree lines on both sides nervously, regretting making this journey in darkness. The stretch of highway was notorious for thieves and the cargo he was carrying was priceless to a man the driver didn't want to cross. When the coach finally pulled to a stop the driver froze and listened to the sounds of the night. Crickets and a wealth of other animals made a variety of noises behind the tree-line, whilst the horses panted, and caught their breath. The driver's heart was thumping in his chest as a thick cloud passed over the crescent moon plunging the highway even further into darkness.

Suddenly the coach's hatch sprung open. "Driver what's with the delay?" a lady's voice that had been trained from years of elocution lessons at the finest school in the land asked. The driver took a deep breath and turned to his passenger, annoyed at the distraction. The driver didn't want to take his eye off the tree-line for a second.

"One moment Madam, the horses are just catching their breath," he replied nervously as he turned his attention back to the tree-line. The horses still hadn't recovered and the driver had a bad feeling in his gut as he scanned the tree-line once more. Suddenly he caught a flicker of movement but it was too late. A bandit sprung out from behind a tree and leapt up onto the coach waving a dagger in the driver's face. The man froze to the spot, more in fear of what the husband of the young lady in the back would do to him rather than the thief himself. The driver stared at the robber who was only a boy. He was tall and skinny with a gaunt face peppered with ginger stubble.

"Money and jewellery," the thief shouted, with a grin on his face. The coach driver shook his head in shock.

"Do you have any idea who's in the back?" he asked the young thief. The bandit's face lit up and he leapt into the back of the coach.

"Well, well, well!" he said in greeting to the wealthy young lady who sat wearing a fine silk dress and petticoat. Instantly the thief took in the rings on the lady's fingers and the golden locket around her neck and smiled to himself. The lady was furious and flashed an evil look the bandit's way.

"My husband will make sure you hang for this!" she warned, as the thief began to remove her valuables. A moment later he leapt from the coach and disappeared amongst the trees. The lady slumped back in her chair. "You'll pay for that," she hissed under her breath before turning to the driver. "Get this coach moving and take me to my husband," she raged at the man who finally whipped the horses forcing them to begin their gallop up the other side of the hill towards safety.

A short time later the stagecoach pulled up outside a large house and the lady climbed out and raced towards her husband who was stood waiting to greet her. "Theodore! Theodore!" she cried as she rushed into his arms. The young man who'd recently been appointed the town's magistrate held his wife tightly.

"What's wrong, my dear?" he asked as she sobbed against his chest, too upset to reply. A moment later the coach driver was at his side and Theodore Rawlings turned and glared at the man. "What the hell's wrong?" he asked the coach driver who stood nervously in fear of his boss' reaction.

"We were robbed at knifepoint," he finally mumbled, as the magistrate's face reddened with fury.

"By whom?" he roared at the driver who quickly described the young thief. It meant very little to Rawlings and could have been one of a hundred different men from the rough and ready town, but the magistrate wasn't going to let the matter rest and had every intention of finding the culprit. Theodore Rawlings didn't know who the culprit was, but he knew a man who would, a man who'd be more than willing to help.

An hour later the young magistrate was sat explaining the events to Samuel Jenkins as a dozen of the leader's family members stood staring at the town's lawman. Rawlings resented the Jenkins family as much as the next man but he had no doubts that they controlled the town. The magistrate was young, smart and eager to earn himself a fortune in the town's cobbled streets. Rawlings understood it would make his job a lot easier if he worked with the clan rather than against them.

"I want the culprit strung up and what he stole returned," Rawlings stated, as Samuel Jenkins twisted the end of his beard with a look of satisfaction on his face.

"If we help you then you'll owe us Jenkins a debt," Samuel reminded the young and naive magistrate who grunted his agreement before giving a description of the thief. Samuel turned to Ronnie who was slumped in a chair in the corner of the room staring at the magistrate and silent for once in his life.

"Skinny teenager with short red hair, any ideas?" Samuel asked his nephew who climbed to his feet. The magistrate stared up at Ronnie in admiration of his huge height and build.

"Sounds a lot like Alfred Bicks. He's a gutsy little toe-rag from the north end of town," Ronnie said as Samuel turned to the magistrate and smiled before turning back to Ronnie.

"Take your men and go find him. Once you've recovered the locket, kill him," Samuel ordered, knowing that such actions would put blood on the magistrate's hands and earn Theodore Rawlings' loyalty forever. Ronnie smiled before marching out of the room.

"To a long a prosperous future together Mr Rawlings," Samuel said raising a glass and toasting the young lawman who was half his age. Theodore Rawlings reluctantly raised his glass, making a pact with the notorious Jenkins family that would last for many years to come.

Chapter Thirty-Two

Early the next morning as seagulls squawked overhead and the town slowly came to life, a small gang of thieves gathered in the corner of Alfred Square where they watched the traders unpack their wares with envy. The thieves varied in ages between thirteen and twenty years old and were shaking off the remnants of another poor night's sleep, cramped up together fighting off the cold in an old fishing shed long since deserted. This morning, like every other morning they were fantasising about breakfast and how they could get their hands on some food. The thieves were friends and often relied on each other for survival, but times were hard and each of them wouldn't hesitate betraying the next if it was worth their while.

Suddenly one of the thieves froze and a hushed warning passed through the group as Ronnie Jenkins was spotted marching across the market square towards them. Glancing around the thieves quickly spotted the huge thugs gang approaching from several directions. Many of the thieves were shaking with fear and panicking. They'd all recently paid their donation into the Jenkins family's coffers, buying them their right to continue operating on the town's streets and they wondered what Ronnie wanted. Most of the men had known him for years and were well aware that he enjoyed hurting people and would often attack people for fun.

"Alfred Bicks, where is he?" Ronnie demanded as he approached the gang of pickpockets, whose leader looked confused as he glanced around looking for Alfie among them.

"I don't know. I haven't seen him since yesterday afternoon," he said as Ronnie grabbed him by the scruff of the neck and lifted him a foot or so off the ground so he could look the thief directly in the eye.

"Is that right?" the huge thug said before throwing the man onto the cobbles where he crashed in a heap. Ronnie turned and addressed the whole group. "Understand that Alfred Bicks is now a wanted man. Anyone who is found harbouring him will face the full wrath of my family!" he warned the men whose day-to-day lives were a battle for survival. "On the other hand anyone with information leading to his capture will be rewarded generously. You all know how to contact me," he said before marching away with his gang of thugs.

The pickpockets stared at each other in silence as any loyalty to their fellow thief Alfie disappeared and they pondered how to get their hands on the reward the Jenkins were offering. Finally somebody spoke and shattered the silence.

"What the hell's Alfie gotten himself into this time?" one of them muttered, mimicking everyone's thoughts.

"I always said he wouldn't live to see eighteen," somebody else cut in before the group began to depart their separate ways to begin searching the streets.

The news of the Jenkins reward for Alfred Bicks spread through the town's streets faster than a gale force wind and quickly reached the ears of Harry Booth's number one enforcer and personal bodyguard. The huge African smiled when he heard the news. Boseda knew Alfie Bicks and knew the youngster was a toe-rag, but a capable one at that with more guts than brains. Boseda wasted no more time and quickly marched out of his boss' headquarters and joined the hunt, hoping he'd find the thief and claim a reward much greater than what Samuel Jenkins was offering.

Hours later, under the cover of darkness an excited Alfie Bicks crept into town. The young thief had never had quite a bounty of wealth like he currently had in his pocket. The locket he'd stolen was solid gold and worth a pretty penny. Certainly enough to keep him fed for months and months to come. Alfie smiled to himself as he turned the corner of an alleyway and froze as he came face to face with his worst nightmare. Staring up into eyes that offered no mercy Alfie fumbled for the knife in his pocket, willing to use it, and not for the first time. It was of no use though. A split second later the huge man threw a right hook that connected with Alfie's ginger stubble and sent the young thief to the floor. The last thing he was aware of was the huge man binding his hands and feet with rope as he drifted into unconsciousness.

Chapter Thirty-Three

When Alfred Bicks regained consciousness he found himself tied to a chair with a gag in his mouth. In a moment of panic he struggled to break free from the thick ropes binding his wrists and ankles, but it was of no use. He quickly scanned the walls of the bare room he was in until he came across a sight that sent shivers down his spine. Leaning against the far wall and smiling in his direction was Harry Booth's bodyguard Boseda.

Alfie tried to talk but nearly choked on the rag stuffed in his mouth. Suddenly a door closed behind him and the young thief tried to turn his neck but failed to get a look at whoever had entered the room.

A long moment passed before the huge African bodyguard stepped forward and untied the gag allowing Alfie to catch his breath. As soon as he'd recovered he attempted to plead ."Mr Boseda whatever I've done I'm sorry," but Harry's right hand man simply put his index finger to his lips and Alfie stopped talking and waited for whatever punishment was coming his way, hoping that the African would make it quick.

Hearing footsteps to his right Alfie craned his neck as a young man strolled into view. The man was in his late twenties with rough skin and dark hair tied back off his face. He wore a fancy suit that had been tailored, but it was the man's eyes that scared Alfie, eyes that were darker than a moonless night. The man leant in close and fixed the young thief with a stare that intimidated him to his very core. Whoever the stranger was he was wealthy and powerful and in many ways scarier than Boseda himself. Staring at his features Alfie could tell he wasn't a Jenkins, but curiously he was in control of Harry's bodyguard and the young thief wondered who he could be.

"Alfred Bicks, isn't it?" Billy Bates asked and Alfie nodded as he struggled to break free of the thick ropes binding his wrists. They held firm and after a moment he gave up and the man continued.

"You robbed a stagecoach at knifepoint last night. A daring move," Bill complimented him. Alfie caught the tone of the stranger's voice and it put him even more on edge.

"I pay off the Jenkins just like the next man," Alfie said staring at Boseda for support. The African stepped forward.

"You pay to pickpockets, not to rob coaches!" he growled, forcing Alfie to glance back at the man in the suit.

"I'm sorry Sir. You can have everything I took," he pleaded. Bill smiled his crooked smile and suddenly there was no doubt the stranger definitely scared Alfie more than Harry's number one bodyguard.

Suddenly Billy Bates pulled the solid gold locket from his pocket and slowly turned it over in his palm looking deep in thought. "It must be worth a fortune," Alfie said before Bill glanced his way with those jet black eyes and silenced him instantly.

"This locket belongs to the wife of the young magistrate who's in charge of this town," Bill said in his croaky voice.

"Damn," Alfie muttered as he dropped his head. A moment later he looked over at Boseda. "I didn't realise that, but the magistrate isn't my problem. I pay the Jenkins, he's their problem," Alfie tried to explain.

Billy Bates chuckled to himself and Alfred Bicks began to believe he wasn't going to leave the room alive. The stranger sat down in front of the thief and Alfie stared into his eyes. If he was going to die he'd at least try and go out fighting.

"The young magistrate is now in Samuel Jenkins' pocket," Bill said. "They've put a price on your head." Alfie Bicks let out a lungful of air and turned a shade paler as he took in the news. Glancing over at Boseda, an ally of the clan, Alfie knew that life was over for him.

"Ronnie and his gang are roaming the streets looking for you and as soon as they've retrieved this," Bill said holding the locket up and swinging it left to right, "they'll kill you!"

Alfie Bicks was staring at the strange man and trying to work out why he wasn't dead already. *'Were they just having some fun before they killed me,'* he wondered, but dismissed that idea. From what he'd heard about Harry's top enforcer it wasn't his style, for him killing was business and never pleasure.

"You have no future in this town anymore. The Jenkins will hunt you down," Bill continued, but Alfie Bicks had heard enough.

"So be it. They don't scare me!" he shouted back at the strange young man who, much to the thief's surprise, smiled.

"That's good I admire courage," he said turning towards Boseda.

The African smiled back. "I told you he had more guts than brains, boss," he said.

A look of absolute confusion had masked Alfie Bicks' face and his jaw went slack. "I would like you to come and work for me," Bill said. "I can offer you a decent living and more protection than you'll find on these streets."

Alfie glanced from the strange young man to Boseda and back again. "But you're Harry Booth's number one enforcer. You work for the Jenkins family one way or another," Alfie mumbled as the huge African stepped forward and stood behind the strange young man, whose eyes were so dark they penetrated into the soul.

"My loyalty lies with this man," Boseda said as he untied Alfie's wrists.

"And who in God's name are you?" the skinny teenager asked.

"My name is Billy Bates and I'm the man who's going to bring the Jenkins' empire to its knees. Are you with me or against me?" Bill asked, extending his hand. Alfie stared at Bill as a smile crept up on his lips before gripping the smuggling boss' hand firmly.

"Billy Bates I'm with you all the way," he said, grinning from ear to ear.

Bill smiled that crooked smile of his and handed the golden locket back to Alfie who took it and held it in his hands before glancing into those dark eyes. "You're giving me this back?" he asked in amazement.

Bill nodded. "As far as I'm concerned it doesn't belong to me," he said before climbing to his feet. "Let's get out of this town."

A few hours later, after creeping out of the town and riding on horseback across the flat and open countryside to the inn where Bill was staying, Alfie sat talking to his new boss when Thomas entered the room. The boy that Bill had found under the jetty froze as he saw Alfie Bicks for the first time. Thomas recognised Alfie. He'd seen the ginger beard and gaunt face before and it didn't take him long to place when and where. The tall skinny teenager before him was the absolute mirror image of the man who'd shown leniency when he'd stowed away aboard his ship, the man who'd terrorised every sailor on earth... the ruthless pirate Alfred Mudd.

"Thomas, this is Alfie," Bill said, pulling him from his thoughts and the orphan pushed the crazy idea from his mind and shook hands with the man he'd one day come to think of as a brother.

*

That night at one of Bill's safe-houses Alfred Bicks was ushered into an old barn that was crowded with the smuggler's men. Bill marched up and down giving orders and making preparation for that night's landing before turning to Alfie and introducing him.

"He's a gutsy young fellow. He'll be protecting cargoes and working by my side as a bodyguard," Bill said to the crowd who appeared pleased with the news. On the other side of the barn Henry Cutler stared at his boss with contempt. The pickpocket who Bill had offered a lifeline to many moons ago was fed up with the young smuggler's success. Envy had turned to hatred and as he watched Bill giving orders he decided enough was enough. Henry Cutler was going to betray Bill and make a small fortune in the process.

Chapter Thirty-Four

Ronnie Jenkins strutted through the town's streets furious that he'd spent the whole day searching high and low for Alfred Bicks and had turned up no results. The teenage thug couldn't understand it. People didn't just disappear and vanish, not without the assistance of his family anyway. Something didn't quite add up but Big Ronnie couldn't place it. In the last few weeks he'd experienced bad luck on several occasions. Ronnie wasn't superstitious. Bad luck had never been a factor during his father's reign as head of the Jenkins family, and such thoughts made him very angry. He wondered if his Uncle Samuel was up to the task of leading the clan and wished there was a way he could take over himself, but knew he'd never win over his family's elders who had huge support for his uncle.

Suddenly he caught sight of a man named Fredericks who pulled him from his dark thoughts. The man was a pimp and a scoundrel who organised the working girls and paid the Jenkins a generous commission to do so. Fredericks would often beat the girls if they didn't make enough money, but the Jenkins didn't care as long as they got their commission.

"Ronnie," Fredericks shouted as he crossed the road and greeted the young thug. Ronnie shook his hand but had no time to waste waffling in the street. The huge teenager was on a mission to find the gang of toe-rags he'd spoken to earlier who were friends with Alfred Bicks. Reaching the market square he spotted them and that look of fear and disappointment on their faces as he approached made him clench his fists in anger.

"We've looked everywhere Ronnie. He must be out of town. As soon as he gets back we'll come straight to you," one of the thieves promised. Ronnie stared at the gang of misfits as anger welled up inside him and they all hung their heads avoiding eye contact with him. A second later he exploded and lashed out with a barrage of punches that left most of the thieves sprawled out in the street unconscious. The few remaining pickpockets begged him for mercy.

"I want Alfred Bicks sooner rather than later!" he raged at them before marching off into Middle Street with his own gang following sheepishly like usual. As he marched along the town's main street mothers came rushing out of houses to grab their children and people crossed the road in fear of him. Big Ronnie Jenkins marched on and watched with pride, ignorant to the fact that respect was a far greater tool than fear. Scanning the crowds Ronnie continued to search for Alfie Bicks, that skinny little upstart he'd been dreaming of catching all day. Ronnie had his own motivations for catching the thief. It was true he needed to impress Samuel and the other elders of his family. He needed to prove to them that he had what it took, just like his father. More importantly Ronnie wanted to impress the young magistrate who he hoped he could work with for many years to come. Ronnie believed he was the next generation of the Jenkins and his uncle was too old and set in his ways to lead his family into the future. Ronnie had no intention of playing second fiddle to Samuel forever, but before he could take over he had to win the support of the clan's elders, his other uncles. Without their approval he'd never be able to follow in his father's footsteps and lead his family.

Reaching a tavern called The Pelican, Ronnie greeted several shady characters who were lingering outside smoking their pipes when one of his own gang approached him.

"Boss I have some news," the man said as Ronnie turned and faced his older cousin.

"What news?" he asked, before the man explained that somebody wanted to speak to him regarding Alfie Bicks. "He claims to know where he is," he said. Ronnie smiled for the first time all day as that smug expression returned to his face.

"Who is this man? And what does he want?" Ronnie asked his cousin.

"He says he wants to work for you boss. His name is Henry Cutler," the man said.

Ronnie followed his cousin to the entrance of the alleyway where Henry Cutler was waiting. The pickpocket who Bill had taken in and employed virtually at the beginning of his smuggling career feared being seen talking to any of the Jenkins family, let alone Big Ronnie himself. Cutler was well aware that the man he envied, the very man he was about to betray had more than a few of his own spies in the town's cobbled streets. Boseda alone would literally tear Cutler to pieces if he heard he'd betrayed Bill and Henry Cutler didn't want to get on the wrong side of the huge African, or Harry Booth either for that matter.

Cutler was an exceptional liar though and was going to be very selective about what he actually told Ronnie. He was going to use all of his skills to negotiate a deal with the young thug. A deal that would reap revenge on an enemy he shared with Ronnie, Ronnie's own Uncle Samuel, whilst also taking Bill's empire down and making himself rich in the process. Cutler was taking a huge risk. Ronnie may just kill him on the spot for even suggesting such a thing, but if he didn't Cutler would end up with everything he ever wanted out of life... money and power.

Cutler's heart began to beat in his chest as he saw the huge teenager enter the alleyway and bark orders at his men to stay and stand guard, before marching towards him. He quickly ran through the script he'd prepared in his head one last time.

"Henry Cutler! Where the hell is Alfie Bicks?" Big Ronnie demanded. Cutler stared up at the young thug in amazement. The teenager was huge, ugly and much more intimidating than Cutler had thought. He took a deep breath knowing that the next sentence would change his life and sever all the bonds he'd made in the last few years.

"You need to hear me out Ronnie. He is being protected by a man named Billy Bates," Cutler said.

Ronnie Jenkins looked baffled. "Protected?" he roared. "Who the hell is Billy Bates?"

Henry Cutler took a step backwards praying that the psychopath in front of him would at least restrain himself long enough to hear what he had to say.

"Billy Bates was a fisherman. A while ago he began smuggling small cargoes across the channel. He operates outside of the town, that's why you haven't heard of him. He is slowly building an army out of your enemies," Cutler said.

Ronnie was silent now, deep in thought. After a long moment he spoke. "I have to say that comes as a huge surprise, but certainly explains a few things. Weeks ago one of my men was attacked and we couldn't find the culprit," he said looking at Cutler for an explanation.

"The culprit was a homeless boy who was sleeping rough in the area. Bill found him and recruited him," Cutler said, as Ronnie suddenly exploded in anger and started pacing up and down in the alley as he clenched his fists. Cutler's heart rate went up a notch. He could see the thug was losing control. Suddenly Ronnie stopped and stared at him.

"And what about Harry Booth, does he know about this?" Ronnie asked.

"Of course not, if he had the slightest of inklings you'd have known," Cutler lied, wanting to make no enemies out of Harry's right hand man.

Ronnie began pacing once more. "I'll kill this Billy Bates and all of his men," he muttered to himself. Henry Cutler watched in panic as the red mist washed over the teenager. He began to regret opening his mouth in the first place. Now though he had nothing to lose and was aware that he'd have to work hard. If Big Ronnie had no use for him then he wouldn't leave the alleyway alive.

"It runs deeper than that Ronnie," he said. "It may sound bad to begin with but it could be the answer to all your prayers."

Suddenly Ronnie snapped out of his trance and stared at the thief. "What do you mean?" he asked, and Cutler quickly explained that he worked for Bill and was trusted completely.

"The first thing I'll do is get that locket back so you can give it to the magistrate," Cutler said, "and then we'll use Bill and his gang to our advantage."

Ronnie stared at Henry Cutler confused. "Meaning?" he asked suspiciously. Henry Cutler took a deep breath to prepare for the pinnacle moment that decided whether he lived or died.

"We use Bill as a scapegoat and let him take the fall for killing your Uncle Samuel," Cutler said. "Then we'll wipe Bill's gang off the map and this whole town and everything in it will be yours."

Big Ronnie Jenkins stared at Cutler for a long moment. The teenager was psychotic but he also had some of his father's brains and Cutler could see the cogs were turning.

"Give me one reason why I shouldn't kill you right here and now," he said coldly and Cutler swallowed hard.

"Because you hate Samuel even more than me," he replied and Ronnie actually smiled. The thug thought about the crazy plan before deciding it was perfect. Ronnie couldn't wait for his turn on the family throne. Samuel had decades left in him.

Finally he turned back to Henry Cutler. "And what do you expect in return?" he asked the traitor who smiled.

"I'm a capable guy Ronnie and I'm sure you'll have a use for me when you're head of your family," he replied.

Big Ronnie rubbed his chin and glanced towards the entrance of the alleyway to make sure none of his gang had heard any of the exchange. Satisfied he turned back to Cutler.

"I believe we have a deal, on the agreement that you bring me the locket within forty-eight hours. After that I'll come looking, you understand?" he asked, shaking Cutler's hand to seal the deal.

A few moments later the odd-looking pair strolled out of the alleyway and went their separate ways. Henry Cutler felt on top of the world, but he was completely unaware of the eyes burning into him from along the narrow street, eyes that belonged to Harry's top man, Boseda. The African debated for a moment on what course to take. '*How much has Cutler told Ronnie?*' he wondered, '*and who did he warn first?*' Deciding that his loyalty must lie in the man who'd employed him all these years he quickly disappeared through the labyrinth of streets. The African was going to waste no time relaying the news to Harry Booth and making sure he was safe. Only then could he think about warning Bill.

Chapter Thirty-Five

Harry Booth was in good spirits, drinking in The Seagull with most of his crew and celebrating the success of several large runs across the channel when Ronnie Jenkins marched into the tavern. Most of the regulars tutted and cursed under their breath at the sight of the young thug who brought trouble wherever he went, Harry Booth included.

'Here we go again,' he thought as Ronnie crossed the pub towards him, shoving people out of his path as he did so. The teenager's eyes were scanning the room, looking for Boseda Harry surmised. The old smuggler was well aware that the young thug had serious issues with his bodyguard.

"Ronnie, can I get you a drink?" he asked cheerfully, as he examined the look on the teenager's face. The young thug wore that arrogant expression even more than usual leading Harry to decide that Ronnie was in a good mood, but that wasn't reason enough for Harry to ever drop his guard. Ronnie Jenkins was just too unpredictable.

The huge teenager nodded his head and a cup of brandy was placed in front of him by a very shaky bartender, who quickly stepped as far away from the pair as possible.

"Where's Boseda?" Ronnie asked, and Harry explained that his right hand man was busy.

"He works hard you know," Harry said, chuckling as he sipped his brandy without taking his eyes off Ronnie. The thug smiled and it gave Harry the shivers.

"He's not working nearly hard enough, from what I've just heard," Ronnie said, smugly. The teenager hated the African nearly as much as he did his Uncle Samuel and couldn't resist the opportunity to rub Boseda's nose in the dirt that somebody had been smuggling on his doorstep and he hadn't realised.

Harry Booth's heart felt like it was going to explode as he stared at Ronnie and a million questions and concerns entered his mind. "What do you mean by that?" he finally mumbled.

Ronnie took a big gulp of brandy and turned to the smuggling boss. "You ever heard of a man named Billy Bates?" he asked. Now Harry's stomach was doing somersaults, but he tried his damndest to remain calm. *'How much did Ronnie actually know?'* he wondered as he took another sip of brandy to delay his response. Harry couldn't know for sure but he assumed Ronnie didn't know of his connection with Bates, if he had he wouldn't be smug, he'd be psychotic.

"I've heard of him, but not for a long time. He used to work as a fisherman but he left the area years ago. Why do you ask?" Harry said, watching Ronnie very closely.

The teenager smiled. "He never left the area Harry. He set up his own smuggling operation further up the coast."

For a moment Harry stared into Ronnie's eyes, then he slammed down his glass on the bar. "He what!" the smuggler roared. "I'll have Boseda gut him like a fish."

Ronnie watched Harry's anguish and smiled. "Don't worry, I'll take care of this problem personally," he said, as he finished his drink and marched back out of The Seagull. There was no way Ronnie was going to let Harry's bodyguard claim any of the glory of catching Billy Bates.

As soon as the tavern's door slammed shut Harry Booth exhaled a lungful of air and rubbed his temples as he wondered what to do. "What a nightmare this really is," he muttered as he turned to the bar and ordered another drink. A second later Harry was relieved to see his number one bodyguard Boseda enter the tavern. Harry had never seen the African looking so worried. He knew his bodyguard had grown very close to Billy Bates.

"How much does he know?" Boseda asked and Harry quickly explained what he'd learnt.

"It was that piece of scum Henry Cutler that sold Bill out," the African raged before turning to his boss. "I need to warn Bill. We owe him that much."

Harry Booth nodded his approval and Boseda marched straight back out of the drinking den. For the rest of the evening Harry thought about the situation. His heart went out to Bill, but the young smuggler was well aware of the risks he'd been taking. Like Boseda, Harry had also become attached to Bill Bates. He was ruthlessly ambitious, but a very likeable character. In the end Harry Booth sighed and accepted that the young smuggler's life was nearly over. Bill for all his courage wouldn't stand a chance against the Jenkins family. They were far too powerful. Ronnie Jenkins was going to tear Bill to pieces and there was nothing anyone could do about it.

Harry Booth sat alone at a small table lost in his own thoughts when he raised his glass. "To the gutsiest smuggler I ever had the pleasure of knowing," he muttered as he gulped down the burning liquor.

Chapter Thirty-Six

Boseda marched to the stables and commandeered a horse before galloping out of town and over to Sandwich. As he raced along dark tracks and across open fields he couldn't get Henry Cutler out of his mind and fantasised about killing the traitor very slowly.

The hour was late but he knew exactly where to find Bill and he also knew the smuggler would be only too pleased to see him. When he finally reached the inn where Bates was staying he spotted several of his men standing guard outside in the street. Boseda nodded as he entered.

The inn's reception was nearly empty except for one person who stood staring at him through vacant eyes. In his hand he held his weapon of choice, an axe. The African had no doubt he could use it, he'd personally taught him.

"Thomas, where's Bill?" he asked the young boy who sized Boseda up before replying. The orphan had become very loyal to his new master in the short time since he'd taken him in off the streets.

"Follow me," Thomas said before leading Boseda through a maze of corridors into Bill's room where he found the smuggler studying a book on the French language. Bill had become obsessed with educating himself; he held the firm belief that knowledge was power and spent most evenings reading. As soon as Boseda entered the room Bill glanced up and stared at the African through those dark eyes, as he placed the book down.

"Boseda old friend, this is a surprise," he said, rising to his feet and greeting the African whose sombre look told Bill trouble was ahead. The pair sat down and Boseda got straight to the point.

"I'm afraid I bring bad news," he said. "Ronnie Jenkins knows all about your smuggling gang." Bill Bates nodded and rubbed his jaw. He appeared to take the news well, all things considered.

"How? Someone must have betrayed me," he asked and Boseda explained about Henry Cutler's meeting with the young thug and Bill cursed under his breath before the room lapsed into silence.

"I'm sorry Bill. He must want the reward the Jenkins are offering for that goddamn locket," Boseda said.

Bill nodded. "He was always greedy," he said, before he sat back in his chair and began to think hard about how to steer himself out of this mess.

Boseda could see the young smuggler was deep in thought so he left him to it, and at least ten minutes passed before the African turned to the young smuggler he'd felt honoured to work with. Much to Boseda's surprise Bill was sitting back in his chair with that crooked smile of his plastered all over his face, and Harry's bodyguard became very curious.

"I have a plan," Bill finally said in that croaky voice, before leaning forward and explaining his intentions. A few minutes later the African sat back in his chair and thought about Bill's idea.

"What do you think?" the smuggler asked and Boseda grinned.

"Remind me never to make an enemy out of you Bill," was all the African had to say on the matter.

Chapter Thirty-Seven

Early the following morning Henry Cutler, Alfie Bicks, Carp and a handful of other men who worked for Bill stood in an old barn that the smuggler was using to hide some of his merchandise. After hauling the heavy cargo several miles and stowing it away they were having a well-earned rest.

"It's solid gold," Alfie Bicks was bragging to the group as he showed off the locket. The men were impressed, even Cutler commented on its beauty, but deep down the traitor was surprised Alfie Bicks could be so stupid.

"What are you going to do with it?" Carp asked, and Alfie turned to the short, tubby man who he liked most out of his new boss' men.

"I'm going to leave it here," Alfie replied as he stashed it away. "It's safer than carrying it on me."

The group all agreed. Every man was well aware that the Jenkins family desperately wanted the locket and were planning on punishing the skinny thief for taking it in the first place, but no-one more than Henry Cutler who had listened intently to every word that Alfie had said and watched exactly where he'd hidden the prized possession.

"Come on then lads. Let's go meet the boss and see what he's got planned for us today," Carp said, earning sighs from most of the gang as they strolled out of the barn. Henry Cutler knew his moment had arrived and he took his time, pretending to gather up his things.

"Are you coming?" Alfie asked as he walked out of the barn leaving Cutler alone.

"Yeah, just a moment," the traitor called after him as he slipped the golden locket out of its hiding place and into his pocket.

'You fool,' Cutler thought, whilst outside Alfie Bicks was walking away from the barn with exactly the same thoughts in mind.

After a two-mile hike the team reached the banks of the River Stour, overlooking the estuary and the English Channel. Bill stood gazing out at the ships that dotted the horizon. He looked exhausted and as they approached he turned and greeted them, before giving out orders for the day. The men could see their boss wasn't his usual cheeky self.

"Are you okay Bill? You look like you've got something on your mind," Carp finally asked, instantly regretting it.

Bill spun around and glared at him. "Maybe I have, but it's got nothing to do with you!" he barked at the man. "Now get to work."

Henry Cutler watched Carp go red in the face, humiliated before he turned and walked away with Alfie in tow, leaving Cutler alone with Bill. The smuggler exhaled a lungful of air and stared back out at sea. Henry Cutler became very curious. He'd known Bill for a long time and could see the smuggler was troubled.

Suddenly Bill turned to him. "Can I have a word?" he asked, and Cutler stepped forward.

"Of course Bill. What's the problem?"

Bill scratched his chin. "I need to talk to someone about this. I've known you a very long time Henry. You're about the only person I know I can trust for certain," he said, gazing out at the ships sailing into the River Stour.

"You know you can tell me anything Bill," Cutler said, and the smuggling boss turned his attention to the traitor he'd given work to. *'You're good,'* Bill thought as he watched Cutler closely. "If you mention what I'm about to say to anyone, you're a dead man," Bill said.

"Come on, this is me you're talking to, of course I won't go blabbing. Now what's on your mind?" Cutler asked. He was very curious now.

"Well," Bill began, "a few days ago Harry Booth was approached by Samuel Jenkins who asked a favour of him. The sort of favour you don't get a choice over." Bill paused as Cutler nodded away as curiosity grew and grew.

"What was the favour?" he finally asked.

"Samuel Jenkins wants his nephew Ronnie dead, the thug's a serious threat to his leadership and a complete psychopath to boot. Samuel can't do it himself because of how it'll look to the rest of his family. It has to be an outsider, so he's forced Boseda to carry out the execution," Bill said. Henry Cutler lapsed into silence as he tried to process what Billy Bates had just confided in him.

"Boseda's going to kill Ronnie in a few days' time, then Samuel will remain leader of the Jenkins for many years to come," Bill said, staring out at the estuary once more.

"It's good news for us, but it means we'll have to watch our backs over the next few weeks," Bill said, as Cutler stood staring out at the Channel, still in shock at the news and wondering what the hell to do about it.

"I feel a bit better now I've got that off my chest," Bill said. "Now you can get to work, but don't you dare tell a soul about what I've just spoken about."

Cutler mumbled an agreement before he climbed up onto his horse and galloped off along the dirt track towards the town of Deal, leaving Billy Bates alone. The smuggling boss stood for a moment watching the traitor disappear with a crooked smile on his face. Suddenly Alfie Bicks and Carp came trundling out of some bushes.

"Did he take the locket?" Bill asked in that croaky voice and Alfie nodded.

"Good work, men," he congratulated the pair.

"What happens now?" Carp asked. Bill turned and fixed those dark eyes of his on the man who'd earned his trust and respect hauling his smuggled merchandise.

"He'll take that locket and what I just told him straight back to Ronnie," Bates said smiling.

Alfred Bicks itched his ginger stubble. "What makes you so sure he believed it?" the skinny teenager asked. Billy Bates chuckled to himself before turning to Alfie.

"Because it was music to his ears. Cutler hates Samuel Jenkins with a passion. It was exactly what he wanted to hear," he said and Alfie nodded, he couldn't fault Bill's logic.

"Now what?" Carp asked the smuggling boss who had turned around and was gazing once again out at the English Channel.

"We go to ground and wait for all hell to break loose," Bill finally said in that croaky voice of his.

Chapter Thirty-Eight

It was gone midday when Henry Cutler arrived in the town of Deal and stabled his horse. Cutler was still in shock about the news Bill had delivered, but he didn't doubt the man. Cutler knew from personal experience that Samuel Jenkins was a coward of a man, and more than capable of ordering the execution of a member of his own family. The traitor had been put in a difficult position. If he told Big Ronnie the news he would have to lie to the man further. There was no way he was going to tell the thug that Harry Booth and Boseda were on Bill's payroll. If he did Ronnie would go on the warpath and everything would be ruined.

Creeping through a network of alleyways Cutler finally reached a spot where several of Big Ronnie's men were waiting and quickly arranged a meeting with their leader. As he followed the foot soldiers through the town's backstreets Henry Cutler was scared out of his wits. The traitor had no idea how Ronnie was going to take the news. Either way he had no choice but to tell him. If he didn't the consequences would be far worse. Ronnie would kill Bill, then get killed himself and who would be left running the town... Samuel Jenkins, and Cutler would be back to square one picking pockets. *'Not an option,'* he thought.

The safest option was to tell Big Ronnie and let him tear his uncle to pieces. *'Hopefully he'll kill him and take control of the clan,'* Cutler thought, as he was led to a shack where the huge thug was waiting. As he entered and clapped eyes on Ronnie, who was sitting at the back of the room in the shadows, he shivered in fear before stepping forward.

"Well, well. Henry Cutler. I hope you've managed to get your grubby mitts on that locket," the teenager said as he rose from his chair and stared at Cutler.

"What's wrong?" he demanded, noticing the look of despair on the thief's face. Cutler was frozen to the spot terrified. The thief had a sharp tongue and could talk his way out of most situations, but he was in well over his head.

"Ummm," he mumbled, "we have a problem. I have some bad news for you."

Ronnie's face screwed up in anger, and he grunted before pulling a dagger from his pocket. Henry Cutler swallowed hard as he stared at its rusty and blunt blade.

"I don't take bad news very well I'm afraid," the young thug said, as Henry began to back away instinctively. Ronnie stepped forward. "Where's the damn locket!" he roared at Cutler who whimpered in fear as he pulled it from his pocket and shakily handed it over to the teenager who held it in his huge palm and smiled, then he glanced back at Cutler and the smile had vanished.

"If I was you I'd take a seat and start explaining yourself. I want to know all about this problem that's clearly worrying you so much," Ronnie said, before the pair took their seats.

"Well I don't really know how to say this, and I hope you don't blame me, after all I'm just a messenger and I'm on your side," Cutler said, as Ronnie played around with the golden locket.

Suddenly the thug looked up at him. "Get to the point!" he barked.

"Well Bill Bates has an inside man in Harry Booth's gang, that's why he's managed to get away with smuggling for so long," Cutler said as he stared at the table, avoiding Ronnie's eyes.

The thug thought for a moment. "I expected as much, Harry Booth is a fool. Do you know who the traitor is?" Ronnie demanded and Cutler explained that only Bill knew the man's identity, which seemed to satisfy the thug.

"Okay I'll find out who as soon as I get my hands on Bill, it's not a problem," Ronnie said, watching Cutler as he took a deep breath.

"That's not it I'm afraid. A few days ago Harry Booth was approached by your Uncle Samuel," Cutler said. "You may not want to believe this, but I promise it's completely true. Samuel has commissioned Boseda to assassinate you. Your uncle wants you dead. You're too much of a risk to his leadership. I'm sorry."

Cutler stopped talking and watched as the red mist descended on Big Ronnie. The colour washed out of his face and he began clenching his fists and muttering under his breath. Cutler tried to talk further but the huge thug had slipped into a world of his own. At least ten minutes passed before Ronnie Jenkins finally looked up at the traitor.

"Get out of town for a few days whilst I deal with Samuel. Only then can we take Bill Bates out," he said, but the young thug wasn't thinking clearly. He'd let anger cloud his judgement and was about to make a huge mistake.

Chapter Thirty-Nine

When Ronnie Jenkins marched into his family's camp that day he was still very confused. All the way home his gang had tried to talk to him and find out what was wrong, but the teenager was lost. He marched along at a fast pace ignoring their questions like he'd been possessed by an evil spirit, and in many ways he had.

The camp was busy as always with dozens of cousins, nieces and nephews milling about. A fire burned away in the middle of a huge clearing and a crowd were gathered around cooking and telling stories, a family tradition amongst the clan.

Ronnie scanned the crowd searching for his Uncle Samuel's face but couldn't place it, eventually turning and marching towards Samuel's shack. Slowly members of the clan were beginning to realise something was wrong. The elders rose from their seats and began to question Ronnie's gang as the thug stormed into Samuel's house. Ronnie's men knew nothing, apart from the thug was furious and they quickly relayed this to the family's elders.

Samuel Jenkins was sitting at his desk making notes in his ledger when his nephew entered the room. The leader looked up. "Ronnie, what's wrong?" he asked, surprised to see his nephew and in such a bad mood.

The words meant nothing to Ronnie who was way past talking. He stepped forward and threw the desk out of his way before punching his uncle in the jaw, sending him sprawling to the ground. A look of utter bewilderment crossed the leader's face as Ronnie leapt on him and began raining down heavy blows.

Suddenly the door burst open and half a dozen men rushed into the room and tried to pull Ronnie off Samuel. The teenager shrugged them off like flies and stopped throwing punches. Now he was gripping his uncle's throat in both his hands and squeezing the life out of him. Samuel began to redden in the face and tried to struggle to break free, but his nephew's huge bulk was bearing down on him, pinning him to the floor.

Suddenly a loud thud was heard as Ronnie was hit in the back of the head with a lump of wood. His grip on his uncle's neck softened slightly and Ronnie was wrestled to the ground. The teenager was still conscious and it took ten men to hold him down whilst his ankles and wrists were bound with thick rope.

Samuel Jenkins lay on his back gasping for air as blood poured from his nose and lips and soaked into his bushy beard.

"You were never right in the head!" he said as he climbed to his feet and spat a mouthful of blood on the floor. "Now get him out of here," he ordered as Ronnie's bulk was dragged out of the room. The teenager was locked away in a barn on a pile of hay where he spent the remaining day and night as a prisoner whilst his family discussed his punishment.

As he lay there the red mist finally evaporated and he began to think clearly. Suddenly he regretted storming the camp and attacking his uncle, a move that would seriously affect his chances of achieving his dream of leading his family like his father. Lying on the hay the teenager realised that he'd let his anger get the better of him, the smart move would have been to kill his uncle anonymously and blame it on the smuggler Billy Bates, but it was too late for that. Ronnie Jenkins had made a huge mistake and would have to deal with the consequences. He wondered what the punishment would be, *'Would they banish me? If they did I'd have to go along with it, but what would I do about Billy Bates and Henry Cutler?'* The traitor's words kept flooding back and repeating, 'Bill's building an army out of your enemies'.

"Well Uncle Samuel let's see how you fair against Bill and his army," the thug eventually muttered to himself. Ronnie Jenkins had decided that the more problems and obstacles his uncle faced the better. If his uncle banished him he'd keep his secret about the smuggler all to himself. "One day I'll be back," he muttered as he drifted off into a deep sleep.

Chapter Forty

Early the next morning the first rays of sun burst through the slats in the barn's walls and Ronnie Jenkins awoke and lay on the hay thinking of his future. At around ten a.m. he was dragged out of his overnight prison and put on trial in front of his whole family. He sat shackled to a chair in front of a raised platform where Samuel and the family's elders sat. The rest of the family crowded around, curious to know the teenager's fate. His own gang stood loyally watching the proceedings, but the vast majority looked at him with fear and disgust in their eyes. Dale's youngest had confirmed what the clan had been whispering amongst themselves for many years. Ronnie was a psychopath and was out of control. He enjoyed inflicting pain and answered to no-one.

When the proceedings began the teenage thug was asked to explain his actions. He wanted more than anything to justify his behaviour and tell his whole family about his uncle's arrangement with Harry Booth to kill him, but now he'd calmed down he was thinking clearly. Ronnie was far from stupid and understood that nobody would believe him. It was well known that Ronnie and Samuel hated each other. The pair had been playing a game of cat and mouse for many years, but it was a private game, and Ronnie knew in his heart that if he ever wanted to lead his family like his father it would have to remain private. As far as the teenager was concerned his uncle had won the battle, but Ronnie knew that in the end he'd make the man pay with his life and he'd win the war.

So instead of explaining his actions he grunted and shrugged his shoulders before the mock-trial broke up and the elders of the family convened to talk of his punishment. Once they'd gone his gang crowded around him with promises to break him out, but Ronnie dismissed them. The huge teenager could have broken free at any moment, but in doing so he'd sacrifice his dream and would never walk in his father's footsteps as leader of the clan.

An hour later the elders returned and took their seats once more. Ronnie sought out his uncle's eyes, but the leader of the Jenkins gang refused to look at his nephew. Ronnie mistakenly assumed this to be an admission of guilt, in reality it was shame. It was his favourite Uncle Derek who rose to his feet and read out the verdict.

"Ronnie, as Dale's son you've always been in line to one day lead this family. At such a young age with such huge height and strength you have all the tools of the trade to follow in your father's footsteps. You have so much potential, but it's widely believed that you've always struggled with your temper. The attack on your uncle yesterday was unprovoked and totally against the Jenkins family's code. We never fight amongst ourselves. Having spoken through the night on how best to deal with the situation we've found ourselves in, it's been decided that you are not only a danger to yourself, but others around you," Derek Jenkins said. Ronnie stared at his Uncle Samuel with hatred in his eyes, vowing that one day he'd make the man pay for this whole spectacle.

"As a result," Derek continued, "it's been decided that it's in the best interests of our family that you get control of your temper once and for all. You have a lot of your father in you and with that in consideration it's been agreed that you will spend the foreseeable future travelling with the gypsy families, like your father before you. McGregor has agreed to take you under his wing and train you as a prize-fighter. Ronnie Jenkins you are banished from this camp and our entire territory for the period of three years."

There was a gasp of shock from the crowd. The last time Ronnie had come across a member of the McGregor clan he'd come close to biting the man's ear off, and Sean McGregor wouldn't forget that in a hurry. Ronnie himself looked fairly composed at the news. The idea of being dragged around the country so every man who thought he was tough enough could take a pop at him for a meagre reward had its appeal.

"And what if I refuse?" he asked, and Samuel Jenkins finally climbed to his feet and looked him in the eye.

"If you break any of these conditions you'll be banished forever, you'll never be accepted in this camp and you'll certainly never lead this family," he stated. Ronnie glared at him before turning to the family's elders who were all nodding in agreement. He gritted his teeth and turned back to his uncle whose face was still battered and bruised.

"I agree to the terms," he said, surprising most of the crowd. Samuel Jenkins nodded and the trial came to an end.

Later that day Ronnie Jenkins was escorted out of the camp down into the town of Deal to a large square south of town to board a coach for the long journey he faced, a journey that would take him out of Kent and far away from the town's cobbled streets. Standing in the square he watched the town's people milling around in streets that were rightfully his and swore that one day he'd return and punish everyone that had wronged him.

Suddenly Ronnie was pulled from his dark thoughts as he spotted the town's young magistrate Rawlings amongst the crowds. The huge thug marched across the road towards him, much to the despair of a dozen of his family members who were under strict instructions from their leader Samuel to make sure he boarded the coach, without causing any further problems.

"Magistrate Rawlings," Ronnie called out, stopping the young lawman in his tracks.

"Ah Ronnie isn't it? I don't suppose you've caught that scoundrel have you?" Rawlings asked, still clearly outraged by the coach robbery. "That locket has been in my wife's family for generations and she's heartbroken," he added. Ronnie smiled and pulled the golden locket from his pocket. The magistrate's face lit up and he went to snatch it out of the teenager's hands, but Ronnie held it out of his reach and Rawlings was forced to look up into the thug's eyes and negotiate instead.

"Don't ever forget you owe me a favour Magistrate, not my Uncle Samuel or my family either for that matter, but me personally, understand?" Ronnie asked.

A hint of a smile crossed the lawman's lips before he answered. "I understand, Ronnie," and the young thug handed him the prized possession. The magistrate fumbled with the locket in his sweaty palms.

"One day, Magistrate, I'll be back to call in that favour," Ronnie said as he strolled across the road and climbed into a waiting coach. As it began to pick up speed and leave the town behind, Ronnie Jenkins thought of all the men he'd punish when he returned. He thought of Alfie Bicks, the mysterious Billy Bates and of course Harry's bodyguard Boseda who he hated with a passion, but above everyone else he thought of his Uncle Samuel.

Chapter Forty-One

Billy Bates went to ground in anticipation of an attack from the Jenkins family. The daring young smuggler didn't know if his plan had worked, but he was fully prepared for war on land and sea anyway. On hearing of Cutler's treachery Bill had immediately arranged for all of his safe-houses to be cleaned out and all of the smuggled merchandise to be moved. Henry Cutler was aware of their original locations, so Bill considered them all to be compromised. The smuggler warned his men not to return to any of the original safe houses for fear of an ambush from Ronnie and his thugs.

Instead the young smuggler arranged to loan a house from his friend Robert Planter, as Bill knew that not even Cutler was aware of his connection to the merchant. The house was out in the sticks where nobody would ever think of looking. For several days Bill waited out the storm, ready for an attack with all his men at his sides, but nothing happened and eventually he grew anxious to hear some news, some word from the town but no messengers came. Every time his gang left the safety of the house to meet his ships and pick up cargoes they were heavily armed with clubs. Billy Bates suspected the Jenkins would hit him where it hurt and go for his merchandise, but every night his men returned, under heavy burden of smuggled goods but otherwise unscathed.

On the third day a messenger arrived and arrangements were made for Bill to meet Boseda. The smuggler travelled on horseback with half a dozen of his men, leaving the sanctuary of his temporary headquarters. Bill was on high alert but Harry Booth's bodyguard quickly put him at ease with news that Samuel Jenkins had been seen in the town. The man was battered and bruised but alive.

"Well your crazy plan kind of worked," Boseda said, smiling broadly and in good spirits. "Samuel is alive, but

Ronnie had a good go at killing him," the African continued. "They've banished him!"

Billy Bates smiled that crooked smile of his. "Ronnie? You know this for sure?" Bill asked and Harry's bodyguard explained that his boss had received a visit from the Jenkins clan's leader, who'd very reluctantly explained it all.

"So Samuel Jenkins knows of me and my operation?" Bill demanded, and Boseda chuckled.

"That's the strange thing Bill. Samuel Jenkins has no idea, the man doesn't even know why Ronnie attacked him," the African said.

Bill laughed whole-heartedly, it was great news. The loss of Ronnie had weakened Samuel's family considerably. Now Bill was desperate to track down Henry Cutler and find out exactly what the traitor had told Ronnie Jenkins, only then would Bill feel safe to come out of hiding. The smuggler set Alfie Bicks to work tracking down the man who'd nearly toppled his operation. Alfie searched high and low but Cutler had vanished, and the skinny bodyguard considered the possibility that Ronnie had killed him. The young thug was certainly capable.

Throughout the whole saga Billy Bates' clippers had been sailing across the channel at full capacity. The young smuggler was ferrying a wealth of merchandise into the country and selling the goods at a healthy profit. The man who'd once earned pittance catching fish was now a wealthy man. The long days he'd spent hiding out at Planter's house had taught him that he needed a headquarters of his own, a home not just for himself but somewhere safe for his men too. For years Bill had worked tirelessly to make something of himself. He'd taught himself many subjects and dreamt of one day having a fancy office like Planter's, with bookshelves and charts and a large table where he could hold regular meetings with his men. Billy Bates decided that the time had arrived to make that dream a reality. A few weeks later, on a cold winter afternoon, he arrived at a big old house nestled high up on the chalk cliffs overlooking the English Channel. Through those pitch black eyes Bill took in the views in every direction, making the house virtually impenetrable from attack. Pulling out his telescope he knelt down on the grass and scanned the channel whilst his men lingered around. The views out to sea were fantastic and the smuggler was pleased he'd be able to monitor the movement of vessels to and fro from the continent. Finally Bill turned to Thomas and watched the orphan as he took in his new surroundings. Bill had come to learn that Thomas liked the safety and freedom of open spaces. After a moment the boy turned to Bill.

"What is this place?" he asked, and Bill smiled that crooked smile of his.

"This, Thomas," he said in that croaky voice, as he pointed towards the house and the land it sat on, "this is our new home." Bill watched as a smile crept onto the boy's face. Thomas took it all in before he marched off to explore. The smuggler watched him go and smiled, he'd never seen the boy look so happy and it was a moment he'd treasure for a long time. Finally Billy Bates turned to the man who was selling the property. "I'll take it," he said and the man smiled awkwardly.

"And how will you be paying sir?" he asked, unsure of whether the shady young character before him had the money to afford such a fine property.

The young smuggler, who'd lived a life of poverty in his younger years, turned to him. "I'll be paying cash," he replied in that croaky voice, before turning to several of his men and nodding. A moment later they placed several large sacks of money at the man's feet, as he gasped in surprise.

Chapter Forty-Two

Within days Bill, Thomas and a handful of his most trusted men moved into the cliff-top house and the ambitious young smuggler who'd lived a life of poverty finally built the study he'd dreamt of having for many years. He purchased a huge oak table that was so heavy it took six men to carry it up the stairs. Bill searched high and low for maps of the area and books to add to his growing collection. For the first time Thomas had a bedroom of his own, and in comparison to the filthy cell he'd once occupied, it was a dream come true. The boy who'd lived amongst the rats and other vermin had never felt so secure, and he knew in his heart that he owed a debt to Bill that he'd never be able to repay.

In the evenings Bill would sit with Thomas beside an open fire, both gazing out at the English Channel as the smuggler talked non-stop, teaching the boy he'd taken in off the streets everything he knew. During the days the odd pair worked harder than ever. Marcus, Bill's number one sailor worked tirelessly ferrying cargoes to and fro from the continent, always delivering the merchandise to Bill's landing teams led by Carp who'd safely transport them to safe houses across the county. The entire operation ran like clockwork. Everyone knew what was expected of them and they delivered for Billy Bates, the man who in many ways had saved them all.

Alfie Bicks concentrated on a different task entirely and spent every waking hour hunting the traitor Henry Cutler, vowing not to rest until the man was punished for his betrayal. Throughout this period Billy Bates stayed well away from the town of Deal and its dangerous streets. With Ronnie Jenkins gone the clan had lost a lot of power, but as far as the Jenkins were concerned they still ruled the area with an iron fist. Billy Bates was happy to let them believe this to be true, for him smuggling was business. The man with the jet black eyes cared little for reputation. The only thing that mattered to him was his men and the money in their pockets. Harry Booth continued to smuggle on the clan's behalf and as far as the townsfolk were concerned the coastline belonged to him. A very select few knew differently though and were all too aware that Harry Booth was just a front man now, someone to attract the attention away from the real man who was running the show and that man was landing more merchandise than ever and making Harry Booth rich in the process.

The Jenkins clan still littered the cobbled streets. The ruthless family had no idea what was happening in their own town. The great Dale Jenkins' death had brought an end to an era. His family's foot soldiers were losing their discipline and their leader Samuel was slowly losing control. More and more the clan were seen wasting their days in the town's drinking dens, boozing on liquor Harry had smuggled into the country, completely unaware of the rug that was being pulled out from underneath their feet.

Harry's number one bodyguard Boseda regularly fed Bill with information and both men were happy to see the Jenkins empire slowly crumbling. The tough African kept his young apprentice Thomas very busy. The boy he'd found under the jetty was a quick learner and excelled at every lesson Boseda taught him. The boy who'd lived through a waking nightmare at the Whitegate Cotton Mill was becoming quite the street soldier. He was still only a teenager, but was solidly built with wide shoulders that rippled with muscle from carrying the heavy tubs of brandy, but it was his vacant eyes that were sunk into a completely emotionless face that scared most men. The boy collected debts on Boseda's behalf and was building quite a reputation for himself in the town's labyrinth of cobbled streets. Few men had the courage to refuse the boy's demands and when they did they regretted it instantly. Usually they coughed up what was owed after glancing at the axe he held at his side and into the boy's vacant and emotionless eyes. The ones who didn't were soon knocked off their feet as the teenager hit them with all his force. Over time Thomas found himself in countless situations where his life was threatened, but the boy never backed down even when he was heavily outnumbered. Even the gutsiest criminals in town knew that the boy in front of them was far more ruthless and violent than his African mentor, and they also knew that one word of complaint from Thomas and Boseda himself would go to war; as a result the boy always collected what was owed.

*

On a warm summer evening Billy Bates' bodyguard Alfred Bicks finally found the man he'd been searching for. Bill's skinny knife-wielding bodyguard had spent months hunting out Henry Cutler, but it was as if the man had vanished. Then one evening Alfie was on his way to a tavern several miles out of town. The red haired young enforcer was a hundred yards from the drinking den when he first caught sight of the traitor, and he stood watching Cutler as he entered the tavern. Alfie's heart raced in his chest as he gripped the knife handle in his pocket and debated what to do next. Alfie wasn't stupid though and knew that Bill wanted to deal with Henry Cutler personally so he decided to be patient and raced off to summon his boss. Hours later when Cutler staggered out of the drinking den into the deserted street and began walking up the road the tall bodyguard was pleased he hadn't given into temptation. Turning to his left he looked at Bill who smiled a crooked smile before stepping out of the shadows with Thomas at his side. Then Bill began following the man who'd nearly cost him everything down the road. The small team quickly picked up pace, moving along stealthily until they were only a dozen or so yards behind him. Cutler was drunk and completely unaware of the predators giving chase until it was too late. The man, who Bill had thrown a lifeline to and given regular work, turned on his feet at the very last minute. He caught a glimpse of Thomas' face before the teenager swung a right hook, which put Cutler on his back. Barely conscious the traitor rolled over, scrambled to his feet and began pleading with his old boss.

"Don't kill me!" he begged, as he stared into Bill's eyes. The smuggling boss wasn't enjoying the moment, as he'd once considered Cutler a friend. But loyalty meant everything to Bill who'd risen out of the gutter with nothing but loyal friends and the rags on his back.

Bill stared at Cutler for a long time. "I won't kill you, but by God do you deserve it!" he finally said. "I put food in your mouth and clothes on your back and this is how you treat me. I'll let you live, but this town needs to know that betraying me has consequences and you Henry will be a constant reminder!" He pulled out the dagger he always carried on him and stepped towards the traitor.

A moment later Billy Bates was marching back along the road with Thomas and Alfie at his sides, as Henry Cutler lay on his back screaming and clutching his face in a futile effort to stem the flow of blood gushing between his fingers from the deep cut running down his cheek.

"One day I'll make you pay," Cutler hissed as Bill and his men disappeared into the night.

Chapter Forty-Three

A few days later...

Bill's best man, when it came to collecting illegal merchandise at agreed drop zones on the shoreline and transporting them to his safe-houses, was strolling into the town's cobbled streets. Carp, who'd been working for Bill for many months, had really proven his worth in the smuggling boss' dark eyes. Billy Bates had given him an opportunity and the red haired young man, who'd been beaten by the Jenkins clan for falling in love with the wrong woman, had seized it with both hands. Times were hard, people were struggling and the youngster was all too aware of how lucky he was. Carp was well liked by Bill who trusted him completely. He was a hard worker and was held in very high regards by Bill's entire team, especially Alfie Bicks who he'd become close friends with.

Working for Billy Bates Carp had begun to feel safe for the first time since the Jenkins clan had taken everything from him. They'd beaten and humiliated him, stolen the girl he loved and forced his previous boss to sack him. Over time Carp's confidence was slowly returning, but as Carp rounded a corner in the town's labyrinth of cobbled streets and entered the market square he spotted the girl he loved and his heart missed a beat. Dropping his head Carp felt vulnerable once more.

She was standing in the corner of the square with a handful of working girls and as their eyes met for the first time in months Carp felt like he'd been punched in the chest. The young man who organised Bill's landing teams struggled to breathe, as he stared at the expression of embarrassment on her face. She looked far removed from the girl he'd fallen for. Now she was wearing a worn out, tatty petticoat with a face full of makeup. For a moment they stared into each other's eyes and to Carp it felt like time was standing still, then she looked away as Frederick, the town's pimp strolled over to where the girls were standing and began berating them for not earning their keep. Carp stood frozen to the spot as everything fell into place and he realised why the Jenkins clan had wanted her in the first place.

As Frederick shouted at his girls several of the Jenkins young ruffians joined his side, the same young ruffians that had beaten Carp many months before. Carp dropped his head in shame and stared at the cobbles at his feet, as he began to make his way across the square. Feeling at the bottom of a pit of despair Carp didn't think things could get any worse, then the Jenkins thugs spotted him and were on him instantly like lions that had spotted an injured antelope. Rushing across the square they mocked him whilst the girl he loved wiped tears from her eyes. There were four of them and they crowded around him shouting insults. He flushed red in the face and tried to focus on getting out of the square and as far away from this nightmare as he could, but as one of the clan stepped in his path and pushed him he staggered backwards and realised that escaping wasn't going to be so easy.

"She belongs to us now!" one of the Jenkins shouted, earning cackles of laughter from his family.

"But if you want her for an hour, we can do a deal," Frederick offered causing more laughter from the clan. Carp looked up and stared into the eyes of the only woman he'd ever loved. The woman he'd been destined to marry and live happily ever after with, raising a brood of children together in a different life. Destiny had offered her up on a plate for him and then taken her away like a cruel joke. Carp watched as more tears ran down her cheeks and then he was pushed again and pulled back to reality.

*

On the other side of the square Billy Bates stood watching the scene unfold in front of his eyes. The smuggler rarely ventured into town, but when he did, he always brought several of his men, just in case trouble reared its ugly head. At his sides stood Thomas, Alfie Bicks and a handful of others who'd proven their worth.

Bill was gritting his teeth, infuriated by what he was witnessing. Carp was a good man with a heart of gold, and he didn't deserve to be treated so cruelly. Billy Bates was a smuggler, a criminal, but Bill was old fashioned at heart. He despised the pimp Frederick and what the man did for a living. Bill knew that Frederick earned a fair income for the Jenkins family and that intervening would be treated as a declaration of war against Samuel and his clan, but for Bill enough was enough. He'd lived in the shadows for too long. Suddenly he was pulled from his thoughts by his tall ginger bodyguard.

"We can't let this happen, Boss," Alfie stated as he turned to face the young smuggling leader. Billy Bates smiled that crooked smile. He couldn't agree more.

"What would you do, Alfie?" he asked his young bodyguard who answered without hesitation.

"I'd teach them all not to mess with us," Alfie said with conviction, and Billy Bates chuckled. The young smuggler admired courage and loyalty in people above all other traits, and Alfie Bicks had both traits in spades.

"You're right, Alfie. Enough is enough. Let's show the clan who really runs this town!" Bill stated in that croaky voice, as he began to cross the busy square with his men at his sides.

Carp knew that he wasn't going to be able to leave the town square without taking another beating at the hands of the Jenkins family. He'd looked away from the girl he loved, as watching her cry hurt far more than any punch he could ever receive. Staring at the Jenkins as they crowded around him shouting insults in his face Carp braced himself for the first punch, knowing all too well that the barrage of blows would continue well after he collapsed to the ground. Glancing around the square he spotted dozens of local faces who were all staring his way, ready to witness yet another cruel attack from the family who'd terrorised the town for decades.

Suddenly though the insults stopped mid sentence as Billy Bates arrived out of nowhere. He strolled past the Jenkins' foot soldiers and straight up to Frederick, pausing when his nose was only an inch away from the pimp's. For a moment Carp's face lit up, but then he realised how much of a dangerous situation Bill had walked into and his heart sank. There were at least half a dozen Jenkins and they wouldn't hesitate leaving Bill in a pool of blood. Any worry Carp had evaporated instantly though as he turned to his left and saw his good friend Alfie Bicks who winked at him. Bill's tall, skinny teenage bodyguard was standing with his right hand in his pocket, gripping the handle of his knife with that crazy look in his eyes. Noticing movement on his right Carp turned to see Thomas who'd moved into an attack position and was standing glaring at the Jenkins only a few feet in front of him as he clenched his fists. Unlike Alfie he held no weapons, but the boy Bill had taken in off the streets was a weapon in his own right. The Jenkins were wary of him, they'd seen him on the cobbled streets at Boseda's side and had heard some of the rumours circulating the town.

"You have a problem with this man?" Bill asked the pimp, as he gestured at Carp. Frederick was speechless for a moment. It had been a very long time since anyone had challenged him.

"Yeah I do!" he finally raged. "Do you have any idea who I am?"

Billy Bates smiled that crooked smile and stared hard at Frederick through those dark eyes of his. "I know exactly who and what you are, you're someone who makes a living out of abusing women," he said in that croaky voice. The Jenkins' foot soldiers had heard enough and took a step in Bill's direction, but it was a step too far. Thomas launched himself at them like a madman. He hit the first man with his signature move, a right hook. It was hard to tell what made the loudest sound, when Thomas' fist connected with the man's jaw or when the man's unconscious body landed face first on the cobbles with a thud. The next man was dispatched with a knee to his chest before Thomas moved onto his next victim. A moment later the boy climbed to his feet, leaving four of the Jenkins unconscious in a heap. A few more stood staring at

Thomas, knowing full well that they didn't stand a chance against him.

Frederick himself looked baffled that such a youngster could inflict such damage. When he turned his attention back to Bill who was smiling broadly, the pimp attempted to pull out a weapon from his jacket. Alfie stepped forward and pinned him up against a wall as he pressed the blade of his knife against the man's throat. The pimp swallowed hard and stared into Bill's eyes.

"The clan'll punish you for this!" he hissed.

Bill chuckled to himself. "The Jenkins are old news, they're nothing. These streets belong to me now," he stated, turning to Carp. "Which one?" he asked and Carp pointed to the girl he loved who was among the small crowd who'd gathered to watch the Jenkins finally get what they deserved. Bill smiled. "She's a pretty girl," he complimented his friend before turning back to the pimp who was still pinned up against the wall by Alfie, who looked crazier than ever.

"This girl belongs to me now. I'll kill any man who goes anywhere near her," Bill stated. The girl was now in Carp's arms where she belonged, and Bill had never seen his friend so happy.

"Let's go," he ordered his men, before they turned and began to make their way out of the square under the watchful eyes of half the town who'd waited a long time to see someone stand up to the clan. From that moment rumours of Billy Bates, the old fisherman with eyes as dark as coal, began to spread through the town's streets, like they would for many years to come.

Chapter Forty-Four

Later that night stories of Billy Bates spread through the countless taverns and drinking dens that littered the town's cobbled streets and working girls praised Bill in whispered tones for standing up to their cruel boss. The town had waited a long time for someone to challenge the Jenkins family. 'The Fisherman' as locals were calling him, was already considered a hero in the town's streets, and would be remembered as one accordingly. The townsfolk admired Bill's courage, but they knew his fate. The Fisherman wouldn't stand a chance against the clan. Locals knew that when Samuel and his army of foot soldiers rolled into town hungry for blood they'd tear Bill Bates to shreds, but the same locals knew very little about The Fisherman who'd apparently left the town many moons ago.

Boseda was sitting in The Seagull listening to the locals gossiping away. Harry Booth's personal bodyguard knew all too well how resourceful Billy Bates could be, and as much as it broke the African's heart, he agreed with what he was hearing. The young smuggler had started a war, and with so few soldiers at his side was destined to lose. Picking up his beaker of ale Boseda drained it in one huge gulp before marching out of The Seagull on a quest to find his master, and discover what action needed to be taken.

*

Meanwhile high up in his cliff-top house Bill sat in his study reading a book. The ambitious smuggler was interrupted when one of his men knocked on the study's door and brought in two trays of supper. Bill put down his book and rubbed his eyes. Since leaving the square earlier that day he'd been racking his mind trying to figure out how to deal with the latest mess he'd found himself in. Eventually he picked up one of the trays and climbed to his feet, before making his way towards

Thomas' bedroom. Reaching the boy's room he rapped on the door before strolling straight in. Billy Bates froze at the sight that greeted him and let go of the tray that hit the floor with a loud smash. Thomas was in the middle of getting changed and had his back to Bill, a back that was covered with the most horrific scars Bill had ever seen. Standing speechless Bill took in the deep wounds and suddenly he understood why the boy never took his top off to swim in the Stour, but chose to stand and watch instead. Thomas grabbed his cotton shirt and pulled it over his wide shoulders before turning to Bill. The boy stared at him through those sunken eyes, and for once the smuggler could see emotion on the boy's face, but it wasn't anger, it was shame. Billy Bates stood in the doorway of Thomas' bedroom completely lost for words.

Over time Bill had grown incredibly attached to the youngster, he was a great friend, but it was more than that. Billy Bates looked on the boy he'd found living under a wooden jetty as a son and he felt responsible. As Bill stood staring at the boy anger welled up in him and for the first time he understood why the boy was the way he was. The smuggler had always believed he'd had a tough life himself, but now he knew that his had been heaven in comparison to Thomas' life, which had clearly been hell. Finally Bill stepped forward and the broken tray and its contents crunched under his boots.

"What happened? Who did that to you?" he asked, and Thomas glanced away. The boy looked ashamed of his past and it broke Bill's heart. Approaching the boy he looked on as a son, Bill sat on his bed. "It's okay Thomas," he reassured him in that croaky voice and the boy's tough façade slipped. Little did Bill know but it would be the only time in the smuggler's lifetime that he'd ever see the boy vulnerable. Turning to Bill, Thomas opened up and began to tell his story. He started from the beginning, and told Bill about his earliest memories as a child at the orphanage where he was relatively happy before going on to his first experience at the Whitegate Cotton Mill. When he explained to Bill that he naively thought the guards were his new friends that were going to look after him, like the others at the orphanage, a lone tear ran down the boy's cheek and Billy Bates gritted his teeth, furious that someone could treat a child so badly. Thomas went on to explain about the torture he had experienced and how he was used as a whipping boy to scare the other children and keep the workforce productive. Billy Bates had risen to his feet and was pacing around the bedroom listening to Thomas' story, as he explained about his near death experience in the murky water of the Thames when the smuggler turned to him.

"They just left you there to die?" he asked through gritted teeth, and the boy nodded before Bill began pacing once more. Thomas considered telling Bill about his face-to-face confrontation with the notorious pirate Alfred Mudd, but decided to keep this detail to himself and take the identity of Alfie Bicks' father with him to the grave. In the end he told Bill that he stowed away on a ship, and when he was caught he was thrown into the sea just off the coast of Deal, which wasn't far from the truth anyway. When he finally finished telling his story he looked at Bill who was still pacing up and down. The young smuggling gang leader looked more furious than Thomas had ever seen him. Marching over to where the boy was sitting Billy Bates knelt down and stared into Thomas' eyes. "What they did to you was wrong, my boy," he said, with emotion in his voice "and I promise you from the bottom of my heart that one day we'll make them all pay."

Suddenly there was a hard knock on the bedroom door and Bill rose to his feet, furious at being interrupted. His anger was obvious when he swung open the door and the man quickly apologised. "We have visitors," he informed them, and Thomas rose to his feet. The moment had passed and the boy's emotionless facade had returned as he marched over to where he belonged, at Bill's side.

"Who?" the smuggler demanded in that croaky voice of his.

"Harry Booth and at least a dozen of his men," was the reply.

*

172

A short while later Billy Bates sat in his study with Thomas, Alfie, Carp and at least half a dozen of his own men, alongside Harry Booth, Boseda and all of their most trusted men.

Bill was anxious, he could see that Harry had something on his mind. "So I'm guessing you heard about the scene earlier in the town square?" he asked, and Harry Booth nodded.

"I can't say I blame you Bill, that Frederick is a piece of dirt, but attacking the Jenkins will have repercussions. I've known you long enough to know that you're not stupid, and you realise that war's inevitable now."

Bill rubbed his chin and nodded. "I wish it could be any other way, but let's face it war with the Jenkins was always inevitable for me. It was always just a question of when," he said, pausing. "I wish I could have walked away earlier today, but that man's a friend," he said, as he pointed at Carp who smiled in return.

Harry Booth was staring at him intently "You'd risk everything for one of your friends and that's why you're such a great leader Billy Bates," he finally said, before turning to his men. "Leave us. I need to talk to Bill in private," he ordered. A moment later they filed out of the door, down the stairs and out onto the cliffs overlooking the sea, only Boseda remained. Harry Booth turned to his huge African bodyguard, the man he'd bought in a market a long time ago, and the man he respected more than anyone else in the world.

"You too," he said, and a moment later Boseda, who could barely mask his surprise, left the room looking puzzled. He was closely followed by all of Bill's men.

Harry stared at the table for a long moment as he gathered his thoughts. When he looked up at Bill he had tears in his eyes. "I've lived a long life in this smuggling business. I've spent the last twenty years sailing to and fro from the continent to make the Jenkins clan rich, but I've also put a fair bit of money away myself. You're right, war was always inevitable for you, for me it was different, but I lack the courage that serves you so well." Bill went to interrupt but was cut short as

Harry lifted a hand and silenced him. "I've landed my last load. I'm too old to fight a war with Samuel and his men, but I can't stand by and watch what they'll do to you. I want to retire immediately. I'm going to gather my wealth and leave this town and all its problems behind," he said, staring at Bill.

The young smuggler thought a lot of Harry Booth. The man who had exclusive rights over the coastline had helped him countless times over the years.

"You make a great leader Billy Bates, you're the smuggler this town needs, and I hope you win this war," he said, as Bill tried to take it all in.

"What about your men?" he finally asked, and Harry smiled.

"They think the world of you, Bill. Earlier this evening when I told Boseda of my intentions I explained to him that he was finally free, he could return home to his people and the life that was stolen from him, and he looked devastated. When I asked him what was wrong he told me that he couldn't leave your side."

Billy Bates sat back in his chair and rubbed his chin as his mind raced. Finally he climbed to his feet and walked around the table and shook Harry Booth's hand. "Thank you for everything. I owe you a huge debt," he said, and Harry smiled. "The only thing you owe me Bill is a promise that you'll look after my men and the people of this town after I'm gone, they're good people and deserve much better than what they get from the Jenkins."

A few minutes later Billy Bates strolled out of his headquarters and stood on the cliffs overlooking the English Channel, as the wind blew a gale and ships bobbed around on her choppy surface. The young smuggler's men gathered around him awaiting orders. He stared out at the stretch of water that had made him rich, before turning to them "We need to gather an army immediately. I want every pickpocket, thief and bandit who holds a grudge with the clan in my pocket. At first light, I want you all in those cobbled streets. Speak to everyone, we have a lot to do and little time," Bill ordered as he turned to stroll back into his house.

"Are we going to war?" Boseda asked, causing his new boss to turn around and smile that crooked smile, as he stood with his black hair blowing in the wind and addressed the crowd. "The time for war has arrived, my men," he bellowed. "It's time to attack the Jenkins clan and let them know that this town is their territory no more! And I promise you that what I've got planned they'll never even see coming," he said.

Chapter Forty-Five

After being attacked in the square the young Jenkins foot soldiers had climbed to their feet embarrassed and humiliated. Nobody had ever been brave enough to attack them before, let alone publically insult their family like the man with the jet black eyes had. The youngsters turned to Fredericks who stood looking infuriated and the older man who'd worked for their family selling flesh to sailors for many years told them to get word to Samuel immediately. It was enough to kick the young thugs into action and they quickly left the town.

When they arrived at the family camp and staggered inside with their split lips and bleeding noses, they may well have had two heads each for the attention they got. As word of the attack spread through the camp tempers rose, but none more than their leader's, Samuel Jenkins who came flying out of his shack demanding answers.

"Who attacked you?" he raged at the small gang who were looking sheepish.

"It was that crazy kid that collects money with Boseda who threw the punches, but it was a man named Billy Bates making all the threats," one of the youngsters said, as half of his family stared at him in silence. Samuel Jenkins twisted the end of his bushy beard.

"And what did he say this Billy Bates?" he demanded of the young thug who stared at the ground as he spoke.

"He said the Jenkins were nothing and the town belonged to him!" he shouted, earning gasps of shock from the men and women gathered. "He also took one of Frederick's girls," the man finished.

Samuel Jenkins paced up and down and racked his brain. He could remember Billy Bates well from many years past when they'd talked in the tavern that night. Bill had been a gutsy young lad, but a fisherman and a nobody none the less.

The whole situation was confusing. Finally, he turned to his family.

"I want the town torn apart for this Billy Bates, and that kid too. Let the locals know there's a price on Bill's head, we'll pay handsomely for any information leading to his capture," he announced as dozens of his kin began preparations to leave the camp and march down into the town's cobbled streets.

*

Early the next day, as the sun made its appearance on the horizon out in the channel, Alfie Bicks strolled into the town. Bill's bodyguard was on edge and kept an eye out for the Jenkins at every corner. He knew the huge family would have heard of the attack and like him would be searching the town, but he also knew the clan were heavy drinkers and would be sleeping off their grog at such an early hour. Reaching the Town's square where he'd threatened Frederick at knife point not twenty-four hours earlier, Alfie Bicks scanned the area and quickly found who he was searching for. On the other side of the square Jimmy Harp stood with a handful of other pickpockets. They weren't hard to spot. All were in their teens and had lived on the streets for many years, as their grubby faces and torn clothes suggested. They were all half-starved too, from a lifetime living on scraps. Alfie watched them observing the town come to life, and knew they were searching for a way to get some breakfast. Alfred Bicks had been incredibly lucky to have been taken in by Billy Bates and knew that if it hadn't been for the smuggler he'd be on the other side of the square, by their side. Alfie had had his fair share of differences with Jimmy Harp, but respected him and understood why he was the leader of all the pickpockets that roamed the town's streets. Over the years Alfie had argued with Jimmy for not going along with his risky ideas, but he'd always known it was because Jimmy was smarter than him and was responsible for them all, and Alfie had accepted that.

Crossing the square Jimmy Harp spotted him a distance away and as the pickpocket approached him with his men at his side Alfie beckoned them down a side street. When they were away from prying ears the tall skinny teenager turned to face them.

"What the hell's going on?" Jimmy asked, stepping forward. The other young thieves dropped back, knowing all too well of their roles in Jimmy's gang. "I hear you threatened Frederick yesterday with a knife. The Jenkins would kill us now for even talking to you."

Alfie nodded and twisted the end of his ginger stubble. "That they would, but their day is over in this town. It's time to stand up to them. Imagine how much easier your lives could be without having to pay their tax," he said, and Jimmy Harp stared at him in shock

"So it's all true, you work for this Billy Bates character? We could never stand up to Samuel and the clan, they have a hundred men and would tear us all to shreds," he replied, as his gang nodded their agreement.

Alfie nodded as well whilst he continued to twist the wispy end of his ginger beard. "You're right Jimmy, the Jenkins have well over a hundred men, but how many enemies do they have in this town?" he asked the young pickpocket who answered immediately.

"Thousands!" came the reply, as Alfie Bicks smiled.

"Exactly, my friends," he said, turning to Jimmy Harp, leader of the pickpockets. "Trust me this once Jim. I promise you that under Billy Bates' rule this will be a different town. You'll no longer have to live in fear day in day out."

Jimmy Harp stood for a long moment thinking about Alfie's words, eventually he spoke. "And what's your plan?" he asked, before Alfie leant down and began muttering in his ear. When he eventually finished the pickpocket stared hard at the ground, weighing up Alfie's words.

Finally, he looked over at Alfred Bicks. "This Billy Bates is even crazier than you, but count us in," was all the pickpocket said.

*

Meanwhile in another part of town Boseda was gathering up every man who'd ever smuggled for Harry Booth. Over the years Harry had given work to many of the locals, and they hadn't forgotten it. Banging hard on the door of a small cottage only a stone's throw from the sea, Boseda waited impatiently for the man to answer. The huge African had a hard day's work ahead of him and time was of the essence. Within the hour the town would come to life and the streets would be full of the Jenkins, which would make Boseda's job that much harder. Finally the cottage's door swung open and its owner, an old sailor named Motler, looked infuriated for being woken at such an early hour. However, after taking one look at Boseda whose huge frame blocked the doorway, the old sailor thought better of voicing his complaint.

"Boseda you old rogue! What brings you to my door at such an ungodly hour?" he asked, and the huge African leant in close. "We have a situation, and we need your help," he said.

The old sailor rubbed the sleep out of his eyes. "What can I do?" he asked Boseda, who wasted no more time.

"Gather your whole crew and meet me this afternoon at 4 p.m. outside of town, near the base of the cliffs at Kingsdown," he ordered before walking away, towards his next meeting.

*

Later that day in the early afternoon Bill's gang had gathered in his study for a meeting. All the faces were there crowded around his huge oak table when the young smuggling leader entered the room and took his seat. "What's happening in the town?" he asked Alfie in that croaky voice.

The skinny teenager wasted no time. "Samuel has put a generous price on your head boss and the whole town is talking about it," he said. Bill tucked a long strand of black hair behind his ear and nodded.

"That's to be expected. How many men have you gathered?" he asked Alfie, who smiled.

"I have all the street-kids. They're scared out of their wits, but they'll fight in your name," Alfie replied.

Bill nodded. "I promise this town will change. I've wanted to help the unfortunate for many years, but couldn't because of the consequences. The street-kids won't regret their decision to help me in the years to come," he said, and Alfie nodded, proud that he'd helped Jimmy Harp and the other toe-rags.

Then Bill turned to Boseda. "And how about your men?" he asked, and the huge African chuckled.

"They're your men now, Boss. I've arranged the meeting like you asked. I'm confident that they'll all be there."

Bill rubbed his chin, deep in thought. "That's good," he muttered, as he stared out of his office's bay window at the English Channel.

*

Later that afternoon Billy Bates left his cliff top headquarters with two dozen men at his side, all armed with thick clubs. Led by Boseda they made their way towards the base of the cliffs and a meeting that would seal Billy Bates' future in the town. The smuggling leader was on edge, nervous that his plan could completely backfire and he'd have to retreat far away from the town and its cobbled streets forever. His nerves improved when his gang finally turned a corner and was greeted with a sight that made Bill smile with pride. Stood milling around, waiting for the meeting to start, were a huge crowd of local faces. Tough men who'd struggled to make a living in the town's streets under the Jenkins' rule for many years. Like Harry Booth the clan had taken the cream of the crop and left the men who'd harvested her with pittance. Bill recognised many of them. A few he'd even fought with in the town's drinking dens, but overall they were good men. As soon as they rounded the bend and came into view the crowd broke from their conversations and stared Bill's way. When they reached the crowd it was Boseda who spoke first.

"Men, I'd like to start by thanking you all for coming," he bellowed at the crowd. "You may not already know this, but change is upon us. Harry Booth announced his retirement earlier today."

Suddenly, the crowd of men began to mutter amongst each other, some shocked by the news. "What are we all to do to earn a living?" somebody shouted from the crowd. Boseda stepped forward once more.

"I'd like to introduce you to a great man. I'm sure you've been hearing his name whispered in the town's streets. Many of you here have known me for a very long time, you're are all aware that I'm a man of honour, and let me tell you this, I'd lay down my life for this man without hesitation. I give you Billy Bates," he roared, as Bill stepped forward to greet the crowd.

For a moment he stared at the crowd defiantly through those black eyes of his and watched as they took in the cut of his jib, and then the first of a barrage of questions came flooding from the crowd. "So what's going on? Are you Samuel's new smuggling boss?" somebody shouted, causing sniggers from Bill's gang.

"No, I have no connection with Samuel Jenkins and the rest of his clan. They're bullies and cowards and I've watched for years as they've bled this town dry," he shouted at the crowd. For a moment they stood speechless staring at him and in that moment Bill wondered whether he'd made a huge mistake, however a moment later a local man who'd smuggled for Harry stepped forward and began to clap and the next minute the entire crowd erupted into chaos as they voiced their support. Eventually Bill glanced at Boseda and the huge African stepped forward.

"Silence!" he roared, and the crowd were silent. "There'll be a time to celebrate, and that time will be when the Jenkins have left this town forever."

Bill stepped forward once again. "At this moment in time I control the largest smuggling organisation on our coast. Within weeks I'll expand and swallow up Harry's old organisation. I can give you all work. Your families will have food in their mouths and roofs over their heads," he shouted in that croaky voice. "But right now I have a price on my head! Thanks to our good friends the Jenkins clan and I need your help."

The crowd stared at him in silence once more. "What can we do?" somebody finally asked and Bill smiled that crooked smile.

"I want to attack them and banish them from this town!" he said, before the crowd erupted into chaos as each man turned to each other and started protesting. Boseda saw his moment and stepped forward once more.

"Silence!" he screamed at them, a scream that echoed off the cliffs and sent gulls squawking out of their nests.

Bill stared at the crowd as somebody shouted from far at the back. "I'd love to make a stand against them, but I have a family. No offence to you Billy Bates, but you have countless bodyguards. After we've attacked them they may not be able to get to you, but they'll pay me a visit, that you can bet on."

Bill nodded. "You're right my friend, but understand this, when we attack them every one of you will have your face covered. I'm happy to lead an anonymous army and with all of you at my side we'll outnumber them three to one. They've made our lives hell for years because they have power in numbers, let's show them that they don't. This town belongs to us now!" he shouted.

The crowd fell into silence and Bill turned to his own men who stood by his side. They were an odd-looking bunch, but Bill wouldn't trade them for anything. At least ten minutes passed by as Harry's old gang discussed Bill's idea amongst themselves. Eventually Boseda marched over to a man named Hutchings who'd been close to Harry Booth, as it was clear they'd elected him as leader.

"Well?" Boseda asked. "Will you make a stand now or live a life under Samuel's rule?"

Hutchings turned from the men gathered and addressed Bill for the first time. "You're playing a dangerous game Billy Bates, but if Boseda here holds you in such high regard then we'll stand and fight at your side," he said, as the crowd erupted in cheers and Bill smiled menacingly.

Chapter Forty-Six

Later that night, when darkness swept over the town, the normally bustling cobbled streets were virtually empty. Locals dared not to venture out and leave the sanctuary of their homes, all too aware that trouble lay ahead. Sailors from the countless ships anchored in the downs still staggered from tavern to tavern, merrily going about their business, completely unaware of the dangers lurking in the seaside town. Frederick the pimp stood in his usual spot on the corner of Coppin St, surrounded by his girls and plying his trade as usual. Deep down the man felt humiliated after the previous day's events in the town's square, but he hid it well as he glanced up and down the narrow street searching for Billy Bates, eager to witness him get what he deserved.

Members of the clan were in the town as well. Like usual they littered the streets, roaming around searching for the man who'd attacked one of their own and eager to extract some revenge. Their leader Samuel wasn't involved in the search. Instead he was sat in one of the town's many drinking dens nursing ale, and surrounded by two dozen of his men. The leader of the Jenkins clan was puzzled by a great number of things, but chiefly why Harry Booth's number one bodyguard Boseda hadn't been to see him. Samuel had tried to summon the huge African hours earlier, but Boseda along with Harry himself were nowhere to be found. Samuel Jenkins wanted answers … he wouldn't have long to wait.

*

Meanwhile Billy Bates had crept into town. The young smuggling boss had marched along the pebbled beach as waves crashed down on the shingle and spray from the sea soaked his jet black hair. Bill was so focused on the task at hand he barely noticed. Reaching the head of the town he turned to the two people he knew he could depend on in a dangerous situation. Alfie stood with a grin on his face and that crazy look in his eyes, whilst Thomas' expression like always was virtually impossible to read. The boy looked vacant, but Bill could tell he was ready for action. The smuggling boss smiled as he marched up the shingle and took a seat on the promenade next to the wooden jetty. Sat with his men in full view of the town Bill knew that it wouldn't take very long for him to be spotted, and he wasn't wrong as a handful of Jenkins who were walking along the shore clapped their eyes on him. Bill watched as they quickly retreated and disappeared into the labyrinth of cobbled streets, knowing full well they were summoning their leader and serious back-up. A moment later Bill's tall skinny bodyguard rose to his feet and disappeared in the shadows.

Billy Bates sat staring at the town with only Thomas at his side, waiting for all hell to break loose and wondering if his plan would work. A few very slow minutes passed before Alfie returned and took his seat at Bill's side.

"Are they all in place?" his boss asked and Alfie Bicks nodded, before Bill turned to the youngest, but most vicious of the trio. "Are you ready?" he asked Thomas, and the boy opened his jacket to reveal his weapon of choice, an axe, before nodding.

*

Samuel Jenkins took another gulp of ale and belched before brushing his bushy beard. The clan's leader had noticed the streets were empty, like a ghost town and Samuel was beginning to wonder why. Suddenly though the tavern's door swung open and one of his nephews came charging into the drinking den, red in the face and out of breath. Samuel was pulled from his thoughts at the sight of the youngster who stumbled in his direction.

"I've found him!" the young ruffian shouted, as half the tavern's customers rose to their feet.

"Where?" Samuel demanded as his nephew caught his breath.

"Up on the seafront with Alfie Bicks and that lunatic kid," came the response, as half the tavern turned to Samuel awaiting their orders.

The leader of the Jenkins gritted his teeth. "Let's teach this Bill a lesson he'll never forget," he roared as his family voiced their support.

Moments later they were all piling out of the door and marching along Middle St. The only noise came from their boots hitting the cobbles and it sounded like an army going to war. Along the way to the shore they picked up smaller groups of their kin. Samuel led the pack and by the time they reached the top of Farrier St and came across the channel spread out before them in the moonlight, they were nearly one-hundred strong.

Samuel spotted Billy Bates immediately. The daring young upstart was sitting with two of his men. Samuel recognised Alfred Bicks and he gritted his teeth in anger. He'd owed the skinny thief a beating ever since he'd stolen the magistrate's locket and the time had finally arrived to hand out some punishment, Jenkins style. As Samuel marched towards the trio with his clan behind him pulling weapons from their jackets, Billy Bates and his two bodyguards rose to their feet. Samuel glanced at the smallest of the three who was only in his early teens and the child stared back at him without a care in the world, which put the clan's leader on edge.

Stopping only a dozen feet from the trio Samuel's men crowded around their leader. "Billy Bates you're a dead man and the same goes for you two as well!" he roared as Bill stared at him through those jet black eyes and the wind whistled around them. Suddenly everyone's attention was diverted as Boseda came bowling through the thick crowd of Jenkins' foot soldiers. The huge African brushed them off like flies as he cleared a path towards Billy Bates, and Samuel stared in shock.

"What the hell is this?" Samuel shouted as Boseda stepped up close to him.

"This Samuel," he shouted back, "this is for all times you robbed and stole from my great friend Harry Booth. This is justice!" He grabbed Samuel by the scruff of the neck and threw him backwards, where he staggered and fell to the floor. Instantly half a dozen clan members rushed forward, but their advance was cut short as Thomas pulled the axe from his jacket and swung it in their direction, causing its sharp blade to miss their faces by mere inches.

For a moment they backed away, as Samuel climbed to his feet, but then their leader who was red faced and embarrassed turned to his family. "Kill them all," he ordered, as the entire clan began to approach Bill who was stood bravely with Thomas, Alfie and Boseda at his sides and a crooked grin on his face.

Suddenly a loud crunching noise filled the air as hundreds of feet marched up the shingle beach behind Bill. The clan stopped in their tracks as the first dozen or so men came into view. Their faces were covered with rags, but it was the thick clubs they held in their hands that caught the Jenkins' attention. Within a few minutes more than a hundred men stood behind Billy Bates, their new leader. Samuel Jenkins stood staring in shock and not knowing what to do, eventually he turned and glanced back at the entrance of Farrier St and Bill could tell he was already considering retreating, but all hopes were dashed as more men came flooding out of the town completely trapping the Jenkins.

The clan, who'd spent a lifetime terrorising the town and its people by stealing their money and leaving them with virtually nothing, were now stood glancing in every direction looking for ways to escape. Samuel Jenkins looked terrified, he wasn't half the man his brother Dale had been and everyone knew it. He stood red faced like a fish out of water as Bill marched towards him, stopping only when he was face to face.

For a long moment Samuel gazed into Bill's jet black eyes before glancing at the floor, as Bill smiled that crooked smile of his. Then Billy Bates stepped towards the clan and addressed them all. "Your time in this town is now over!" he shouted in their direction as he marched up and down.

"Tonight you'll leave this town and tomorrow you'll abandon your camp, never to return. Many of my friends here would like nothing more than to see your blood spilled on these cobbles tonight, but if you agree to my terms I promise not to hurt a hair on any of your heads! From this day forth this town and that coast," he shouted as he pointed towards the shore, "belongs to me and any man who dares to defy me will die very slowly."

Samuel Jenkins was still staring at the floor as he gritted his teeth and clenched his fists. "Do you agree to my terms?" Bill asked, and Samuel looked up and into the young smuggler's eyes once more.

"Well you seem to have won the battle, but you'll never win the war. I agree to your terms Billy Bates," he shouted as spittle flew from his mouth, "but one day my nephew Ronnie will make you pay for this!"

Boseda stepped forward into Samuel's path. The huge African had waited a long time to teach Ronnie Jenkins some manners. "I look forward to that day!" he said, as Samuel sneered at him. Then Samuel Jenkins turned and led his family out of the town for the last time.

As soon as they were gone the crowd erupted into chaos as cheers of celebration filled the air. Bill stared at the scene in front of him and let the men have their moment. They'd all risked a lot by standing at his side, and he'd never forget their loyalty. Eventually he climbed up onto the sea wall and the noise died down as the townsfolk stared at the young man who'd stood up to the Jenkins clan, a young man who up until twenty-four hours ago few had even heard of.

Glancing at the crowd who were stood in awe Bill asked them all to remove their masks. "You have nothing to fear no more," he shouted in his croaky voice, which was received with more cheers of support. A moment later the crowd stood staring at him and Bill returned their gaze. He watched the street-kids with their grubby faces, kids as young as ten who'd risked their lives on his behalf before turning to Harry Booth's gang of hardworking men who were truly worth their salt, as the evening's events had proven.

"Men my name is Billy Bates, for those of you who don't know me I'm as fair as the day is long. Tonight you all stood at my side, and I'll never forget your loyalty. Like most of you I was raised in poverty and I know how it feels to struggle not knowing where your next meal is coming from," he said, staring at Jimmy Harp, the leader of the street kids who was taking in every word. "But let me tell you from now on we struggle no more. Tonight we celebrate!" he said as a dozen of his men began placing tubs of brandy and hampers of food along the sea wall in front of them. Bill climbed down as the crowd erupted in cheers of celebration and within minutes men were guzzling brandy and feasting on the banquet their new leader had provided. It was a scene the town had never experienced. As they celebrated the start of a new era and toasted the town's new leader, Bill stared out at the English Channel and remembered Samuel's threat that one day Ronnie would make him pay. Billy Bates had no doubt that one day Ronnie Jenkins would return to the town and at least try.

Chapter Forty-Seven

Ronnie Jenkins travelled for several days towards the gypsy camp where he'd spend the next three years as punishment for his attack on his Uncle Samuel. The journey was exhausting, even for the huge teenager whose physical strength was more than most men's. When he finally arrived he marched in with his head held high as small crowds of the tough gypsies glared his way. Amongst them he spotted the man he'd bitten at the Kent show a few years earlier, and he felt far from welcome in their camp. Ronnie had thought he'd be able to relax once he'd arrived and recover from the long journey, but the teenage thug was quick to realise that the next three years were going to be much harder than he'd imagined.

For Ronnie's entire life he'd been a somebody amongst his own clan, he'd been Dale Jenkins' son, but he'd also had his huge stature to set him aside from the rest. On arrival at the gypsy camp he walked towards McGregor's shack with his bag on his back and realised that suddenly he wasn't so special. Ronnie Jenkins was many things but he was far from stupid. He understood only too well that his family name meant very little now and unlike his own clan, his new family wouldn't hesitate punishing him if he stepped a fraction out of line. When he was a short distance from McGregor's shack he spotted the gypsy leader with his arms crossed in front of him watching his approach. McGregor was surrounded by his men who all glared Ronnie's way as they sized him up. Every one of them had heard of his father, who was a legend amongst fighters and every one of them would love to claim the glory of beating the great Dale Jenkins' son in a fist fight. The gypsies were wary of him too though, and not just because of his size. They were all aware that the Jenkins had banished him because he was out of control, and as far as the gypsies were concerned the Jenkins clan were a rough crowd. Ronnie knew his vicious reputation had proceeded him as he approached McGregor and all of his men walked away leaving the pair alone.

The man who'd earned the title 'King of the Gypsies' with his fists stared at young Ronnie for a long moment, as Ronnie threw down his heavy bag.

"So they've sent you to me, the problem that even your own clan can't deal with, and believe me I've known your family for a long time and they can deal with most problems," McGregor said as Ronnie looked him up and down and anger rose within him. He gritted his teeth and clenched his fists, but didn't mutter a word. When he was a boy, his father who he'd idolised, had once described the gypsy leader as the best fighter he'd ever had the honour of battling. Ronnie understood that the tough gypsy in front of him was cut from the same cloth as his father, and that was enough to earn Ronnie's respect, but it did little to help his temper.

The gypsy leader watched the teenager struggling from deep within, trying to battle his emotions, a battle Ronnie was losing. "What the cat got your tongue lad!" he barked at Ronnie as he purposely stepped forward into Ronnie's personal space and squared up to him.

The huge teenager was trying his hardest to control himself for the memory of his father, but he could feel the anger brewing and the red mist beginning to cloud his mind. He stared at the floor and took some deep breaths trying to remain in control as McGregor continued to taunt him.

"What's wrong, boy? You not got the courage when you haven't got a hundred of your clan backing you up?" the gypsy leader snarled and Ronnie finally lost control.

Glancing up from the floor and into McGregor's eyes the huge teenager launched a punch at the man, but his right fist connected with nothing but air. The gypsy leader who'd spent a lifetime in the ring easily ducked Ronnie's sloppy hook before bringing one of his knees up, which connected with the teenager's chest, knocking the air out of him. Ronnie Jenkins looked confused by the speed with which the gypsy had moved, as he collapsed to the floor for the first time ever. Struggling to catch a breath Ronnie flailed around on the floor as his pride told him to get back up and his body refused. The huge thug who'd terrorised the town of Deal was completely immobilised for the first time in his life and he felt vulnerable as he stared up at Sean McGregor, the toughest of all the gypsies who knelt down beside him.

"You know lad I'll help you, but not because I owe you or any of your clan a thing, but because of your father, God rest his soul. Dale Jenkins was a great man, and it's not a term I use lightly. He was a man of honour, you understand?" McGregor asked. Ronnie was lying on his back staring at the gypsy leader who was as calm as the English Channel on a windless day. Ronnie realised that McGregor didn't fear him like everybody else. The gypsy had known all along that Ronnie would lose his temper, but had also known the teenager wasn't a threat to him, and Ronnie Jenkins understood exactly why his father had spoken so highly of McGregor.

"I understand," Ronnie finally managed, as the gypsy smiled for the first time showing a mouth with very few teeth.

"So are you gonna get control of that temper of yours and one day be a great man like your father before you?" McGregor asked. Ronnie Jenkins swallowed his pride as he stared up at the tough gypsy.

"I promise to try my hardest," he said and the gypsy leader extended his hand and pulled the teenager to his feet.

*

Ronnie began his training with McGregor that very day and the gypsy leader punished the youngster from the very start. Every morning at sunrise McGregor would wake him with a bucket of cold water and the bare knuckle champion would begin his wicked training regime. On the first day Ronnie was shocked by how hard McGregor was pushing him, but he never backed down. During those moments of physical pain Ronnie would grit his teeth and think of his enemies, his Uncle Samuel, the smuggler Billy Bates and even the African Boseda, all of which he vowed to one day punish. As the days wore on the teenager became accustomed to McGregor's tough training sessions. For several weeks the gypsy leader concentrated on stamina and strength, forcing Ronnie to run mile after mile carrying heavy weights. At night Ronnie would collapse on the hay exhausted and sleep, only to awake and begin the savage cycle once more. Slowly the teenager began winning over the gypsies as they slowly accepted him into their camp. Many of the men were fighters themselves and during the day would train by his side. Like Ronnie himself they never refused a single order from their leader, who treated all men as equals and never showed leniency to anyone. Most days they'd all spend the morning training together, before the rest would disappear into an old barn for the afternoon leaving Ronnie to train alone.

After weeks and weeks of pushing his body to the limits Ronnie's muscles swelled in size, and the teenager looked much scarier than ever before. Occasionally in the midst of a heavy training session he'd catch the other fighters staring his way, and he'd note the look on their faces. Initially he'd found it hard to place, but eventually he realised it wasn't fear but respect.

Then one day McGregor woke him and instead of starting the day with their usual run the gypsy leader led Ronnie into the barn. Strolling through the barn's doors for the first time Ronnie stood and took it all in, as he glanced from the punch bags made from straw and thick canvas to the ring that sat proudly in the middle. He turned to McGregor and the tough fighter smiled.

"This, lad, is like a church to our kind," he said and Ronnie chuckled. "Now show me what you can do on one of the bags. You're a big lump, but can you throw a combination like Dale could?"

Ronnie Jenkins approached the bag, and not for the first time. His father had introduced him to a punch bag over a decade before. Dale Jenkins had tried everything to figure a way of controlling his son, but had ultimately failed.

McGregor stepped behind the back of the punch bag, which was made from canvas and straw and hung loosely from a wooden beam by thick rope. He pulled it towards him and held it into his chest before nodding at Ronnie. "Give me everything you've got!" he demanded, as Ronnie stepped forward and threw several sharp jabs with his left before following it up with a brutal right hook that connected with the punch bag at such speed that McGregor staggered backwards.

The tough gypsy smiled. "You certainly have the strength lad, but fights aren't won on strength alone," he said as he stepped forward once more and gripped the bag as Ronnie hit it with a combination of punches that made the beam above their heads creak and the gypsy wonder whether the old barn was going to collapse. "The question is do you have the discipline? If I enter you in a fight will you do exactly what you're told?" McGregor continued, causing Ronnie to stop for a second and look him in the eye.

"I'll do whatever you ask of me," he promised as he hit the bag once more at full force. It took McGregor a moment to recover before he looked Ronnie in the eye. "That's good lad, your first fight's next weekend. Then we'll see if you really have what it takes," the gypsy leader said, causing Ronnie to smile eerily before he continued to hit the bag with all his might.

Chapter Forty-Eight

One week later Ronnie left the camp with McGregor and another two dozen of the gypsy fighters. Travelling on horseback they rode north for several days across barren fields and through thick woodland until they finally arrived at the Chester Fair, a huge agricultural event where farmers traded animals and talked late into the night about the best tactics to reap bumper crops. The gypsies played an entirely different role in the fair, they'd come to fight, entertain and earn good money. McGregor's gang were not alone. Fighters had travelled from all corners of the country to compete and earn a reputation with their fists. The actual bouts were held in a huge barn, inside a makeshift ring where a hundred or so men would gather to watch the blood be spilled. Ronnie was scheduled for the first evening and as he climbed into the ring he gritted his teeth, knowing he was about to take a serious beating for the first time in his life. McGregor hadn't brought Ronnie on the long journey to compete like all of his other fighters, what Ronnie faced was far worse. The gypsy knew that Ronnie wasn't quite ready. What McGregor wanted was for the huge teenager to prove himself and show he had the discipline that every fighter needs. Only then would McGregor teach him everything he'd learnt from a lifetime spent bare-knuckle fighting.

As the crowd stared at Ronnie for the first time, taking in his huge stature and rippling muscles, they all stood silently. Every one of them had heard of his father and nobody fancied their chances against the teenager. But then as Ronnie's hands were tied tightly behind his back with thick ropes and the master of ceremonies began heckling the crowd.

"Who'll fight this giant?" he screamed at them. "One two minute round with his arms tightly fastened and one without! If you're still on your feet you'll be five pounds richer," he continued and the crowd grew braver. Finally someone stepped forward, a big ugly man with a large belly called Abraham.

"I'll knock this boy unconscious," he screamed as the crowd went wild and he was ushered into the ring where he stood clenching his fists.

On the other side of the ring Ronnie stood facing his opponent, as McGregor whispered in his ear. "Every man can hand out a beating, but only the toughest can take one. Remember what I've taught you and keep moving," and then suddenly the bell rang, the crowd went wild and Abraham ran straight forward and swung the first of many punches at Ronnie's jaw. The first punch caught Ronnie on the left cheek and he staggered backwards, but before he could react another punch connected with his right cheek sending his head swinging in the air. Abraham was taking no chances and understood that he had two minutes to knock his opponent unconscious before his wrists would be untied and the fight would be fair. Left hook then right connected with a bam as the teenager was knocked all over the ring. The crowd were screaming with excitement and even McGregor's own fighters were pleading with their leader to stop the fight.

"He's getting killed out there," one of them shouted at the gypsy leader who turned to him angrily.

"That's Dale Jenkins' flesh and blood out there, believe me he can take it," he shouted back.

Meanwhile the clock was ticking down as Abraham continued to hit Ronnie with all his might and the teenager staggered around the ring whilst blood poured from his nose, lips and deep cuts around his eyes. McGregor stood watching his young apprentice getting beaten half to death with a smile on his face. He could see that Ronnie had zoned out, which was what he was expecting, and as the bell rang McGregor stepped into the corner knowing that it was the next round that was important. Abraham screamed in frustration as he returned to his own corner, knowing that he'd just hit his opponent non-stop for two minutes and the teenager was still on his feet.

Ronnie Jenkins approached his corner. "I'm going to kill him!" he hissed through gritted teeth as one of McGregor's men poured a bucket of cold water over him and another untied his wrists. The teenager looked possessed as the gypsy leader stepped towards him.

"No you're not lad! You remember what I told you about discipline. Fools rush in Ronnie where angels tread lightly," he shouted before slapping Ronnie around the face. The entire arena held their breath expecting Ronnie to retaliate but instead he stared hard into the gypsy's eyes. "You just do what we planned!" McGregor warned as the bell rang and Ronnie turned to face his opponent. Abraham was running towards him once again, but this time Ronnie Jenkins was able to defend himself. However, instead of attacking him and reaping revenge like everyone expected, Ronnie side-stepped him and then for the next sixty seconds the crowd stood amazed as Ronnie ducked and weaved around the ring avoiding every one of Abraham's punches without throwing any of his own.

McGregor stood proudly watching his young apprentice before stepping forward. "Now!!" he roared with all his might, catching his fighter's attention who smiled menacingly. Suddenly Ronnie hit Abraham with a jab that stopped him dead on his feet in the centre of the ring where he stood dazed for a fraction of a second. When the next punch in Ronnie's combination found its mark, a right hook, Abraham's head looked like it was going to come off at his neck. He flew through the air and landed in a heap in the corner of the ring where he lay unconscious. The crowd went crazy until the master of ceremonies finally got control of them.

"So will anyone else accept the challenge and fight this man?" he shouted as they all shook their heads sheepishly. Ronnie stood leaning his huge bulk against the ropes, lost in thought, not of his achievements that night or even of his late father but of the town of Deal, and revenge on his Uncle Samuel and the smuggler Billy Bates, both men he'd one day punish.

Chapter Forty-Nine

Three years later…
The Kings Head Tavern, London

The drinking den was situated in an alleyway, only a short distance from the River Thames. On a usual night it was a crowded place full of merchant sailors and dockside workers from the countless wharfs beside the mighty river. On this dark winter night the streets were empty and the tavern's only customers were guards from the cotton mill a few streets away. Suddenly the door blew open and a man entered. The landlord hadn't seen him before, but that wasn't unusual. Taking in his ripped and tatty clothing the landlord took him for just another sailor from one of the dozens of merchant ships docked on the Thames. As a gust of cold air blew into the drinking den it caught one of the guard's attention who was sat in the corner.

"Shut that bloody door!" he barked at the newcomer, who flashed an evil glare in the guard's direction. Feeling outraged at the stranger's audacity the mill workers began to stir and mutter to one another.

The landlord took a deep breath, fearing trouble ahead. He knew the guards well, they were nasty people and he felt sorry for the stranger as he stepped up to serve him. "Beaker of your finest rum sir," the man said in a croaky voice as he fumbled around in his pockets. The landlord quickly poured the drink and placed it on the bar nervously. Now the tavern was silent, the newcomer had the guards' full attention, including their boss', the warden of the mill who alongside his colleagues was glaring in the stranger's direction.

"If I was you my friend I'd drink up and leave," the landlord whispered as the stranger picked up his glass and drained it in one gulp, before placing it back down on the counter and chuckling to himself.

Suddenly the mill's warden Mr Anderson climbed to his feet and his colleagues followed suit. Panicking the landlord leant in close to the stranger who glanced up at him, suddenly causing him to stop in his tracks. The man had weather beaten skin and the darkest eyes he'd ever seen, they were jet black and as the stranger smiled a crooked smile the landlord felt shivers race down his spine. Now the mill's warden was crossing the empty tavern with his two guards at his sides. The landlord knew them both, their names were Simmonds and Roberts and they followed their boss everywhere, hanging on his every word in a pathetic attempt to impress him.

"Listen I don't want any trouble!" the landlord said, pleading with the guards, who paid little attention to him.

"If I was you I'd take a walk," the mill's warden barked at the newcomer who turned to face the men.

"And if I don't?" he asked the warden who was gritting his teeth in anger now.

"I'll take you outside boy and teach you some manners!" the man responded. Billy Bates smiled, but like the bald pock-faced warden in front of him he gritted his teeth as he gripped the handle of the dagger in his pocket. The smuggling boss was tempted to kill the warden where he stood for torturing the boy he thought of as a son, but the landlord seemed like a nice fellow and Billy Bates wasn't planning on leaving any witnesses alive.

"Well, I'll choose the second option," he said, as he barged passed the warden and stepped out into the narrow empty street. Infuriated the guards grabbed their jackets and caps and rushed out after him. Bill marched along the deserted alleyway in the thick fog as he listened to the footsteps of the guards giving chase. Several oil lamps were burning away, but giving off very little light, as Billy Bates turned on his toes and faced his pursuers. The vicious guard, who'd tortured Thomas in order to keep control of the workforce inside his precious mill, marched up to Bill with his men at his sides. All three had pulled the thick batons they used to beat children from the belts on their waists and were gripping them menacingly.

"How dare you?" Anderson barked at him. "Do you have any idea who I am?" he said, stopping when he was only half a dozen feet in front of the smuggler.

Billy Bates smiled that crooked smile of his and all three guards stared at him with looks of confusion, looks that were quickly replaced by expressions of anger.

"I know exactly who and what you are," Bill said. "You're a coward and a bully who gets pleasure out of punishing children."

For a moment Anderson looked surprised, but then he exploded in anger and raised his baton over his head to strike Bill. Suddenly he froze at the last moment as a deep voice caught him off-guard.

"I wouldn't do that if I was you," the deep voice ordered, and Anderson turned and froze in his tracks at the sight of a huge African man who'd appeared from nowhere and he wasn't alone. At his side was a tall and rather gaunt red headed youngster who was glaring his way.

Anderson took a deep gulp of air and turned back to Bill and his arm dropped to his side.

"Not so brave now?" Billy Bates asked, but he didn't wait for a reply. "I'd like to reunite you with someone," he said as he stepped to the side.

Marching out of the fog like the devil himself, Thomas stood and stared at the men who'd tortured him a lifetime ago through those deep sunken eyes of his. Thomas was a child no more though. Now he was a young man and after years of carrying the heavy loads of smuggled cargo his wide shoulders had swelled in size.

Anderson turned a shade of white as memories flooded back to him. The wooden baton fell from his hand and clattered to the ground as he staggered backwards a few steps. Thomas stepped towards him.

"It can't be, you're dead we ..." the warden mumbled, ending mid-sentence. Thomas took another step in his direction and pulled an axe from the inside of his jacket. Anderson let out a gasp and stared at the ground terrified. Simmonds and Roberts tried to make an escape but were quickly apprehended by Boseda and Alfie. Finally Anderson looked up into Thomas' vacant eyes, the man whose very soul he'd destroyed with a whip many years before.

"Please show me mercy," Anderson pleaded, as Thomas raised his axe.

"Mercy is something you should have shown me," he stated before swinging his axe in the warden's direction.

Chapter Fifty

Billy Bates and his most trusted bodyguards arrived back in the town's cobbled streets the very next day. As the carriage entered the outskirts of town it pulled to a stop at the insistence of a handful of the smuggler's men and an urgent message was relayed to Bill that Jimmy Harp wanted a meeting. Sensing trouble Bill ordered the meeting to be arranged immediately before his horse and carriage continued its journey into town. Bill sat wondering what Jimmy wanted as he stared out at the streets that belonged to him through those jet black eyes of his and watched as local people waved and bowed in his direction. Bill smiled that crooked smile. A long time ago he'd dreamt of being held in such high regards by the townspeople, and his dream had come true.

Suddenly the carriage pulled up outside The Seagull, one of many taverns in the town Bill now supplied with his smuggled liquor. Alfie Bicks and Boseda climbed out of the carriage and Bill listened as they greeted more of his men whilst the smuggler turned to the boy he looked on as his own. Thomas sat daydreaming, reliving the moment when the warden and his guards had met their end the smuggler surmised.

"You okay, boy?" Bill asked, pulling Thomas from his thoughts. The child Bill had found living under a jetty smiled.

"Better than ever," he replied as Billy Bates climbed out of the carriage and onto the street, where he took in the sights and smells of the town's main thoroughfare.

The streets were bustling as people rushed to and fro. Many tried to approach the smuggling leader and offer their thanks for the many generous gifts he'd bestowed upon them, but as usual nobody got within striking distance of him as the crowds were forced back by his bodyguards. Since that confrontation with Samuel Jenkins and his clan when the town had stood behind Bill, the smuggler had channelled a large percentage of his profits straight back into the town. Billy Bates had watched Dale Jenkins control the cobbled streets through fear, but the smuggler agreed with Harry Booth that the townsfolk deserved better. Billy Bates wanted to try something completely different and earn the town's loyalty not through fear but through respect. The smuggler's men regularly delivered food parcels to the people who needed them. Bill had even commissioned the construction of a large barn to house all of the street kids.

Bill stood taking in the chaos before turning on his heels and marching into the tavern.

The Seagull was virtually empty, apart from a small crowd gathered around a table in the corner who were staring Bill's way. The crowd were made up of Jimmy Harp and several members of his gang. The days when they'd trawl the streets with empty stomachs looking for pockets to pick were long gone. Now Jimmy and his men worked for Billy Bates as spies, they were his eyes and ears around the town, constantly watching and reporting back to the man who'd put a roof over their heads.

Reaching the table Bill greeted Jimmy and his men warmly before taking a seat. "What can I do for you boys?" he asked and Jimmy wasted no time getting to the point.

"Bill we've seen Jenkins in the town on several occasions over the last few days," Jimmy warned his boss who looked up and into the youngster's eyes.

"Where and when?" he demanded with that croaky voice of his as he rubbed his chin.

"There were half a dozen of them and they were watching the town, it looked like they were searching for someone," Jimmy replied, as Bill sat in silence, deep in thought.

On several occasions since their eviction the Jenkins had been caught boozing in the town, and on each occasion Bill's men had explained with their fists that they weren't welcome.

Turning to Boseda, Thomas and Alfie who'd joined them Bill warned them all to keep vigilant and report back to him immediately if any of the clan were seen again in the town.

Finally he turned to Jimmy Harp and thanked him for reporting the news before dismissing the street-kids and any notion of a threat, a mistake Bill would regret for the rest of his life.

*

Many miles away from the town's cobbled streets and further along the Kent coast Samuel Jenkins was drowning his sorrows in a small tavern out in the sticks near to where his family had settled after fleeing the town of Deal. The clan who'd ruled the whole area with an iron fist decades before were now scattered across the country. The huge revenue that Dale's empire had brought into their family's coffers had finally dried up, forcing most of the youngsters to seek employment elsewhere. After years of terrorising the area very few locals would employ them. So the young Jenkins men had been forced to travel great distances to find work whilst the women and children had stayed at their new camp. A few of the men had stayed too; some were too old to work whilst others clung onto a dream that one day the Jenkins would return to their glory days.

Samuel Jenkins blamed himself for the fate of his family. "If only I'd had the courage Dale had," he muttered to himself as he drained his beaker of ale and demanded another. The tavern's landlord quickly fetched a fresh drink. He knew Samuel Jenkins well. The man sat on the same stool and drank himself into a stupor most days. Walking over the landlord placed another beaker on the table in front of him, just as the door swung open and four men entered. The landlord recognised them too. They were relatives of the drunk, that was clear to see from the virtually identical features they shared, but it was clear there was no lost love between them by the expression on their faces.

Taking another gulp of ale Samuel placed his beaker down, whilst his nephews pulled up chairs around him. The same nephews who'd sided with young Ronnie years before.

"Boys," he slurred, "can I get you a drink?" he offered, but they shook their heads as they stared at the man who'd ruined their family. "Oh I've returned, to lead this family and I'll lead them straight into the town of Deal to claim my father's territory back!"

"Suit yourselves!" Samuel grumbled as he slurped more ale, dribbling some down his chin where it soaked into his bushy beard. "So your little leader will be back in three months," Samuel slurred. "I received a letter from McGregor only a few days ago."

Daniel Jenkins smiled his uncle's way, but didn't rise to the bait. "Yeah my leader will be back soon Samuel, that uncle you can be sure of," he said, climbing to his feet and staring the landlord's way who stood behind the bar polishing glasses.

"Take a walk," he barked at the man who paused from his task and stared Daniel's way, quickly deciding that standing his ground wasn't worth losing his life over, he placed his cloth and a glass down and walked out of the tavern with his tail between his legs.

Turning back to his Uncle Samuel, Daniel Jenkins smiled. "Talking of Ronnie I have a present from him," he said. Now Samuel Jenkins was glaring at his nephew Daniel, who he'd held a grudge against, along with all of the others who'd followed Ronnie around like disciples years before.

"A present from Ronnie?" Samuel asked as he twisted the end of his beard confused.

Suddenly the tavern's door opened once more and a man entered the fray. Crouching down to fit his enormous frame through the small door Samuel watched in horror as dread washed over him. The man stood for a moment staring Samuel's way with an evil grin on his face. Sammy Jenkins swallowed hard as he took in the man's huge height and rippling muscles. He'd heard McGregor had been training his nephew hard, but nothing would have prepared him for the sight of Ronnie. The teenager had grown into a man, but not just any man. Ronnie Jenkins now looked like a freak of nature that belonged in a circus.

"Uncle Samuel," Ronnie said as he strolled over towards the table.

"You're back already," Samuel mumbled, looking paler and much more sober.

"Oh I've returned, to lead this family and I'll lead them straight back into Deal to reclaim my father's territory back," he stated, as Samuel rose to his feet in a fury and pointed Ronnie's way.

"They'll never follow you! Not if I have anything to do with it," he shouted angrily.

Ronnie Jenkins grinned as he reached in his jacket and pulled out a blunt and rusty looking dagger. Samuel's look of anger turned to fear in the split second it took Ronnie to step forward and plunge it into his uncle's heart. Samuel let out a gasp as blood trickled out of his mouth. He looked up from the handle of the dagger imbedded in his chest to his nephew's face.

"Why?" he mumbled. Ronnie Jenkins stepped forward, smiling like a madman and Samuel realised that the time he'd spent with McGregor had only made him more dangerous. His nephew simply wasn't right in the head.

"Because uncle, I need the whole of our family behind me in order to wipe Billy Bates off the map, and that'll only happen if they think Bill killed one of their own. Now they'll follow me," Ronnie said as Samuel fell to his knees and died.

Then Ronnie Jenkins turned to his cousins who stood rooted to the spot terrified. "Now get his body loaded up on the cart and back to the camp! You all know the story, Bill Bates and his men attacked Samuel," he said to his gang who were stood in shock.

Only Daniel had the courage to speak. "What's next boss?" he asked as Ronnie turned to him.

"It's time to settle a score and weaken Bill's gang in the process. I've wanted to teach Boseda a lesson for a long time. Once the African's dead we'll wipe Bill and his whole gang off the map once and for all," he said.

A moment later one his cousins built up the courage to speak and turned to Ronnie. "But what if our elders find out the truth about who killed Samuel?" he asked, as Ronnie exploded in anger.

"What they'll do to you is nothing in comparison to what I'll do to you! Now get moving!" he shouted as they snapped into action.

Chapter Fifty-One

Later that day when Daniel Jenkins and the rest of Ronnie's gang arrived back at the Jenkins' camp, news of Samuel's death spread like wildfire. The men, women and children rushed out of their shacks and stared at the wooden cart that carried Samuel's body that was wrapped in bloody rags.

"There were over two dozen of them," Daniel informed the elders of the clan, who looked on their slain brother with tears in their eyes. "But it was Billy Bates who stuck the knife in and he told us to relay a message that he wouldn't rest until our family were no more," Daniel continued, as gasps of shock came from the women and their men held them tight to reassure them. Daniel watched as fear spread through the group, quietly confident that Ronnie's plan was working perfectly. "Even this far from the town of Deal we're not safe. It's time to welcome Ronnie home," he pleaded to the elders who were crowding round Samuel's body mourning. "It's time we fought back! And we need Ronnie's help," Daniel said, receiving shouts of support from the rest of Ronnie's gang.

After a long moment the eldest of the original nine brothers, Derek Jenkins who was now clan chief by birth right turned to him. "Tomorrow you'll begin your journey to McGregor's camp. Ronnie belongs here with us now," he said, "but first we must bury Samuel. God bless his soul."

Derek Jenkins ordered his brother's body to be removed from the cart. Most of the clan stood rooted to the spot, devastated by the news of Samuel's death. Daniel Jenkins turned to his small gang and smiled. He had no intention of travelling the vast distance to the gypsy camp, as he knew all too well that his leader Ronnie was much closer to home.

*

On a pleasant summer evening a few days later the cobbled streets of Deal were busy as usual. Sailors from all corners of the globe staggered from tavern to tavern, working tirelessly in their attempt to drink the town dry of grog, whilst the working girls batted their eyelids at them and local fishermen crowded around telling stories of that catch that got away. As usual Billy Bates was nowhere to be seen. The smuggling leader kept visits into the town down to a minimum and was much more comfortable sat in his study reading a book than he was boozing in one of the town's many taverns. Billy Bates didn't need to venture into the maze of cobbled streets to know what was happening. The town was crowded with his spies who informed him of everything.

Meanwhile Bill's tough African bodyguard was strolling back towards his house after a hard day's work when suddenly he stopped dead in his tracks as he caught a glimpse of one of the Jenkins foot soldiers. The African recognised him as one of the thugs that'd terrorised the town at Ronnie's side. Feeling outraged Boseda crossed the road and marched towards the youngster, but at the last minute he turned on his feet and saw Boseda bowling towards him. Suddenly he began to run, but the African wasn't going to let him get away as he sprang into action and gave chase. Running through a network of alleyways Boseda thought he'd lost him as he disappeared from sight for a fraction of a second, but then a second later he saw him rush into an alleyway that was a dead end and Boseda slowed down, smiling to himself as he marched towards his prey.

Daniel Jenkins stood trapped in by brick walls on each of his sides. Eventually realising there was no escape he turned and faced Boseda, who admired his bravery.

"Well, well," Boseda said, stepping towards him, "why do you risk everything venturing into this town? You know your family isn't welcome anymore."

To Daniel Jenkins' credit he stood his ground. "This town belonged to my family a long time before you ever stepped foot in these streets," he hissed, "and they'll belong to us once more."

Boseda turned his head to the sky and roared with laughter. "I give you your due boy! You've got guts," he said as he stepped forward and clenched his fists.

Suddenly though a voice came from the entrance of the alleyway. "Guts run in my family," the voice warned. Boseda spun around and stopped dead in his tracks at the sight that greeted him. Stepping out of the shadows and blocking the alleyways entrance his old rival Ronnie stood smiling menacingly, then a moment later the gigantic thug began marching towards him.

The African was shocked at the size of the youngster. Ronnie was a goliath in comparison to the rest of his gang who crowded around him.

Gritting his teeth Boseda realised how stupid he'd been to fall for such a simple trap, but glancing at the brick walls trapping him on all sides he knew the only way out was through Ronnie and his men.

Years before Boseda had relished the idea of going toe to toe with the out of control teenager, confident he'd win. But now as he turned to face Ronnie he had his doubts.

"So you now work for Billy Bates?" Ronnie asked as he took off his jacket, ready to fight.

Boseda did the same, he wasn't sure whether he'd beat Dale's youngest, but he'd have a good go. "That I do Ronnie. Harry retired just after your family decided they didn't want you anywhere near them," he replied, hoping it would wind Ronnie up and put the odds in his favour.

Ronnie Jenkins chuckled to himself. Years before Boseda's tactic would have worked, but that was before McGregor had taught him everything he knew about physical conflict and eventually Ronnie had broken the gypsy's jaw in return, before fleeing the camp and McGregor's men who wanted his blood spilled.

Ronnie's gang crowded around the two giant men, excited and eager to see their leader battle Harry Booth's old bodyguard. Over the last few years they'd heard the rumours that Ronnie was unbeatable in the ring. McGregor had dragged him all over the country, battling against the best of the best and Ronnie had destroyed them all. Then when Ronnie realised there was nothing more the gypsy leader could teach him he'd turned on the man.

Boseda stepped forward bravely and wasted no time as he rushed in throwing wild punches that Ronnie easily out-manoeuvred. Only one punch caught Ronnie and split his lip, and as he tasted blood he went berserk. Suddenly he punched the African in the chest, which made Boseda buckle and collapse to the floor in pain. The African tried to stagger to his feet and defend himself, but for Ronnie there were no rules of conduct. The thug kicked Boseda square in the jaw, which knocked him back to the ground and he fumbled around barely conscious as Ronnie rained down blows.

Watching and shocked at their cousin's viciousness Ronnie's gang stood waiting for their leader to climb off Boseda's body. Eventually when he rose to his feet Ronnie had blood all over him and the African was lying on the floor, completely still. The child that had been stolen from the African coast by a slave ship had finally returned to his ancestors.

Chapter Fifty-Two

Early the following morning one of Jimmy Harp's street kids strolled into the alleyway and found Boseda's lifeless body lying in a pool of congealed blood. Letting out a gasp of surprise others were soon attracted and as the street urchin rushed off a crowd had gathered. Word of Boseda's gruesome murder quickly spread through the town. For locals it wasn't just any old murder. Many of them had stood by Billy Bates' side solely because he'd had the support of Harry Booth's fearless bodyguard. Now with Boseda dead many were already regretting their stand against the clan. People were scared and vulnerable. The local lawmen who were normally all too happy to turn a blind eye to most offences felt differently about murder. Troops were called in to catch the killer and reassure people the town was safe. The locals knew differently though. The cobbled streets had experienced three long years of happiness in the clan's absence, but now they were back with a vengeance.

The previous night the Jenkins family had been seen in the town, and not just the waifs and strays. Ronnie Jenkins had marched along the town's main thoroughfare with at least fifty of his kin, assaulting locals and making threats along the way. People had stood frozen to the spot in shock, before they'd rushed into their cottages and bolted their doors.

Within a day of Ronnie's return blood was running through the cobbled streets and the town was scared out of its wits. Most had known Ronnie when he'd been just a boy standing in his father's shadows. Everyone knew he was an absolute animal who took pleasure from inflicting pain. Now he'd returned bigger and stronger than ever before, with his entire clan at his beck and call.

News of the African's murder reached Bill Bates early the next morning. Jimmy Harp had rushed out of the town and straight to the smuggler's headquarters, perched high up on the chalk cliffs overlooking the channel.

Bill had been in a great mood when he'd opened the door, but after taking one look at the young pickpocket he knew something was amiss. Ushering Jimmy inside and up to his study Bill sat across from the youngster and when Jimmy informed him of the African's demise tears ran from Billy Bates' dark eyes. A moment later he brushed them away.

"Gather your gang and bring them all here. It'll at least be safer than down in the town's streets," he said, before Jimmy rose to his feet and left Bill alone with his thoughts.

Around an hour later Alfie Bicks strolled into the study and found his boss staring into space. "You okay Bill?" he asked, pulling the smuggler from his thoughts. Turning to face his tall ginger bodyguard Bill sighed.

"I need you to organise a meeting Alfie. Gather everyone who's earned a crust from me in the last few years and get them to meet at the bottom of the chalk cliffs at 3 p.m.," he muttered as Alfie nodded and disappeared from the study. Then Bill reluctantly rose to his feet and strolled towards Thomas' room, knowing he couldn't put off telling the boy any longer.

Billy Bates was devastated by the news of Boseda's murder and not just because of the blow it dealt to his smuggling organisation. Boseda had been a great friend, but Bill knew he hadn't been half as close to the African as Thomas had been. The pair who'd shared a slave past had a special bond. Boseda had spent a long time training Thomas after they'd found him under the jetty, teaching him every skill in his lethal arsenal.

The smuggler knew Thomas struggled expressing his emotions and would take Boseda's death badly, but Bill had no idea how the boy would deal with his grief. Rapping on the door Bill strolled into Thomas' room and took a seat on his bed as the youngster stared at him through deep sunk emotionless eyes. Staring at the floorboards Billy Bates let it all out as tears flowed down his cheeks.

Eventually he stared up at Thomas who was staring back at him, looking possessed as he gritted his teeth and clenched his knuckles so hard they'd turned white. "I need to avenge Boseda's death and kill Ronnie Jenkins," the boy stated, as Bill let out a faint gasp of surprise before nodding his agreement.

*

When Alfie Bicks left Bill's house he climbed onto his horse and galloped down into the town. Alfie wasn't taking any risks though and tethered his horse before making his way onto the cobbled streets on foot. With a cloak pulled up over his head he was hardly recognisable as he rushed from one tavern to another organising his boss' meeting. Several hours later he was back at Bill's side, marching towards the bottom of the cliffs where a large crowd were gathered. Approaching the group Billy Bates watched as they talked amongst each other, he could see the men were scared before he stepped up to address them.

"Thank you for coming," he said, "as I'm sure you're all aware the Jenkins family are back, including Ronnie," but Billy Bates was drowned out as one of Harry Booth's old smugglers stepped forward, a man called Hutchings who'd once again been elected to voice the crowds opinion. The man looked over into Bill's eyes before glancing at the ground.

"We're not standing up against Ronnie, Bill, I'm sorry you've been good to us all, that we're not debating, but Ronnie is an animal and making a stand against him is suicide. I'm sorry," he said, and then suddenly the crowd began to disperse as they made their way home to safety.

Billy Bates stood staring at the crowd with his head held high. The vast majority of his men were abandoning him at his time of need, but at his sides stood Thomas, Alfie, Carp and another two dozen of his own men whose loyalty was unquestionable. When most of the crowd had gone only a few clusters here and there remained. Jimmy Harp stood surrounded by his gang awaiting Bill's orders. The smuggler nodded his respect to the street kids whose bravery far outweighed their age. Turning his beady eyes Billy Bates noted every single man who'd stayed. The smuggler would never forget their faces and vowed to reward them all if he outlived the week, which was something he was beginning to doubt himself.

The small crowd who were still present gathered around Bill, the man who'd risked his life for them all and a man who they'd stand by until the very end. The smuggler himself was staring out at the English Channel watching the vessels bobbing around on her choppy surface, lost in his own thoughts. After a few minutes he turned to them.

"What's the plan boss?" Alfie Bicks asked, as he twisted the end of his ginger beard and Bill smiled that crooked smile.

In some ways the smuggling leader was glad of Ronnie's return. He'd miss having Boseda at his side and would blame himself for the African's death until the day he died, but at least it had taught him which of his men he could truly rely on. He vowed that he'd never give any more work to the men who'd betrayed him, as far as Bill was concerned they'd made their choice.

Finally Bill addressed the crowd. "Men we have a problem, and a problem which offers only one solution. We need to execute Ronnie Jenkins, he's a lunatic and he'll never give up his quest to fill Dale's boots and run this town." As Bill paused the silence was filled by cheers of support, but the smuggler quickly silenced the crowd. In Bill's eyes murder was never a cause for celebration.

"The rest of the Jenkins family and even his own gang are nothing without him, they proved that three years ago when we ran them out of this town," Bill said, pausing to find a particular face amongst the crowd.

"Jimmy," Bill said, catching the youngster's attention. "Where are Ronnie and the clan now?"

Jimmy Harp stepped forward. "I've had lookouts posted all over the town since first thing this morning when the body was found. The clan vacated the town late last night. It's likely that they panicked and fled to the safety of their camp. Ronnie and his gang are a different matter they're hiding out in the northend of town. The King's soldiers arrived from the barracks hours ago though so Ronnie won't venture too far into town," the leader of the pickpockets said.

Bill listened intently as he paced up and down deep in thought. He'd always believed that knowledge was power and the service the street-kids provided him was worth its weight in gold. Finally he stopped dead in his tracks and faced the crowd once more. "Jimmy take your men and infiltrate the north end of town, I want your spies everywhere," he ordered, as Jimmy nodded.

"How will we relay information back to you, boss?" he asked, and Bill turned to him once more.

"You know a farm called Prosperity?" he asked and Jimmy nodded. "We'll hide out there and when the time to attack arrives we'll creep into the north end and silence Ronnie once and for all," Bill said, receiving shouts of support from the crowd.

As the cheers died down Bill addressed the crowd once more. "Men, I appreciate the loyalty you've shown to me today, and believe me I'll never forget it, but tonight we'll be relying on the element of surprise that Jimmy and his gang here will provide. If we travel in a large gang then Ronnie's gang will spot us, or even worse the soldiers of the crown," he said in that croaky voice, before turning to his most trusted bodyguards. Thomas stood staring at him, with an expression that displayed little emotion, but Bill had no doubt that the boy was ready for war. Alfie on the other hand had that crazy look in his eyes and looked excited at the prospect of conflict.

"I only need half a dozen good men. When we hit them, we'll hit them hard and then vanish into the night. I want every one of you to go to ground. Get your families and take them to my headquarters or any of our safe houses and wait out the storm. Understood?" Bill asked, and his men voiced their support once more, but Billy Bates had no idea of the mistake he was making.

Chapter Fifty-Three

The sun was just beginning its slow descent towards the horizon ending a day of pandemonium in the town's cobbled streets, as soldiers of the crown in their bright red uniforms marched up and down searching for a man responsible for a murder, a man named Ronnie. All day long the soldiers had heard dreadful stories about the Jenkins' psychotic leader and they now feared him in equal measure to the locals who were scared out of their wits. The soldiers had turned the town upside down in their search, but hadn't found a trace of the clan's presence. Many of the soldiers believed he'd fled the town, which was the smart thing to do, but they didn't know Ronnie Jenkins. The more experienced men were beginning to make preparations for a long night.

Contrary to popular belief Ronnie Jenkins was still in the town, unlike many of his kin who'd fled after he'd beaten Boseda to death with his fists. Ronnie feared nobody though. He'd spent a few years away from the streets that he felt belonged to him, now he was here to stay. He was standing near the shoreline close to the ruins of the Tudor castle at Sandown, a little north of town, watching the ships sail in the channel. Surrounding him were ten of his men, men who'd followed his every word since they'd been kids. Most of them were as scared of their unpredictable leader as the townsfolk, but they hid their fear well.

A short distance away and watching their every move stood another kind of leader completely. Jimmy Harp was as selfless as they came and would go hungry himself to provide for anyone of his men. It was this very reason why Jimmy's gang of street urchins looked at their leader with a level of respect Ronnie Jenkins could only dream of. Staring hard at the gigantic figure whose men appeared like dwarves around him, Jimmy was suddenly distracted by a flicker of movement out of the corner of his eye. Turning his attention along the shoreline Jimmy spotted a large gang of men marching in the Jenkins' direction with determined expressions on their faces and as Jimmy took a closer look he realised they were sailors from one of the countless merchant ships anchored off shore. Intrigued at this latest twist Jimmy Harp took a risk and crept even closer just in time to witness one of the sailors point in Ronnie's direction.

"That's him all right!" the man shouted, causing Ronnie to turn his attention away from the channel and smile eerily at the crowd in front of him. The sailors had been drinking, Jimmy could tell even from a distance by the way they staggered and the silly grins on several of their faces. They continued to march towards Ronnie and his men, much to Jimmy's surprise who couldn't believe what he was seeing.

Suddenly the group stopped only a short distance from the clan and one of the sailors stepped forward. "We dropped anchor out there years back," he sneered, "and were attacked in one of this town's grog shops," the sailor continued. Ronnie stepped towards the crowd of sailors with a massive grin on his ugly face, a grin that only served to put the sailors on edge. The thug's gang didn't move a muscle, except for one. Daniel Jenkins stood at his cousin Ronnie's side, issuing threats and stirring up the sailors who'd had already had a gutful of Dutch courage and didn't really need it.

"I'm not in the mood for this!" Ronnie warned. "Now scatter or I'll make sure you regret it."

The sailors held their ground though, aware that they outnumbered their enemy, and then one of the biggest stepped forward towards Ronnie. "Or what, boy?" he shouted.

Ronnie Jenkins' lips creased into a slight smile for a fraction of a second, and then in one swift movement he pulled his dagger out and leapt forward, plunging it straight into the sailor's heart. The man's bravery slipped away faster than his life as he stared at Ronnie's hand gripping the handle of the dagger buried deep in his chest. A moment later Ronnie retrieved the blade and the man dropped to the ground dead. The rest of the sailors had turned rather pale and stood staring in shock at the lifeless body at their feet, before Ronnie warned them all to scatter or face the same fate. The men rushed off, leaving their dead friend in a pool of blood as Ronnie placed his dagger back in its sheath.

Daniel Jenkins stared at his brothers and cousins who stood rooted to the spot and clearly scared before turning to Ronnie his leader, who was staring back out to sea once more without a care in the world. "We need to get off the streets Ron and hide out for the night. There is a tavern called the Black Bull a few streets away. Let's get there and wait out the night," he pleaded. Ronnie turned his attention to Daniel and grunted his consent before the gang strolled away from the shoreline.

Jimmy Harp rubbed his chin for a moment and let out a deep sigh before climbing to his feet. The leader of the town's street kids thought the world of Billy Bates, the man who'd put a roof over their heads and food in their mouths. Jimmy feared that when the pair finally came face-to-face Ronnie Jenkins would cut Bill to shreds without a second thought. Now Jimmy Harp was aware that inevitable confrontation was only a short while away he had a horrible feeling in his guts, a feeling he tried to push out of his mind as he began his journey to Prosperity Farm to inform Bill of where Ronnie's gang were hiding.

*

Billy Bates stood in a field staring at a large pond and debating his future. The field itself was part of a farm which belonged to a friend of the smugglers, a man named Havelock. Many years before when he'd been just a mere farmhand Havelock had helped Bill transport his smuggled cargoes by loaning mules to bear the heavy weight of contraband from the shoreline to his many safe-houses. In return Billy Bates had rewarded the farmhand generously by loaning him the money to buy the farm the smuggler now stood on. Billy Bates and Havelock shared many qualities; they'd both been raised in poverty, but were hard working and ambitious. Since the first time they'd met they'd got on like a house on fire. On this day though the farmer could see that his friend was troubled, more troubled than he'd ever seen him. Havelock had heard the rumours around town that Ronnie Jenkins was out for his blood and most of the town had abandoned him. The farmer felt bad for his friend as he watched Alfie Bicks, Thomas and a dozen others stood in silence at their leader's side, staring at the flat surface of the pond.

It was Carp who looked up first and spotted Jimmy Harp and a bunch of his toe-rags making their way across the field, but it didn't take long for news of their arrival to spread through the group. Billy Bates marched towards them. "What news do you bring?" the smuggler demanded in that croaky voice of his, before Jimmy informed the gang of what he'd witnessed and the smuggler's men failed to conceal their shock over the sailor's murder.

"They're off the streets now and hiding out in The Black Bull," Jimmy said, as the crowd broke into discussion about how best to proceed. Eventually Jimmy Harp turned to Bill. "Ronnie's completely out of control boss, he'll kill you if given half the chance. Why not go to ground and let the soldiers deal with him?" Jimmy asked.

Billy Bates rubbed his chin deep in thought for a long moment before replying. "Jimmy I appreciate your concern. I'm many things, but I'm not a coward. Anyway Ronnie and his gang will sneak out of town tomorrow, but they'll come back. Dale Jenkins ran this town for many, many years. Ronnie isn't going anywhere and until he returns we'll all be looking over our shoulders from one day to the next," he said, turning to Thomas and staring into the boy's vacant eyes, knowing only too well that he wouldn't rest until Ronnie Jenkins paid the price for murdering Boseda.

"No!" Bill stated. "Going to ground isn't an option. We need to attack The Black Bull and take Ronnie out once and for all," he finished before he began to march across the field towards the north end of town and a meeting with destiny.

*

Ronnie Jenkins was pacing up and down inside the tavern as the landlord sat tied to a chair terrified. The gang of thugs had forced their way into The Black Bull only a short while earlier. The curtains had been pulled tight and a sign had been placed on the door informing any potential customers that the establishment was closed for the night. The landlord wasn't concerned about losing the night's takings. Like everyone else in the town he'd heard of the trouble brewing between Ronnie Jenkins and Billy Bates, the fisherman turned smuggler. The townsfolk were talking of nothing else and few believed that Billy Bates would survive to tell his tale. The landlord stared at the floor, praying he'd see the sun rise once more over the channel and smell that salty air. The rest of Ronnie's gang sat in silence watching their psychotic leader pace back and forth as the floorboards creaked under his weight. The landlord assumed that like himself they were wondering just what in God's name was going through his head, and he wasn't far wrong.

*

Billy Bates was marching along a deserted street en-route to The Black Bull with his men at his sides. The smuggler had spent many years in the north end of town in what felt to him like a lifetime ago. Only a few streets away was the shack he'd shared with Benjamin Swift, his best friend who'd begged him not to become a smuggler and warned him countless times that it would only end in trouble. As Bill reached The Black Bull and his men crowded around him he wondered whether Benny had been right all along. A second later he gritted his teeth and pushed the painful memories of his childhood friend out of his mind as he turned to the task at hand.

The tavern's door was locked and bolted and the curtains were drawn, but to Bill it was obvious someone was inside by the flickering glow of candlelight coming from within. Arriving at his side Jimmy Harp informed Bill that his men hadn't taken their eyes off the front door since Ronnie and his gang had entered an hour before and the smuggler nodded.

Turning to his men who were gripping their bats anxiously Billy Bates wished them all the best of luck.

"We'll smash the windows. When they come out they'll come out fighting so expect the worse," he warned before turning to Alfie and Thomas. "Concentrate on Ronnie and try and make it quick," he advised, as he picked up a large pebble out of the gutter and prepared to launch it.

Chapter Fifty-Four

As the pebble flew through the air it felt like time itself had stopped for the smuggler's men who gripped their weapons nervously, ready to do battle in Billy Bates' name. As the stone hit the window the pane shattered into a thousand pieces and the empty street erupted into mayhem. The Black Bull's heavy door swung open and Ronnie came flying out of the tavern like a bull that had seen red. He stood for a fraction of a second and took in the group of smugglers as he stared from one man to the next, until his eyes settled on Billy Bates.

"Well, well, well. I've waited a long time for this!" he said with a menacing grin on his face, as his men poured out of the tavern and into the street behind him. Alfie Bicks spotted an opportunity and the tall red haired teenager wasted no time. Launching himself at Ronnie with his dagger gripped in one hand Alfie hoped he'd deliver a fatal blow, but Ronnie side stepped him at the last moment and delivered a blow to the jaw that sent Alfie sprawling to the ground, and then the battle really kicked off. The street that only a moment ago had been dead to the world was now a scene of horror as both gangs rushed towards each other waving clubs and knives in the air. Screams and grunts of pain pierced the night as men from both sides collapsed to the ground wounded.

Ronnie Jenkins stayed firmly on his feet swinging wild punches like a man possessed and swatting his enemies away like flies. Bill's most ruthless bodyguard didn't take his eyes off of Ronnie, the man who'd killed his friend Boseda, as he dispatched several of Ronnie's gang in an attempt to get within striking distance of their leader. Remembering the African's wise words Thomas put all of his skills to the test and was making real progress, but then suddenly a pained shout filled the air in a croaky voice the boy would have recognised anywhere. Thomas spun around and watched Billy Bates stagger and fall backwards clutching his chest whilst Daniel

Jenkins stood in front of him still gripping the dagger he'd slashed him with. Struck with fury Thomas launched himself at Daniel Jenkins with a combination of punches that left him lying on his back unconscious. Focusing his attention on the man who meant everything to him, Thomas rushed to Bill's side and helped him climb to his feet. The smuggling leader was grunting with pain as he gripped the wound on his chest with one hand whilst he leant on Thomas for support with the other, and he was dragged away from the battle.

Thomas who'd focused on nothing else but exacting revenge on the man who'd killed Boseda searched frantically for somewhere to hide the man who'd provided him with a life worth living.

Meanwhile Bill's men continued to fight it out with Ronnie's gang. They rushed at the huge thug and hit him with clubs and bats that broke like matchwood across his huge frame, but Ronnie remained on his feet swinging wild punches and dispatching the smugglers to the cobbles with ruthless efficiency. Then suddenly the giant thug glanced up and caught sight of Thomas half-carrying Billy Bates to safety. Observing the way Bill was leaning on the boy for support Ronnie guessed his enemy was injured and grinned wickedly before dealing with the remainder of Bill's men, who either fell to their knees or scrambled away. Signalling several of his clan Ronnie Jenkins began to follow Thomas' path and after a few hundred yards he caught sight of the pair smashing their way into a shed used by fishermen to store their equipment. Looking up at the sky Ronnie laughed like a lunatic as he marched towards the shed. The thug had waited a very long time to extract his revenge on Bill Bates, the man who'd had the audacity to banish his family from the town and Ronnie planned on making the man suffer before he killed him.

Meanwhile Thomas placed Bill down on a large pile of fishing net before glancing around to double check that he hadn't been followed. Peering through the shed's door his heart sank as he saw Ronnie and two of his men marching in his direction. The boy who'd lived through hell at the Whitegate Cotton Mill as a mere child cursed in frustration as he gritted his teeth and clenched his knuckles until they turned white whilst racking his brain for a solution to the dilemma he'd found himself in.

Suddenly Billy Bates gripped his shoulder and he turned to face the man he thought of as his saviour, the man who'd found him living amongst the rats under a wooden jetty and had offered him a warm meal, a comfy bed and a future.

"Listen to me Thomas and listen good!" Bill demanded. "You leave now and don't turn back, get to our house. My money is hidden under a loose floorboard near the window in the study, take it all."

"No," Thomas mumbled as he watched a lone tear run down Billy Bates' weather-beaten cheek.

"Listen to me Thomas!" Bill said in a raised voice as he clutched the wound on his chest and winced in pain. "You go, and go now and that's an order."

Thomas stared hard into Bill's dark eyes. "A long time ago you told me that someone saved you. They took you in, put a roof over your head and food in your mouth, and asked for nothing in return." he said, and Bill nodded with a confused look on his face.

"You told me that you'd have done anything and everything for that person," Thomas stated as he rose to his feet and pulled his axe out of his jacket. Now Ronnie Jenkins and his men could be heard outside as they made their way towards the storage shed.

"No don't do this, it's suicide! Run and live a normal life," Bill pleaded, and Thomas stared at him for a moment longer through his deep sunk and emotionless eyes.

"Any chance I ever had of living a normal life was beaten out of me a long time ago," he said as he barged his way through the door of the shed and disappeared into the night, leaving Bill cursing in anger.

Outside in the street Ronnie Jenkins stood staring at him with a strange look on his face, as Thomas marched towards him. "Kid you're crazier than me!" Ronnie said as Thomas rushed at him and swung his axe at the thug's chest missing him by mere inches. Then the pair began circling each other, as both men waited for that perfect moment to launch an attack. Watching Ronnie closely, Thomas witnessed a smile creep up on the thug's face and all his hopes sank as he heard footsteps behind him. Glancing around in despair he watched as four of Ronnie's gang surrounded him with wooden clubs gripped tightly in their hands. Turning his attention towards their leader Thomas watched Ronnie step backwards, even closer to the shed's door as he laughed a deep laugh from the bottom of his stomach and his wide shoulders rolled backwards.

"Well, well, well it has to be said I admire your style, but I'm sure one day we'll continue this battle in hell," Ronnie said as he turned on his heels and marched towards the shed.

Thomas screamed in frustration, a scream that echoed into the night as he flung his axe to the ground and launched himself at the Jenkins thugs throwing wild punches in an attempt to fight his way towards the shed and save Bill's life. As the first of many blows struck him causing him to stagger and nearly collapse, Thomas realised he wouldn't make it after all and it was all over for Billy Bates.

*

A short distance away Alfie Bicks opened his eyes and slowly climbed to his feet. He was battered and bruised, but in the land of the living once more. Staring at the scene of devastation he stepped over several bodies as shattered glass crunched underneath his feet. For a split second he thought the battle was over but then he heard shouts and screams from a few streets away and he rushed off to join the fray once more. Rushing through several alleyways and passing countless tatty shacks Alfie rounded a corner and came across a sight that made both his heart miss a beat and his face light up with pride. His friend Thomas stood getting beaten badly by four men with clubs, but the boy stayed on his feet and continued to fight back even with the odds stacked so against him. Creeping up on them Alfie picked up a lump of wood before launching an attack that left two of Ronnie's gang unconscious and another fleeing into the night.

"Where's Bill?" Alfie asked and a second later Thomas was rushing towards an old shed with Alfie in pursuit.

*

Lying on his back in agony Billy Bates prayed that Thomas would see sense and make an escape before it was too late. The smuggler had accepted his fate, he'd brought it all on himself when he'd chosen to smuggle merchandise across the channel and cheat the Jenkins family many, many moons ago. Staring around the shed at all the fishing equipment he smiled to himself. "This was always my destiny," he mumbled to himself, and then he looked up and froze.

Ronnie Jenkins stood in the doorway, smiling like the maniac he was. Summoning his last ounce of strength Bill scrambled to his feet and burst through the shed's back door only to land on his hands and knees in another empty street. Rolling over onto his back Bill tried to scramble along the cobbles, as he watched Ronnie appear once more.

"You know Bill I admire you in many ways, you've got courage and brains to boot, but thinking this town would stand up against me was a huge mistake," he said, pulling a rusty looking dagger from a sheath around his waist. "The respect they have for you would never outweigh the fear they have of me," he continued as he stepped forward. "When it comes to the crunch fear is a much more powerful tool. My father taught me that."

Deciding that he wanted to die facing his enemy Billy Bates climbed to his feet once more. "Your father despised you Ronnie, just like everyone else in this town," Bill said as Ronnie stepped even closer.

"Any last words Bill?" Ronnie hissed through gritted teeth, but Bill just glared at him through those dark eyes of his. Raising the dagger and preparing to plunge it into the smuggler's chest, he stepped even closer. "See you in hell, Bill," Ronnie said, but then a fraction of a second later the huge thug was hit with a lump of wood that snapped across the back of his head. Bill watched in slow motion as Ronnie's eyes rolled into the back of his head and he fell forward knocking Bill to the ground and landing in a heap on top of him.

Bill lay trapped with Ronnie's enormous bulk pinning him to the ground for a moment before he struggled to roll the giant off of him, and then Bill rose to his feet ready to thank the man that had saved him, but the only thing that greeted Bill was an empty street and the sound of his saviour's boots hitting the ground as he fled. Disorientated and confused Bill stared at Ronnie's limp body and blood oozed from a deep wound on the thug's head. A long moment passed before Bill heard Thomas shout his name and he turned to see the orphan stagger towards him with Alfie Bicks at his side. Both men had taken a severe beating and were worse for wear, but Billy Bates was ecstatic to see his friends alive.

"You killed him," Alfie said as he stared at Ronnie's body lying motionless at Bill's feet, and his boss smiled a crooked smile. Then suddenly the first of many whistles filled the air as the soldiers arrived in the area. Bill Bates turned to the two odd-looking young men he'd choose over anyone to stand at his sides. "It's time to go to ground," Bill said in that croaky voice, as the trio hobbled off and disappeared into the night.

Chapter Fifty-Five

That night Billy Bates staggered home to his cliff-top headquarters, badly wounded but otherwise alive. At both of his sides and supporting his weight were his two best men Alfie Bicks and Thomas. Both had experienced their fair share of problems in life, just like Bill himself, but both had the courage to face their enemies and stand loyally at the smuggler's sides when countless others had abandoned him in his moment of need and fled in fear.

The build up to that eventful night had changed everything for the fisherman who'd grown into the most powerful smuggler on the coast. It had taught Billy Bates many things, but above everything it had shown him who was truly his friend and who wasn't. It was a question of fear and respect, a lesson Bill would never forget. In the years ahead Bill would come to describe each of those friends who'd stood at his sides as one of his own.

As the weeks passed by the wound on his chest began to slowly heal, but unfortunately Bill wasn't alone. When soldiers had arrived on the scene and stumbled across the bodies that lay scattered in the street outside The Black Bull it didn't take them long to follow the path of destruction to the murderer they'd been frantically searching for. Initially when they'd come across Ronnie sprawled out on his chest with a deep wound on the back of his head they'd assumed that he was dead, but after a handful of soldiers struggled to haul his gigantic frame onto a cart the thug came around. The story that spread through the cobbled streets was that it took a dozen soldiers to hold him down whilst others stood in shock before they leapt into action and chained his limbs with thick shackles. The soldiers were so surprised at his strength that word soon spread and after a few weeks locked away in the clink, a decision was made that Ronnie's strength would be put to good use helping to expand the British Empire overseas and he was placed on a slave ship and banished to the colonies.

Ronnie Jenkins' arrest wasn't the only story to find its way through the town's streets. News that Ronnie who'd terrorised the town for years had challenged Billy Bates and had been left in a pool of blood for his troubles circulated the town from ear to ear and tavern to tavern for many weeks during the aftermath of that fateful night. Locals began to truly fear Billy Bates, the ex-fisherman with eyes as dark as a moonless night. Only Bill and one other knew the real truth that he hadn't even laid a single hand on Ronnie Jenkins, and for a very long time he racked his brain in frustration trying to figure out who'd saved his skin.

The smuggler wasn't seen in the town for a long while, and spent many a long day with a book in his palm and his dark eyes staring out to sea whilst his wounds healed. His cargoes continued to hit the Kent coast day in day out and his men were kept as busy as always, whilst the townsfolk held their breath in anticipation of his return.

Eventually when Billy Bates strolled through the heart of town surrounded by a dozen of his most trusted men, who in turn were surrounded by Jimmy Harp and his gang of street kids, many tried to offer their respects and beg for his forgiveness for abandoning him in his moment of need, but the smuggler continued to stroll on as his gang blocked their paths.

*

The years began to pass by and Billy Bates continued to smuggle merchandise across the channel he'd grown into a man on. Time hadn't been good to Bill and the years he'd spent living on a knife edge had left their mark. Billy Bates knew he was growing too long in the tooth for the smuggling game. Glancing at his sides he wondered who'd lead his men after he'd gone. The two most likely of candidates were both far too aggressive for the task. Alfie Bicks, whose ginger stubble had grown into a mighty ginger beard that dangled from his gaunt face down to his chin, was always far too eager to brandish his dagger rather than use his brain. Thomas, who Bill thought of as a son, had issues he'd never overcome, issues that life had forced upon him when he'd only been a boy. The orphan had experienced things as a child that no child should ever experience, and those experiences had left a scar on his soul that would never heal. As time passed Billy Bates began to wonder if he'd ever find anyone to take his place and manage the empire he'd risked everything building, and then one night everything changed.

Chapter Fifty-Six

It was on a warm summer night when Billy Bates decided to take a risk and oversee a landing operation of his merchandise on the shoreline in person. It was a task he'd carried out thousands of times in his youth, but hadn't overseen in years. That week he'd heard news on the grapevine that had hurt him deep inside like a knife twisting in his guts, and that news was that his childhood friend Benny Swift who'd taken him under his wing many years ago had fallen ill and was no longer able to work on the fishing fleet. Bill had spent several days wondering what he could do, knowing he couldn't stand by and do nothing. The smuggler owed Benny everything.

Standing in the brush and staring out at the channel that was quickly falling into darkness Bill spotted Marcus' clipper moving towards the shore and he quickly pulled out his spout lantern and flashed a signal out to sea, whilst his bodyguards crowded around him. Earlier that day as his men gathered around the meeting table in his study and the smuggling leader had announced he'd be joining Carp's team for that night's action, both Alfie and Thomas had sat in shock before voicing their concerns, warning that it was an unnecessary risk.

Bill had turned to them angrily. "I lead by example, I always have and I always will!" he'd barked at them in that croaky voice of his, they both knew better than to argue with.

Hours later as the rowboat began to ferry Bill's smuggled merchandise towards the shore and Bill marched onto the shingle that crunched under his boots he spotted a lone figure sat on the shore staring out to sea. On closer inspection he noticed it was a boy of twelve or so with blond hair blowing in the wind. Not willing to take a risk and allow someone to witness the operation Billy Bates marched straight over, ready to tell the youngster to scram.

When he was only a few yards away the boy turned his head and stared at Billy Bates through blue eyes that made the fearless smuggler freeze in shock. Suddenly a million memories came flooding back into Bill's mind of his early teens, of long days out at sea and even longer nights fantasizing about the future that lay ahead with the boy who'd taught him everything. Memories of years spent when he'd never felt alone. The smuggling leader stared at the youngster sat on the shingle and the boy stared back defiantly. To Billy Bates it felt like time was standing still, as he took in the boy's handsome features and decided that he looked just like his father had at the same age. His father who Bill had spent a lifetime thinking of. His father who was more talented at steering a ship over the treacherous sandbanks than anyone Bill had ever met during his long career. Suddenly Billy Bates was dragged back to reality as a dozen of his bodyguards appeared at his sides and stood staring at the boy menacingly, but Jacob Swift held Bill's gaze and suddenly everything fell into place and the smuggler was hit full force with a shocking realization that nearly took his breath away.

Images of that eventful night when Ronnie Jenkins had nearly killed him came flooding into his mind. Firstly of him marching towards The Black Bull and passing near to the shack where he'd had many good memories. Then of him pleading and Thomas staring at him through those emotionless eyes of his and saying, "You once told me someone saved you and you'd do everything and anything for that person," before turning and marching towards Ronnie and his gang. Finally, the image of Ronnie being hit around the back of the head and falling forwards, as Bill's saviour fled.

Suddenly Bill came back to reality and glanced out to sea as he gathered his thoughts. For years he'd wondered why nobody had approached him and claimed the credit and potential reward for saving his skin and as he turned to the boy sat on the shingle he finally knew why. To Benny Swift nothing really mattered apart from Jacob. The boy was the only reward he'd ever need and he wouldn't have risked the Jenkins retaliation and the possibility of denying the boy a father as well as a mother, for anything.

Finally Bill managed some words. "You're Swifty's lad, aren't yar?" he asked in a hoarse voice.

"Yeah, my name's Jacob Swift," the boy replied.

"I heard your father's fallen ill. I'm sorry to hear that, he's a good man – one of the best – and he knows that ocean," Bill said, as he paused and stared out at the channel and the rowboat that had nearly reached the shore. "Second to none," he muttered under his breath. Glancing at the boy he asked if he wanted to earn some coin and the boy climbed to his feet and tucked a strand of his shoulder length blond hair behind one ear. As he held Bill's gaze, a gaze that normally intimidated even the most hardened of men, in that moment Billy Bates thought of all the people that depended on him for a living and knew he'd finally found the boy who would lead them.

To be continued...

Out Now!

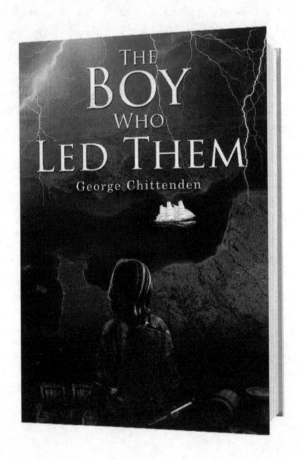